BATTINGHAM CASTLE

Dorrance Publishing Co
585 Alpha Drive
Pittsburgh, PA 15238
Visit our website at www.dorrancebookstore.com

ISBN: 978-1-6470-2321-8
eISBN: 978-1-6470-2794-0

BATTINGHAM CASTLE

by

Sue Fisher

DORRANCE
PUBLISHING CO
EST. 1920
PITTSBURGH, PENNSYLVANIA 15238

Chapter 1

*T*he Earl of Battingham, Lord Troy Bowling, was riding in his carriage
with his groomsman, Bailey. Lord Bowling was only twenty-five
years old. He had inherited his title when his father had passed
away when he was only twenty years old. He was a very good-looking
man with shoulder-length blonde hair that turned blonder the more sun
he acquired. He had hazel eyes that sometimes looked blue and sometimes
green depending on the clothing he would wear. He kept fit from all the
work he had to do. He had the responsibility of over five hundred acres of
land rented to tenants and the Castle of Battingham. He lived with his
mother and sister at the manor house.

It was a hot summer day and the Earl was looking out the window at
the woodlands around them. His thoughts went to his estate. Since his father passed away five years ago from a broken neck when he had fallen
from his horse, all the responsibility fell on his shoulders. Sometimes it felt
like too much, but his family was very important to him. He had to take
his responsibilities stoically and do the best of his ability to ensure his family was well taken care of.

All of a sudden there came a sound of gun fire, bringing him out of his
reverie. The Earl tried to see out of the window for some sign of what was
happening. Suddenly the carriage came to a halt.

"Get down from the carriage," came a demand from outside.

"What is the meaning of this?" demanded the Earl as he climbed down from his carriage. "What is it that you want?"

"We were told you have a trunk of gold coins," said the leader of the group of men surrounding the carriage. All the men were wearing bandanas to hide their faces.

"My dear man," answered the Earl laughing. "If I had a trunk full of gold coins, I surely wouldn't be driving around the countryside without an armed guard."

"Are you saying the information is false?" argued the leader.

"Unfortunately, yes, I'm saying you were misinformed. It's not this carriage that has any gold coins. Please take a look and you can see for yourselves."

The Earl dramatically gestured for the men to dismount and check out the carriage. The leader motioned for two of the group to examine the carriage for a trunk. They dismounted and made everyone stand back from the carriage while they checked the entire carriage.

"There's nothing here," said the one horseman.

"Mount up and get out of here," replied the leader angrily. "Sorry to have inconvenienced you, your lordship. You can be on your way now."

The group started off in an easterly direction and left the Earl and his entourage alone.

The Earl walked to the front of the carriage. The driver was shaking from the ordeal.

"Are you alright, Fredrick?" he asked.

"Yes, my lord. I'm just a little shaken from looking at those guns," Fredrick replied.

"You did an excellent job and we can get on our way back to the manor," the Earl replied as he got back into the carriage.

Bailey joined the Earl.

"It was a good idea to hide the gold under the seats. No one would ever look there since they are usually not hollow," Bailey chuckled.

"When we get back to the manor, pull the carriage to the outbuilding.

You will have to figure out how to get the trunk to my office unseen. And remember, there are eyes everywhere."

"Yes, my lord. I will figure out a way to get it there unseen," Bailey answered and leaned his head back to think over the different ways to accomplish this order.

To the east of the road through the woods, the group of five bandits stopped and dismounted. They sat around in a circle.

"I don't know that I trust his Lordship," stated the leader.

"We checked the entire coach," whined the bandit who led the search of the coach. "We didn't see anything that could have held that much gold."

"Aye," the second bandit concurred. "There was nothing that looked like a trunk of any kind. There was not even a trunk for clothes. His Lordship must have been traveling close to home. Maybe he buried the trunk somewhere."

"That's a possibility, but doubtful," responded the leader. "Cleavus, you still work at the manor?"

The bandit called Cleavus nodded his head.

"Keep your eyes open. Especially watch the Lord's groomsman. If anyone knows something, it will be the groomsman. The information was not false. The coins were in the coach somewhere. Let's get back to our abodes and will meet when we find out something. You all know the signal to look for."

They all mounted their horses and went in different directions. The signal was a wind flag out in the northwest pasture. It didn't fly all the time, as they found out, so the leader started using it as the signal to call a meeting.

The Earl returned back to the manor and entered through the servants' entrance. The manor was an old castle which had been fixed to be a warmer manor house. The outside was still made of the old stone but the inside was made into smaller rooms which could be made warmer with the fireplaces. There were four torrents at each end of the house. His office was in one torrent with his assistant's office and the other three torrents were made into extra bedrooms. He entered the kitchen and snuck up behind the cook, reached behind her, and took a piece of bread from the table. Marple swatted at his hand without turning around.

"If you know what's good for you, you will leave the food alone. It's for the family," she stated.

"I am the family," Troy said behind her.

"Oh!" she exclaimed as she turned around.

Troy grabbed her around the waist and twirled her around. He laughed and gave her a kiss. She had been the cook at the manor since before Troy was born. He loved sneaking up behind her and taking some of her delicious food.

She swatted at him again as she laughed with him. "Go on your way so I can get a meal together for the rest of your family and your guests."

"Guests?" he questioned. "We had no guests when I left. I was not expecting any guests."

"Then go and pester them and find out who it is. Leave me in a moment of peace." Marple shooed him away. He left laughing.

When he reached the drawing room, he could hear people talking. He turned towards the steps leading to his offices on the other side of the manor but was not fast enough. His sister let out a yelp and came running towards him.

"You're back," she yelled as she grabbed him around the neck and hugged him. "Come in with us and see who has come for a visit." She started pulling him towards the drawing room.

Penny was becoming a beautiful young lady. She would turn seventeen in another month or two. She had long light blonde hair and eyes of blue. She was gaining a full-bodied figure. Today she was wearing a light pink straight-lined dress. When one looked at her walking, one could see the outline of her body under her garment. When she wore a gown that buffeted out into a circle, it was so low cut as to not hide much. But that was the fashion, even if Troy didn't like it. She was his little sister and he loved her very much. He would do anything for her.

He laughed at Penny. "Penny, dear," he said giving her a kiss. "I have some business to attend to and will join you after I have finished my business."

"Oh, you are no fun," she said with a fake pout. Penny was such an admirer of her brother. She loved him with all her heart. He could do no wrong in her eyes. "Go then, but hurry back."

"I will, I promise." He strode off to take care of his business.

When he got to the offices, he went looking for his Chief Financial Assistant. He found Donald Blake in his office.

"I'm glad I found you still here. I want you to call the sheriff. We were held up on our way here. They didn't find anything, but I want to report the incident. We have to do something to stop these highwaymen."

"Absolutely!" replied Mr. Blake. "I will send someone immediately to fetch the sheriff. Were you able to hide the shipment?"

"Yes, it was well-hidden. They searched the carriage but didn't find anything. Now Bailey only has to figure out how to get it into the manor. I have faith in Bailey's ingenuity."

"I will let you know as soon as the sheriff arrives."

"Very good, now I have to go and find out who our guests are."

"I am not sure you will be all that happy to find out, your lordship."

"Oh, should I leave again without saying ado to our guests."

"It wouldn't hurt anything if you did. I don't think you're going to be that happy when you see who has arrived."

"Pray tell me who can be such odious people that I would want to leave rather than to see them?"

"They are the Baron of Louder and his daughter, Lady Lucy."

The Baron of Louder was their neighbor to the northwest of their lands. The Baron was pompous at most. He was short and pudgy with graying hair that was becoming less and less on his head. He always had his handkerchief out, wiping his mouth. His daughter could have been a beautiful woman if she didn't wear so much grease on her face. She had long dark hair which she wore mostly in ringlets around her head and brown eyes.

She always wore a fake birthmark on her face which wouldn't have been so bad if she had worn it in the same place each time, but she changed the placement of the birthmark every time she reapplied it to her face. She had a plump body and didn't mind showing it off. Her dresses were even more low cut than society permitted. She wore dresses which pronounced the shape of her body. If she would have taken more time with her appearance, she could have been quite beautiful.

Troy groaned, "You are right. Maybe I can make my escape and make up some excuse as to why I had to rush off again." Just then, he heard the voice of Penny in the hallway. "I think I'm too late."

The door opened. Penny walked in followed by Lady Lucy. Penny's pink gown, even though it showed the outline of her body, made it appear she was flowing across the floor as she walked. Their mother had taught her well as how to walk. Lady Lucy on the other hand was dressed in a purple gown with such a low-cut bodice it left little to the imagination. Her hair was full of the usual ringlets that tried to make her look much younger than she actually was. At nineteen, she was one year older than Penny and four years younger than him. Lady Lucy has been trying to catch Troy as a beau for the last year. Troy was not falling for it. He wanted to wait for someone to love. A love like his parents had. He did not feel that for Lady Lucy.

"There you are, dear brother," Penny stated as she took his arm. "We have come to capture you and return you to the drawing room. Look who has come to visit. She and her father are going to be staying a long while with us."

"Lady Lucy," Troy bowed to her and took her hand to kiss. "What a pleasant surprise." Behind him he heard a cough which he ignored. "Donald, you will get on to that request as soon as possible?"

"Yes, my lord. You will hear from me shortly."

"Good. Ladies, shall we retreat to the drawing room?"

Troy followed behind the two ladies and went down the stairway to the drawing room. His mother was sitting in a chair by the fireplace. She was wearing a beautiful dark blue silk gown with white trim. She was tall and still young, even though she was a widow. She also had blonde hair but was starting to get a few strands of gray. She has the blue eyes Penny had inherited. She was entertaining Baron Louder. Troy went over to his mother and gave her a kiss.

He turned to Baron Louder and shook his hand. "What a nice surprise to have you come for a visit. Baron."

"Yes, I do hope you don't mind the intrusion," said the Baron. He could be quite an overbearing person but sometimes he was actually polite. "We wanted to get away from our manor for a while and decided to prevail upon your hospitality."

"You are welcome in our home anytime," Troy said. "How are you feeling, Mother?" he asked.

"I'm well, Troy. Thank you for asking. I'm hoping you will get me a little sherry before dinner is served." She said looking to him with a smirk on her face. She knew how he felt about the Louders.

"Of course," he said, walking to the counter in the corner of the room. "Can I get anyone else something?"

Lord Louder said he would have a drink. Everyone else declined. He handed the sherry to his mother, the drink to Lord Louder, and then took the seat in the chair on the opposite side of the fireplace, facing his mother. Penny was seated on the couch next to the Baron and Lady Lucy had seated herself on the loveseat. She seemed a little perturbed he did not sit next to her. He had poured himself a small glass of bourbon and sat sipping it while watching the assembly before him.

Penny spoke up. "Lady Lucy was just telling us of their trip to London. They were invited to a ball at the palace. It sounds so exciting. Please continue telling us all about it."

Lady Lucy brightened up and said, "It was so spectacular. There were candles everywhere, even in the gardens. The musicians played all the modern waltzes. It was so much fun. I danced the night away. There are quite a few eligible men in London." She looked at Troy as she said this.

"I'm sure you would have quite the pick of any number of eligible suitors with your beauty and grace," Troy said being polite but ignoring her not too subtle barb towards him. Just then it was announced that dinner was being served.

Chapter 2

*A*s they were walking to the dining room, Mr. Blake came to tell Troy he had another visitor. Troy excused himself after he walked his mother into the dining room and sat her at the table. He went to the front entrance and shook hands with the sheriff.

"Thank you for coming so quickly," he started. "I wanted to tell you as soon as possible about the attempted robbery of my coach along the highway coming home this afternoon."

"I was in the vicinity. We've had a rush of robberies lately. Can you give me any details?"

"Only that there were five of them. They covered their faces so we couldn't identify them. But they knew I was carrying a trunk of gold. They didn't find it though. It was well-hidden."

"That's good. I wish more would be as cautious as you. Did you see what direction they went after the encounter? Did you recognize anyone's voice or any distinguishing marks?"

"No, but I think I would recognize the voices of two of them if I heard them again. The leader of the group instructed two of the men to search our carriage. One of the men informed the leader they could not find any trunk in the carriage. I believe I would recognize their voices. When they left, they went towards the east. That could have been a ploy to throw us off their true direction."

"True. They sound like they are very resourceful at hiding their identity. Thanks for the information. We will keep a look out for the bandits and hopefully will get a lead to arrest them soon. I will call upon you for help if we can find any of them."

"Best of luck to you," Troy said, shook hands with the sheriff, and returned to the dining room.

Lucy was continuing her talk about the ball. Troy could see Penny's eyes fill with the enchantment Lucy was building. He decided to change the subject before Penny could insist they go to London for the season.

"How is your estate flourishing, Baron?" he asked.

"Quite well," the Baron answered, "I don't really keep up that much with what is going on. I have a good overseer who keeps up with the nitty gritty of the everyday problems. He just lets me know of any big problems that need my attention."

"That must be nice but are you sure you are not being taken advantage of? I have one of the best overseers, but we work hand-in-hand on the daily workings of our properties."

"My good man, your lordship, I do know how to handle my own affairs."

Lady Matilda spoke up before Troy could get himself into more trouble. "I'm sure Troy didn't mean it in that manner, Baron. Did you, Troy?"

"No, Mother, I did not mean any ill will towards the Baron. I was simply stating that there are so many people in the world today that would rather cheat and steal than make an honest living. Why, just this afternoon my own carriage was attacked by bandits. One can never be too cautious."

"Oh, dear," Penny sounded concerned. "I do hope no one was hurt."

"No one was hurt. I simply let the bandits search the carriage and when they didn't find anything they wanted, they left."

"I do hope you reported the incident to the local authorities," the Baron said.

"Yes, that was all taken care of," Troy laid down his napkin. "If we are done, would you ladies like to retire to the drawing room? Baron would you like a cigar and some cognac?"

"Yes, I definitely would," he answered.

Troy completed his duties of the evening. He sat and talked small talk with his family and his guests. When it was time to retire, he helped his mother to her room.

"Please come in Troy and have a little talk with me before we retire for the night."

"Sure Mother," he went into her room and took a seat in a chair out on the balcony. Her balcony was set up with several chairs arranged in a circle with a small table in the middle of the circle. "What is it you would like to talk about?"

"Well first, my dear, Lady Lucy brought up something I have been thinking about. I would like to talk to you about your sister, Penny." His mother sat on the chair facing him.

"What, in pray tell, has she done now?" Troy asked.

"Nothing, my dear. She can be a handful at times, but for now she has been quite well behaved. I'm worried about her future. Lady Lucy's talk has reminded me that Penny is getting older. There are not many possible husbands in this area of the countryside for her. The estates are so far and few between. I'm thinking we need to spend some time in London and get her started on her debut into society. She will be eighteen next month and it is time to think about her future. She won't make a very good old maid."

Troy groaned inside when he heard the word "London" but made no outward discerning remarks. "Mother, she is far from being an old maid. But I do see your point and yes, we must ensure her a good future. Could we not have a party here at the manor and invite everyone in the district?"

"Not really, I have been giving this some thought of late and there are not many eligible men in the district."

"I give. I see the importance of making a good connection for her. How about I let you work on setting a date and time for us to go to London in time to prepare for her debut? The season has just finished for this year so it will give you plenty of time to prepare for us to go. You know so much more about this sort of thing than I do."

"I agree with you. You would be useless in making this type of plan for your sister." Lady Matilda laughed at the thought.

Troy loved hearing his mother laugh. She used to laugh all the time when his father was alive. Now she laughed very seldom. He said softly, "You do not laugh that often anymore, Mother. I miss the sound."

"Yes, your father made me laugh all the time. I do miss him so," she sighed. She perked up and looked at Troy. "Now I have something else to talk to you about. You need to find a wife for yourself. You need to start having children to ensure there are heirs to carry on the family name and business."

Now he groaned out loud. "If you are indicating I start looking at Lady Lucy, I refuse. I'm only twenty-five years old and have plenty of time to find someone suitable to have a family."

"What is wrong with Lady Lucy?" his mother asked. "A combination of our two families will make a strong partnership, not just for a strong family but also financially. Lady Lucy is an only child who lost her mother."

"Yes, but you are forgetting the most important fact of all. I do not love her. You and father spoiled me by having such a loving relationship. I cannot think of marring anyone I do not fall completely in love with."

"Your father and I had a special relationship. One that doesn't happen very often. Most marriages are marriages of convenience. I feel you will be disappointed and end up with no heirs. I worry about you. You do need a woman to help take care of you."

Troy got up and went over to his mother. He knelt in front of her and took her hands. "My dearest Mother, I only want what you and my father showed me is possible. I cannot even think of marrying without love. You and father showed Penny and I how special and important love is in a relationship. I believe Penny will not marry unless she is in love also. Although she was much younger than I was when father passed away."

Lady Matilda looked into his eyes with tears in her eyes. "I only want the best for you and Penny. I miss your father so much. It's like only yesterday that he was here with us. Sometimes it is very lonely."

She started crying and Troy took her in his arms and held her.

"I know. I feel the same way," he soothed her.

He stayed with her until she was calm again. Then he said he would let her retire for the night and went to his own room. There were ten bedrooms on this floor. The third floor held the rooms for the servants. Bailey was waiting for him to help him get ready for bed. He waved Bailey off and went to the window to look out.

"Was our project taken care of?" he asked Bailey.

"Yes, my lord," he replied. He chuckled a little, "Thanks to the unexpected arrival of your guests. I had their carriage brought to the outbuilding and when their luggage was brought into the house so was our little cache. It worked beautifully."

"Never thought I would be thankful for a visit from the Louders," he laughed with Bailey. "Good work. You can retire now. I can get myself ready for bed."

"Is there anything you need before I retire? May I make you a drink?"

"That would be nice, a bourbon please," Troy said as he walked over to the chair by the fireplace. He sat down and pulled his boots off to let his feet relax. "Ah, that feels so much better." He took the drink from Bailey, "This will help me relax even more. Thank you, Bailey and have a good evening."

Troy sat for a while and nursed his drink. His mind went back to his discussion with his mother. He missed his father terribly just like his mother. He did not expect him to pass away so young. He felt like most children that his parents would live forever. Troy did not feel he was ready to take on all the responsibilities that were thrown at him at the age of twenty. But he didn't have a choice. He had to step up and take charge even if he wasn't sure what to do. Even after five years, he felt inadequate. Now his mother has reminded him of another responsibility, his sister's future. What was he supposed to do? Should he start putting out feelers? How strict should he be when she started meeting eligible suitors? Should he be the chaperon or was his mother or someone else? There was so much to learn. Was it time to look for a ladies' maid for Penny? Troy knew his mother had one. He would have to have an in-depth talk with his mother on this subject. As far as his own life went, when he had time to look for someone suitable, he would look. But as he told his mother, he refused to settle. He wanted what he wanted. Time would tell as to which direction his life would take.

He was starting to get tired and started getting ready for bed. He had pulled his shirt out of his trousers and had started unbuttoning his shirt, there was a soft knock on his door and the door was being opened slowly. Troy was expecting Penny or Bailey, but Lady Lucy entered wearing a very revealing night gown with no shawl or cover. She came over to him and kissed him. Being male, he could not help having some reaction to what he was seeing and feeling when she took his hands and put them on her body.

He pulled away, surprised, "I'm so sorry, Lady Lucy," he said, turning away from her. "I cannot oblige you with what you are wanting." He was very naïve and was not sure what she wanted. But his body was reacting in ways that surprised him.

"Why?" she asked demurely. "Don't you like what you see?"

"Lady Lucy, that is not the question. You are very beautiful. I can't take advantage of you without the protection of marriage. But marriage is not in my near future. I have too many responsibilities to still learn before I can even think of adding a wife." He picked up a blanket and turned around to help cover her.

'Please," she begged, clinging to him.

"Lady Lucy, please do not lower yourself to this. Please cover yourself and I will walk you back to your room. I will not mention this to anyone and pray you do the same."

She grabbed the blanket from his hands and wrapped it around her. "I can find my own way back to my room. Your assistance is uncalled for." She turned around and stomped out of the room.

Troy sat down on the bed. So much for getting any sleep now. He went back to the chair and picked up the drink he had not finished and downed it. He was not looking forward to the morning and breakfast. He went out on his balcony and sat for a while contemplating what had happened tonight.

He had only been around his mother and sister as far as girls go. There were girl servants but he had never paid them any mind. He was not sure what went on. He was very confused as to what really Lady Lucy was expecting of him. He was going to have to find out what went on before it happened again. He was firally tired enough to retire to bed. He ended up having bad dreams all night.

Chapter 3

*T*roy *was up early the next morning* and was off to check on one of his tenants to the south of the manor who, he had heard, were having some problems. After riding about an hour, he spotted a few small cottages in a group in the distance and made his way there. Some men and children were already in the fields. He dismounted from his horse and went over to talk to the men.

"Good morning," he said to the first and oldest of the men.

The man bowed and said, "Good morning, me lord. What is it we can do for you this early morning?"

"Come with me, Mr. Bloom, and we can have a little talk."

Troy led the way a distance from the field. There were a couple of tree stumps and he sat down on one of them and gestured for Mr. Bloom to sit upon the other.

"I have heard that you are having problems here and I want to help in any way possible. Can you tell me what is going on out here amongst the tenants?"

"Ah, me lord," Mr. Bloom stated looking down at the ground. "We have been having problems with some thieves. Some of our cattle and sheep have been stolen. It'll be that hard for us to pay the rent this time. We were taking some cattle and sheep to market in Leicestershire. Now we don't have enough to pay our rent. We have to save the rest to feed our families or we will starve during the winter."

"Have you a description of the thieves?"

"Nah! They come in the night. We tried to keep watch but they seem to know where we are at all times."

"Have you talked to the sheriff from this region?"

"Yes, but there is little he can do since we don't have any information other than that the cattle and sheep are missing."

"We will organize a watch and see what we can do. As far as the rent goes, don't worry about it. I'm well enough off at the moment and have no need of your money. Is there anything I can do to help you? Are there any needs for you or your family or any friends?"

"Thank you, me lord, we are managing on our own. Would you like to come in and have some breakfast with the family?"

"I would love to spend some time with you and your family. Lead on man, I am famished from the long ride."

Troy let Mr. Bloom lead him to the cottage. He was pleased to see the cleanliness of the outside as well as the inside of the cottage. There were a group of children around the room.

"Are these your children?"

"Yes, and two more are out working the fields. This is my wife, Marmmie."

Marmmie turned around and curtsied and said, "Good day to you, me lord. Please have a seat and I will get the food on the table."

"You are very kind to share with me. Children, come and sit. Your mother is setting a fine table."

The six children looked to range in age from about fourteen to ten. Two of them looked exactly alike and must be twins. They all looked at Lord Bowling and then at their father. Mr. Bloom nodded towards the table and the children sat.

"I don't believe your children are usually so quiet. Let me start with you," he said, motioning to what looked like the youngest. "What is your name, young man?"

The child looked at him with wide fearful eyes.

"Come here," Troy encouraged him. When the child ɪ
picked him up and sat him on his lap. He said softly, "I wis
precious as you."

"Do you have a son?" asked the boy in a timid voice.

"Not yet. I'm not married. But when I do have a child, I hope he or she
will be as precious as you are."

Troy tickled the boy under the chin and got the child to giggle. That
broke the ice and all started talking. Troy kept the youngest on his lap and
let him eat from his tray of food. He spoke to the other children and found
out about each one. Troy had such a wonderful time with the Blooms that
he lost all track of time. It was nearing eight o'clock. He finally realized he
would have to return to the manor. He waved his goodbyes and told Mr.
Bloom he would send help.

He rode back to the manor in thought. Were the robbery attempt and
the stealing from the tenants connected? This was something he was going
to have to look into. He would gather some of his best and most trusted
men and have them start investigating the surrounding areas. Maybe they
will be able to get to the bottom of what was going on. He rounded a curve
in the path through the woods and entered a meadow. He could see the
road in the distance and saw a carriage moving swiftly away from the
manor. He rode on and came to the entrance of the manor.

"Whose carriage was that on the road?" Troy asked.

"Your visitors did not stay long. They had breakfast, packed up, and
left."

Troy chuckled a little. "I wonder if the little escapade from last night
encouraged Lady Lucy to leave quickly."

"An escapade from last night?" questioned Bailey with raised eyebrows.

"Never mind," Troy answered. "It was not important. They are gone
and it's a relief to have our peace back. Where are my mother and sister?"

"I believe Lady Matilda is resting in her room and Lady Penelope is in
the library. Is there anything I can do for you at the moment?"

"Yes, there is. Find Matlock and have him gather up about ten of the most trusted men at the manor and have them meet me in an hour by the outbuilding."

"Will do, my lord." Bailey bowed and turned and left the foyer.

Troy went to the library. He found Penelope reading a book. He went to her and kissed her.

"There is my favorite sister," he said.

"I'm your only sister," she replied laughing.

"But still my favorite." Troy took a seat on the settee across from Penelope. "Did you say something to Lady Lucy this morning?"

"I have not seen Lady Lucy this morning. What did she say and why did they leave so quickly?"

"She made some derogatory remarks concerning you and told her father they were leaving promptly. The Earl was quite taken aback and kept telling her she was being rude. She didn't care. She wanted to leave as soon as possible."

"I have no idea what was going on with Lady Lucy. I do have some questions for you though. There is an area of human behavior that I am quite unfamiliar with and maybe you can shed some light on it for me."

"Sounds intriguing, does it have to do with Lady Lucy?"

"Maybe a little as she is a girl. What I'm concerned about is how girls think. For instance, it has been brought to my attention that you are about to turn eighteen and that is apparently the age to start looking for a husband for you. How do you feel about that?"

Troy was thinking of the way Lady Lucy was acting last night and was hoping Penelope would never act that way. He couldn't tell Penelope about what had happened. He was so uncertain as to how girls acted and he had no father to talk about this.

"For one thing, I'm not sure I should be talking to you about such a subject. It is quite a private subject that I do not know if I can talk to you as a male. I know that you are my brother, but some things are too delicate to discuss between boys and girls and this is one of them."

"I understand, but I am very limited in my knowledge of girls and how they work. I only have you and mother as examples and I consider the love I have for you both as something natural. I guess I am wondering about the feelings between a man and a woman. Like the love between mother and father."

"You are really getting into a very delicate area. As a girl, or soon-to-be woman, I don't really know myself. I haven't explored that part of life as of yet."

"You haven't had any notion of any of the gentry from the area?"

"Good heavens no, they are all boys I grew up with and played games with. I could never think of any of them seriously. Maybe I still need to grow up."

"Well, how would you like to make you debut in London next season?"

"Are you serious?" she asked excitedly.

"Mother mentioned it to me and I think it's an excellent idea."

Penny jumped up and hugged and kissed Troy. "I would love to go to London. When are we going?"

"You will have to talk to mother about that and maybe help her make all the plans. There will be a lot to do."

Penelope went straight up to their mother's room, skipping all the way. *Maybe she does have to grow up a little,* Troy laughed.

He was still confused about the ways between a man and a woman. He was very sure of himself as far as handling things for the household and financials but when it came to men and women he was totally confused. It appeared Penny was too. He was embarrassed that he reacted to Lady Lucy last night, but he also knew instinctively that he could not do as she wanted. He knew that would be the wrong thing to do. So now he was more confused than ever. He felt embarrassed to talk to his mother and was hoping his sister could give him some insight into the female complexities. He was wrong. She was younger than him and had just as much to learn as he did. He just knew he wanted to learn more about relationships and how he should go about nourishing them. He felt he would just have to explore like Penny would need to when they went to London.

He walked out to the outbuilding to talk with the men gathered around. As he approached the men, he spotted someone loitering close by. It was a new employee he did not recognize. He went to Matlock and asked him about the person. Matlock went out to drag the man by the neck back in front of Troy.

"Why were you hiding outside beside the window opening? It looked like you were trying to eavesdrop on our conversation."

"No, your Lordship," the man took off his hat and kept his eyes down. "I was just looking for something to do."

"You know you are supposed to go back to the servants' quarters when you complete your chores and wait to be assigned again," replied Matlock.

"Yes sir, I will go right now." He took off running in the wrong direction.

"I would keep a close eye on that one. I know he is new and might not know where everything is but that was strange behavior."

"Yes, my lord. I agree."

Troy gathered the group together. "What I am about to say has to be kept in the strictest confidence. You can tell no one else. Otherwise it would be impossible for us to get to the bottom of what is going on." He went on to tell the group about the problems happening in the area. "Matlock will be in charge of organizing you into groups and you will be watching over the tenants, investigating what has been happening and hopefully will find the culprits. Work together and maybe we can help the community rid itself of this unwanted element."

All the men agreed and Matlock started to organize them into smaller groups. Troy left and knew he had picked the right person for the job.

Troy was working in his office when word came to him that his mother wished to speak to him. He finished what he was working on and went down to his mother's rooms. She had a suite of rooms. Her sitting room was separate from her bedroom. She also had a wash room behind her walk-in closet. He knocked and was told to enter.

"Good morning, Mother," he said walking over to her as she sat on the settee. He bent and gave her a kiss. She patted the place beside her to indicate for him to sit. He sat and took her hand. "What is it I can do for you, Mother?"

"Penny came to see me this morning. Penny is in need of a personal maid. Until now she had been fine without one, living in the country there has been no reason for her to have one. However, she is old enough to need a lady's maid and since we will be going to London, it will be a necessity."

"Another thing I must worry about! Where would I even start looking for a lady's maid? I would not know what to look for. If I can find some women who want to be a lady's maid, will you help me find the right one?"

"You can advertise in the newspaper and of course I would not expect you to pick someone. Just get some women for us to interview and leave the rest up to me and Penny. Now since you have sent Penny to me concerning London, there is so much I have to do. She wants to leave yesterday," she laughed. "I will have to teach her the art of patience."

"You are the perfect person to teach her," he said and decided to broach the subject that had been bothering him. "Mother, may I speak to you about something that has been confusing me? I'm not going to go into details but I am curious about something."

"Of course you can talk to me. I don't think there is any subject we can't talk about."

"This is of a very delicate nature and I do not want to go into it very far. I'm sorry but it is terribly embarrassing. I had an experience with a woman wanting something from me and I am not sure all women are like this. It is so hard to know because I have no one to talk to about such things. I am embarrassed to be talking to you but am hoping you can enlighten me just a little. I'm very afraid Penny could be like this and I am hoping she will not be."

"Your father thought he had lots of time to tell you about men and women, so unfortunately he never broached the subject with you. With both men and women, you get to an age where feelings become very intense. The trick is controlling them. We women must just say, "No" and control ourselves. Men are a little different. Your father told me it is much harder for you to say, "no" but it's not impossible. And men have a tendency to show when they are excited which can be very embarrassing to them. I still remember when your Father courted me. Emotions can get out of hand and neither the man nor woman understands completely what is going on. Women only have their feelings and most times a woman has a hard time realizing what she is feeling. Your father did say a dunk into a cold river would help when a certain part of his anatomy would show up at an inopportune moment," she laughed. "What is important in life is being honest and respectful of others. Treat women with respect and you should have no problems. Remember it is just as hard for them to say no as it is for you. When you find your mate, you will enjoy a lifetime together. Love her and respect her and you will be fine. It will become natural as long as you love each other. I do hope you find that love."

"But how will I know? I know nothing of love or how it feels. I saw you and Father looking at each other as if there was no one else around. I saw you give small kisses and were always holding hands when you were together. There appeared such a closeness to the two of you. I want that but don't know how to get it."

"My dear, if it is meant to be, you will find the one and only meant for you. I do know that it is important for you to have the heir to keep the family going and I only hope it will not take too long for you to find your mate. I only hope that you will find your one true love."

"Thank you Mother, for helping me." He kissed her on the cheek again.

She placed her hand on his cheek. "Oh Troy, you had to grow up so fast. I'm so sorry all or this has fallen on you. But do not worry; I will continue to do my duty towards both my children."

Troy got up and bowed to his mother and kissed her on the forehead. "As usual, you have helped me tremendously."

He turned and walked from the room. He didn't drink very often but right now he wanted a drink and wanted to think about some of what his mother told him. He went to the library to see if it was empty. It was. He strode over to the cabinet and pored himself a bourbon on the rocks and sat down behind the desk. He turned the chair to look out the window.

So according to his mother, it is not unusual for women and men to have strong feelings. That is probably good for him to know. That explains why he had a strong reaction to Lady Lucy the other night and it probably explains why she came to his room in that manner. However, she has not learned to control her feelings as of yet. Knowing how he felt, he was able to understand. It was really good to know he could jump into a cold river and help himself if that ever happens again. So he was beginning to understand a little about this thing between men and women. But with so much going on right now, he didn't have time to dwell on this issue. He felt good he had some understanding for future reference.

Chapter 4

*T*roy went in search of Mr. Blake again. They had a small office behind the library they used sometimes. He found him in the downstairs office; Troy informed him that he wanted to advertise for a lady's maid. Mr. Blake said he could do that for him. He took the information and went about completing the task. Troy turned and went back to the library.

Just then, he saw Matlock ride up to the manor. He got up and went to open the front door before the butler could get there. He stepped outside.

"You are in a hurry, Matlock. Have you learned something?"

"Not yet, my lord." he said dismounting. "But I heard we may have a problem over by the woods to the east. Someone heard some screaming. We must hurry to see what is going on," he jumped on his horse and waited for Troy to get his horse and follow.

Troy followed as fast as he could. The Castle of Battingham was centrally located within the five hundred acres owned by Lord Bowling however, the ride still took them an hour and a half to reach the area even riding their horses at full force.

They reached a clearing within the woods. Troy was aghast at what he saw. A woman was tied to a tree screaming and five men were surrounding her, one on a horse and four on foot. She was trying to get loose. The men dancing around the woman were tugging at her clothing. Her breasts were almost exposed with her bodice nearly completed torn. When they heard the horses of Troy and Matlock, the men on the ground jumped on their horses and all five rode off in different directions. Troy jumped off his horse and went to the woman. Matlock took off after one of the riders.

Troy started to untie the woman. He got her away from the tree and tried to hold her so she would not fall.

"Take your hands off me!" she screamed.

"I am just trying to make sure you are alright," Troy answered and was trying to cover her up.

"How dare you assume I could not take care of myself," she ranted. "Just because I'm a woman you assume I need your help to get out of trouble."

Troy was trying to be patient with her. "Madam, I assure you whether you are female or male, I would try to ensure you aren't hurt. I would have helped any man just as easily as I am trying to help you!"

"Oh!" she slapped his face, stomped her foot, and turned around.

She turned so fast she swooned and fell into Troy's arms as he rushed to catch her. She had fainted. He took a quick glance at her and thought she was the most beautiful woman he had ever seen. She was tall and well formed. She had ash blonde hair with a darker complexion. Her skin was the color of gold. He didn't get to see her eyes of yet, but she was definitely the most beautiful woman he had ever seen. He grabbed a blanket off the horse and covered her in his arms.

Just then Matlock returned. "Sorry, my lord, I lost him."

"That's okay for now. Help me get this woman up onto my horse with me and you can go get some of the men working for you and try to retrace the riders' tracks and see where they went."

"Yes, my lord."

Troy got onto his horse and Matlock handed him the woman. Both rode off towards the manor. When they arrived, Matlock jumped off his horse to help Troy dismount with the woman. Troy took her into the manor house and straight into the drawing room. Lady Matilda and Penny were both there.

"My dear Troy! What in the world are you doing with that woman?" Lady Matilda exclaimed.

"Help me, Mother," he said as he laid her on the settee.

Matilda jumped up and rang for the housekeeper. Mrs. Trumble came as soon as she heard the bell.

"Go get Sarah and have her prepare the room next to Penny's."

Mrs. Trumble left immediately. Penny went over to the woman on the settee.

"Explain yourself, Troy," Lady Matilda demanded.

"Matlock came to get me. Someone had heard some screams from the woods to the east. When we arrived, this woman was tied to a tree and four men were on foot surrounding her. One man was on a horse. When they heard us, they took off. I went to help the woman and Matlock tried to follow one of the men on horseback. When I untied her, she turned on me for helping her then she just fainted, I think. I don't know if she fainted or there is something wrong with her. I got her back here as soon as possible. Shouldn't we call the doctor?"

"Let's get her upstairs and then we will call the doctor," Penny replied.

Troy picked up the woman and took her to the room indicated. Then he left to have the doctor sent for. Lady Matilda and Penny took care of the woman and prepared her for bed. They removed the woman's torn clothing and placed a new gown on her and covered her up. The woman started waking up. She groaned and tossed around and finally opened her eyes. She tried to sit up but couldn't make it.

"Where am I?" she asked in a terrified voice.

"You are at the Battingham Castle," Lady Matilda answered from across the room. "And who might you be? My son says he rescued you from a band of men who had you tied to a tree."

The woman started crying. "I have no idea who I am. I have no idea how those men caught me and tied me to the tree. I woke up when those men took me to the clearing. I must have been in and out because I only remember bits and pieces. Then those two men came rushing into the clearing and one of them untied me from the tree," she sobbed.

"You don't have any memory of who you are or where you are from?" asked Penny incredulously.

"No, I don't. I have no idea at this moment. Maybe it will come back to me, I hope." She lay back on the bed. "Maybe if I get some rest." She started crying again and hid her face in the covers.

"Mother, you go back to the drawing room and wait for the doctor with Troy. I will stay here with this woman," Penny said. "She does need to rest until the doctor gets here."

"Alright, Penny, but ring if you need anything."

Lady Matilda waited with Troy in the drawing room however she did not inform him that the woman woke up and claimed to have no memory. She was a little skeptical of that idea. Someone who finds themselves in the Battingham Castle may just want their memory lost. However, her tears and the terrified expression on her face did seem genuine and Lady Matilda was moved by them.

When the doctor arrived, Matilda took the doctor up to the room. She stayed in the room while the doctor examined the woman.

"How do you feel, my dear?" asked the doctor of the patient.

She looked so disoriented. "I believe I'm feeling better," she said. "But I can't remember anything." Tears filled her eyes.

The doctor gave her a sedative. After the examination, Lady Matilda met with the doctor out in the hall.

"I can't seem to find any bump on her head that could cause amnesia," the doctor reported. "However, it could be caused by trauma. It doesn't necessarily have to show up in a physical manner. It could be in her mind. A trauma can be just as devastating and cause amnesia as by a physical event. We don't know what happened and so we don't know the cause."

"Can she be faking it?" Lady Matilda asked.

"Of course she can. But time will tell whether she is faking or not. If she is faking, she will make a mistake sometime, somewhere. For right now, I gave her a sedative so let her get lots of rest and I will be back in a few days to check on her."

"Thank you, doctor. I'll walk you to the door."

Once the doctor was gone, Lady Matilda went into the drawing room to be with Troy and Penny.

"What did he say?" questioned Penny.

"He can't find any sign of a bump on the head or anything. However, he says that she could have had a tormenting experience and that is why she can't remember."

"What do you think, Mother?" Troy was looking at her.

"I think time will tell whether she is faking or not. She appears to be sincere but we will have to wait and see," replied Lady Matilda. "May I have a sherry, Troy?"

"Oh, you two are so skeptical. That poor woman was attacked by five men and you mistrust her! I'm going up to sit with her." Penny turned and ran from the room.

"So you don't trust that this woman really can't remember?" Troy asked.

"Let me put it to you this way, if you were a servant and found out you were brought to Battingham Castle, what would you do? I might be very wrong. Her clothing was of quality fabric, not of what a servant would be wearing, but I feel we need to be very cautious. We just have to watch her for a while. Get her well and send her on her way."

"But if she really can't remember, where would we send her?"

"We will just have to wait and see what happens in the future. Like I said, she could be truly traumatized and does not know who she is. Time will tell."

"Let's hope and also hope no harm will be done in the meantime. I'm going to go see if Matlock has returned." Troy left the room.

Penny was sitting with the woman. She was sleeping when all of a sudden she screamed and thrashed around. Penny jumped and ran to sit on the side of the bed. Troy had heard the scream in the downstairs hallway and took the stairs two at time getting to the room as fast as he could. He threw the door open.

"What happened?" he shouted as he took in the sleeping figure in the bed and his sister sitting beside her.

"She must have had a bad dream. She just let out an appalling scream in her sleep. She is still sleeping but she appears to be taunted by dreams. Can you sit with her while I go and get her some hot tea? I won't be long."

"I'll stay but do hurry. It is not proper for me to be here alone with her."

Penny kissed him on the cheek and ran from the room, leaving the door open. Troy was looking at the woman. She truly was a beautiful creature. He had never seen anyone quite so beautiful, except for his mother and sister. The woman started stirring again. She started thrashing around. Troy became concerned she would hurt herself so he sat on the side of the bed and tried to hold her. He brushed some hair from her face and she seemed to relax at his touch. He picked up her hand and was rubbing it with his thumb and she went into a deeper relaxed sleep. He started having some of those feelings he had felt with Lady Lucy, which was ridiculous since this woman was completely covered. But he had to admit he was having some stirrings of some emotions. Penny returned just then. She put the tea by the bedside.

"She seems to be relaxing more now."

"What did you do to get her to relax?" Penny asked.

"I just sat here with her," Troy answered. He did not want to admit he had touched her. "I will leave you alone with her. Let me know if you need anything." He gave Penny a kiss on the cheek and left.

Troy went to his room and tried to relax himself. His mind kept wondering back to the mysterious lady. He was not sure what to think of his own reaction to her. He couldn't get her out of his mind. She was like a whisper of a ghost that was always there in the back of his mind. He went down to have dinner with his mother. After dinner, he went looking for Matlock. He found him in the stables.

"Did you have any success on your mission?"

"No, my lord," Matlock answered. "There were horse tracks but they did not lead anywhere. They mainly went around in circles. These bandits are inventive. And I am not sure I picked up the right tracks. The area is heavily traveled."

"I'm sure," said Troy thinking of the area and knowing it was close to a road. "One of these days we will catch a lead and perhaps start finding out some clues as to who these bandits are. In the meantime, we must keep trying."

They didn't notice, but just outside the door a man stood listening and smiling at what he had heard. His boss was indeed smart. He walked away confident that the gang he was with was a good one. But his boss wanted information on the woman and as of yet he had heard no mention of her. He was sure she was in the castle, but that was all he was sure of. That would be all he would be able to report back. He went to the grub house for some dinner. He would go tonight and meet his boss and give him a report on what he heard.

Troy walked back to the manor after talking to Matlock. He was frustrated that no signs have been found as to the culprits. This was a time for patience, but his patience was getting thin. He had no idea of any other line of action. They would just have to continue searching until they found something. He went to his office and tried to do some work. He was not successful. There was too much on his mind at the moment. He went downstairs and stopped at the door to the mysterious woman's chambers. He knocked and Penny told him to come in.

"She is still sleeping," Penny announced. "The doctor must have given her a strong sedative for her to sleep so long." Penny yawned.

"You are tired," Troy said putting his hands on her shoulders and rubbing them. "Did you have some dinner?"

Penny shook her head no and patted his hands.

"If there would be a way I could stay with her, I would and let you get some dinner and rest."

Penny looked up to him, "We could have Sarah stay here with the two of you to chaperone," she suggested. "That way there would be no impropriety."

"If you feel that would work, then by all means, please call Sarah and have her stay here with the two of us."

Penny pulled the cord to ring for a servant. Sarah answered the call. Penny explained to her what was needed of her and she agreed to stay. Penny went over and kissed Troy on the top of his head.

"You are so good. I love you so much," she said and slipped out of the room.

Neither one noticed that the woman had started waking up and heard what Penny had said. *So these two were lovers,* she thought. *So be it. He is very handsome and the woman who had just left is a very lucky woman indeed.* She fell back into a deep sleep.

Troy sat watching the woman and wondered about her for quite some time. Then he started dozing off. Very early in the morning, the woman awoke and just laid there watching him. As if he could sense her looks, he woke up himself. He looked at her and saw her eyes were open. They were the color of golden sunshine. They were beautiful.

"Good morning, ma'am," he said.

"Good morning," she replied. "I do want to thank you for saving me yesterday. But I'm at a disadvantage and have no idea who I'm speaking with."

Troy chuckled, "Yes that is quite a disadvantage. Let me introduce myself. I am Troy Bowling the Earl of Battingham. And you are?"

"I don't know," she seemed surprised. "My mind is blank and I have no memory of anything except what happened yesterday."

"Exactly what happened yesterday?" Troy asked.

"All I remember is that I woke off and on until reaching the clearing and the men tied me to that tree. Those awful men were surrounding me, pulling at my clothes, and making taunts at me. Then you came and rescued me. But before that I have no memory." She blushed at the memory of what she said to him and what she looked like when he rescued her.

Troy also made no mention of what she had said to him upon being rescued or what he apprised of her exposure. "The doctor examined you yesterday and found no bumps or bruises on your head, so it is strange that you were not awake before being tied to the tree. And that you have no memory of the events leading to that?"

She was trying to sit up and then realized the situation. "Oh, I'm here alone with you? I am completely ashamed." She pulled the covers up to her neck.

"No, we are not alone. A maid, Sarah, is watching us. We made sure no improprieties were committed to your honor."

"Thank you," she said weakly.

"Are you hungry or thirsty? I can have some nourishment sent up for you."

"Thank you, I am a little hungry and thirsty."

"I will go down to the kitchen while Sarah finds you some suitable garments to wear and we will have a simple breakfast, if that is alright with you."

"That would be fine with me, your Lordship."

Troy stood up and bowed to her, spoke to Sarah, and left the room. Troy went to the kitchen, found Marple, and asked for some breakfast to be brought to the room of the mysterious woman. Then he went to his room and freshened up. Sleeping in a chair was not conducive to looking one's best. His clothes were all rumpled and he felt unkempt. He felt so much better after cleaning up. He then went back to the mysterious woman's chambers.

Chapter 5

*T*roy *knocked on the door.* He was surprised to hear Penny's voice tell him to enter. Penny and the woman were seated at a table by the window in front of the balcony leading from the chambers. His breath caught in his throat when he saw the vision of the woman sitting demurely at the table. She was dressed in a day dress of Penny's. It was a light blue with a low neckline showing her cleavage. It had short sleeves and hung straight from an empire waist. He forced himself not to react and went to Penny and gave her a kiss on the cheek.

"Good morning, love," he said. "Is it alright for me to join you two lovely ladies?"

"Of course, silly," Penny replied. "You sent up more than enough food so please join us."

"We do have a few things to discuss with this enticing woman sitting with us," Troy commented.

"Please do not act like I am not in the room," said the woman. "I do understand my predicament and am not happy with the situation." She gave Troy a testy look.

Penny laughed. "Oooh, I think you have met your match. I'm going to enjoy this."

Troy gave his sister a heated look. He did not like the woman's ungrateful attitude. "I was not trying to imply that you were absent. However, we don't even know what to call you," he said, staring at the woman.

"Do you have any idea what your name is?" Penny asked sweetly.

"I don't have any memory of my name, but somewhere I do remember the name Aspen. Whether that is my name or not, I don't recall."

"Then we shall call you Aspen. At least until we know for sure what your real name is," Penny replied.

"Then Aspen it is," commented Troy. He loved the sound of that name. It fit the picture of the woman.

"We have other things to think about also," Penny replied. "We are going to have to find you a wardrobe. You cannot continuously stay dressed in my clothing, although I don't mind sharing until we find out who you are."

Aspen blushed. "Definitely not. But I don't know where to start. I don't know anything."

She looked so forlorn, Troy's heart melted. He was trying to keep himself apart from the situation but was being pulled in with his too soft heart. He would have to distance himself more from the situation.

"Why don't we enjoy this wonderful meal and work out the details later," he said softer than he wanted to.

"That's a wonderful idea," Penny said as she patted Aspen's hand. "I will help you with whatever you will need. Don't worry."

They finished their meal and Troy took his leave. He kissed Penny on the cheek and bowed to Aspen.

"Your beau or husband seems a little testy this morning. However, it could be my fault since he slept in the chair all night."

Penny laughed. "Oh Troy is not my beau or my husband! He's my brother. He really is quite sweet most of the time."

They started talking together.

Troy went to his mother's chambers. He knocked on the door and was allowed in. He went over and kissed his mother on her cheek.

"I hope you had a good night's rest."

"I did and I hear yours was not as comfortable as mine." She looked at him understatedly.

"I see word has gotten around as to where I spent the night. I only sent Penny off to get some dinner and a good night's sleep. Sarah stayed in the room with me all night so no improprieties were committed."

"That was good thinking on someone's part. You don't want to be put into an unseemly situation. You must protect your own reputation as well as the woman's."

"I understood that and Penny suggested Sarah stay in the room with us all night. So no one can say I was a cad."

"It would be hard to see you as a cad. You are a sweet, dear boy. Sometimes too sweet or soft for your own good."

"I know my faults, Mother. We have found a name for the woman. She says she has a vague memory of the name Aspen but is not sure that is her name. We have started calling her by the name of Aspen. However, it appears that is not the only problem. Penny has realized that Aspen also needs a wardrobe if not many other things. That is quite out of my league so I will leave all of that to you and Penny."

"Yes, I see the predicament. Penny and I can handle that part. You don't have to worry about any of that."

"Thank you. That is a load off my mind. I do have some work to do, so I will leave you for now." He stood and went to give his mother a kiss on the forehead. "I will see you later." He turned and left. He went up to his office and started going through the books again. This time he made himself concentrate on what he was doing.

Lady Matilda finished her breakfast, called her maid to help her get dressed for the day, and headed towards Aspen's chambers. She found Penny and Aspen talking and laughing. Penny jumped up at seeing Lady Matilda and ran to her and gave her a big kiss on the cheek.

"Please come and join us Mother," Penny said as she took Lady Matilda's hand and lead her to a seat by the table.

Aspen stood up and curtsied to Lady Matilda.

Lady Matilda nodded towards Aspen and sat down. "Well, I hear you have a name now. Aspen is it?"

"Yes, my lady. The name is familiar to me but I'm not sure it is my name. However, it will do for now until I can recover my memory."

"I am Lady Matilda. Yes, that is a very pretty and unusual name," stated Lady Matilda.

"I don't know how unusual it is. It sounded vaguely familiar. I do want to thank you for all you have and are doing for me," answered Aspen.

"You are in dire straits and are in need of our help right now. Maybe your name will help us find out some information concerning you, since it is so unusual," Lady Matilda replied.

"That would be wonderful. I don't like not remembering anything," said Aspen with a genuine look of fretfulness.

"Well it appears that we have a few other problems to sort through first," Lady Matilda said.

"You talked to Troy, Mother, didn't you?"

"Yes, my dear. Troy came to see me after he left you and Aspen this morning."

"Aspen and I have been talking and we have come up with an excellent idea until we resolve all the problems surrounding Aspen," Penny started. "You know you wanted to search for a lady's maid for me. Well Aspen has agreed to be my lady's maid."

"That is interesting," said Lady Matilda. "How do we know you have the qualifications for being a lady's maid? How do we know that you are not a lady yourself? Your destroyed clothing was made of rather rich material."

"I don't know that I am familiar with all that being a lady's maid entails but if there is something I don't know, I'm sure I can learn. As far as being a lady myself, I don't know about my clothing as I have no memory of anything. I have no idea who or what I am or where I came from so for the time being I would consider it an honor to help out in any way possible. I do appreciate all you are doing for me and want to repay you in any way."

"That is very commendable." Lady Matilda started seeing the woman in a slightly different light. Maybe she was telling the truth. "I agree with the arrangement for the time being. However, I'm thinking more in the lines of companion for Penny. Sometimes Penny needs to be reminded she is a lady. I will let you, Penny, take Aspen in hand and make all the arrangements. We also have the seamstress coming today to start our wardrobes for London so we can include some things for Aspen. For now, I will leave you two and go and take care of my daily duties as the lady of the manor. I will see you two later."

Lady Matilda rose and gave Penny a kiss on the cheek. Aspen curtsied again and Lady Matilda left the room. Penny and Aspen started dancing around in joyous anticipation.

Troy was finished with his books for today. He went to look for Matlock. He was so relieved to be done with the all the problems going on within the manor. He saw a carriage come up the lane and saw a woman withdraw from the carriage. Her carriage was filled with boxes of material for the chore of making clothes for the ladies. He assumed it was the seamstress who was due today. He went to the stables where he could not find Matlock. He then went to the outbuilding and could not find Matlock. Lastly, he tried the grub house and found Matlock in conversation with some of the men.

"Have you heard anything yet, Matlock?" Troy asked him.

"I was just talking to some of the men. The man we caught the other day loitering around the outbuilding before the meeting has been leaving and no one knows where he goes. He is doing his work so there is no complaint there. But he does not tell anyone when he leaves and is acting very strange."

"Maybe he has a woman on the side," said Donovan, one of the trusted men.

Matlock and Donovan started laughing as some of the other men gathered around. Troy laughed along even though he did not understand the comment. Troy did not want to act so naïve so he kept his laugh quieter.

"He sure could have," Matlock answered. "But I would really like to follow him and make sure."

The other men left and left Matlock and Troy alone.

"Let's take a walk, Matlock, and have a talk," Troy said.

They walked away from the castle and into the woods surrounding the castle.

"I do think we should have this new man followed to ensure he is not a bandit," Matlock started.

"I agree with your account of the problem. But I would like to ask you a few questions. I am embarrassed by my lack of knowledge but have no one to talk to. I do hope you don't mind me asking you some questions."

"There is nothing you can't ask me, my lord. I know your father passed on before you had a chance to grow up. Ask your questions and I will try to answer them."

"It was the comment Donovan made about this new guy maybe having a woman on the side. What did he mean by that? A wife?"

Matlock chuckled, "No, my lord. Have you not had feelings or stirrings when you look at a woman? Have you not taken notice of some of the pretty servants in the manor house?"

"I have had some stirrings, but I presume these are natural. Mother said Father told her that he used to take a cold dunk in the river when he got those feelings and reactions. I have spent most of my time with other men. The only women I'm used to being around are my mother and sister. I have had very little time to notice the servants in the house."

"Jumping in a cold river does help to hide the bulge you get when you see a pretty girl walk by. But there is not always a river around. Did you not know there are a certain type of women who relieve men of their feelings outside of wedlock?"

Troy turned beat red. "No, I was not aware of such a thing. I have been told you must wait for the right woman and only do your marriage duties together. I had no idea there were such women in this world."

"You have been very sheltered," Matlock replied. "But I will say that the gentry are less likely to use this type woman than the rest of us."

"Do you mean you have been with this type woman outside of wedlock?"

"I will admit nothing. I don't want anything getting back to my wife." Matlock laughed and put his arm around Troy. "Don't worry, my lord. I'm glad I could answer your questions and if I see you in the river, I will understand. And I will not tell anyone about this conversation. If you do need any more help, please just ask me. I can be like a father to you. I can tell you much more about women, when the need to know comes up."

"Thank you, Matlock. It has really helped to have this talk and I feel I'm not so misguided about these matters now. I'm glad I will have someone to talk to."

Troy and Matlock walked back towards the manor. Matlock had his arm around Troy's shoulders and they talked amiably on their way back.

Chapter 6

With everything going on at the manor house, Troy tried to stay far away. It amazed him when he saw Penny and Aspen together. Their arms were always joined together with their heads close and they were usually laughing. He still had stirrings when he saw Aspen and had thought of going to the river several times, but he was able to keep his distance and calm himself. He wanted to be the one to follow the new man when he left the premises but Matlock pointed out that the new man would know immediately who he was, so they picked someone the new man had never seen. They were waiting for reports. They wanted to follow him for long enough to know whether he was honest or a bandit.

Troy was finally in the manor for the whole day. He went to his office and looked through the applications of women wanting to be lady's maids. He put those aside to hand to his mother. He decided in the afternoon to join the women in the drawing room. They were all there. As usual he lost his breath for a second when he saw Aspen. He walked over to his mother and bent to give her a kiss.

"How are you, Mother?" he asked as he went to give Penny a kiss on the forehead and a bow to Aspen. "I brought you some applications for the position of lady's maid."

"Thank you. I will look through these and I am fine, Troy. We have not seen much of you lately."

"I have had a lot of work to do. I have to ensure we have enough money to pay for all of Penny's wardrobe for London." He laughed and Penny gave him a playful scowl. "How have things been going within the manor?"

"Everything has been going along as planned," replied Lady Matilda. "We have set a date for leaving for London. We will leave in three months' time. The house will be open before we arrive but we will have plenty to do to finish the undertaking. Then we will have to start the pre-debutante parties and such. Once we get there it will be a whirlwind of affairs."

"Maybe we will have to sit down sometime, Mother, and you can explain what is involved in a London season. You know as the male of the family all I know is how to keep track of what is going on with our tenants, our financials, and such. I never went for a season in London."

"I do agree dear, you do need an education."

Penny jumped up and grabbed his hands. "Poor Troy, has never been to London." She twirled him around. "I will have to teach you the latest dances. Won't I, Aspen?" She kept twirling Troy around.

"Yes, you will definitely have to teach him to dance," Aspen said, laughing.

Penny stopped in front of the doors going out to the garden. "Oh, let's go out to see the roses and other flowers and trees. The gardeners have done such an excellent job. You haven't seen it yet," she said as she pulled Troy outside. "Come on, Aspen," she called as Aspen held back from following.

Aspen went after them. Penny brought them all to an area with roses and trees with a bench to sit upon. She told Aspen to sit and then made Troy sit.

"I need to go get a shawl. I'm chilly. I'll be right back." Penny ran off toward the manor.

Troy and Aspen were sitting so close he could smell her scent. Troy wanted to bend over and kiss her but knew that was totally wrong. He tried making small talk to her.

"How is it coming with the recovery of your memory?" he asked.

"Why do you ask? Am I not recovering fast enough for you?" Aspen disdained.

Troy was taken aback with her intensity. "I did not mean any such thing, Aspen. I was merely wondering how you are doing."

"Well, why not ask how I am doing rather than inquire about my memory?"

"I don't understand how I got you so upset in just a few minutes. Please try to explain to me how I got us off on the wrong foot."

'Well if you don't know, I can't help you." She rose from the bench and started walking away.

Troy jumped up and grabbed her arm. She twirled around on him.

"Keep your hands off of me," she said forcefully.

"I'm truly sorry and didn't mean any harm. Please Aspen, stay and talk to me," he sat back down and motioned for her to do the same.

She reluctantly returned to her seat.

"I was merely inquiring about how you are doing. I think you are good for Penny. She has only had me and Mother. Your memory is important for you to find where you are from. You may have a family worried sick about you."

"That is true, I had not thought of that. I'm just afraid you don't believe I have lost my memory. Every once in a while, I get a feeling of something familiar but it is fleeting. It doesn't last long and it is sporadic so I can't put any pieces together."

"I'm sorry to hear that, I know you would love to go home to your family."

"Yes, but in the meantime I am having a very good time with Penny. She really is precious and very kind."

"She is very special to me. I won't let anyone or anything hurt her," Troy said.

"I knew you didn't trust me," Aspen exclaimed. She jumped up and ran towards the house and this time Troy didn't try to catch or stop her.

He walked slowly back to the manor house. Lady Matilda was still sitting in the chair by the fireplace and working on some embroidery.

"I guess I just keep putting my foot in my mouth with Aspen." Then he said without thinking, "I think I need to go down to the river," and he left.

Lady Matilda sat there with her eyebrows raised, then she smiled knowingly. This was going to be interesting.

Matlock was riding by the river just as Troy was getting out.

"Lady problems, my lord?" he asked laughing.

"I think I need one of those talks, Matlock. I don't understand anything that is going on," he said.

"With women, very few men can understand them. What seems to be the problem?" he dismounted and went over to Troy.

"Well, for one thing I can never say the right thing. It appears anything I want to say comes out wrong or she takes it the wrong way. Then on the other hand all I can think about is her heavenly scent and I want to pull her into my arms. Only my mouth makes her angry and she keeps storming away from me."

"Well, it could be that time of month which normally makes women get upset easier. Or, true love," Matlock sighed. "It sounds to me that you have been bitten. Once bitten there is nothing for you to do but give in."

"What are you saying, 'I've been bitten'? By what?"

"By the love bug. You are in love, my boy."

"No way. I don't even really know her and she doesn't even know herself. It is the mysterious Aspen. The way she is always so angry with me, how can I be in love with her? She hates me and what are you talking about, 'that time of month'?"

"You don't know about the time of month? You are lacking in your education about women. We will leave that for now. Never tell a woman her anger is because of that time of month. But one mechanism that women use is pretending to be angry. They are angry with the feelings they get when they start getting them for a man."

"My mother mentioned that men and women get such feelings but men show their feelings physically which I have found out. But you mean she might love me back?"

"Too early to know. The game is just beginning." Matlock laughed again. "It will be quite a ride for you my boy. It appears you have a real spitfire."

"I don't believe this is love. If this is what love is about, I don't want any part of it."

Troy got back on his horse after he was finished dressing and rode off. He could hear Matlock still laughing in the distance. He got home just in time for dinner. Penny and Lady Matilda were seated at the dinner table.

"Where is our lovely Aspen?" he inquired.

"Whatever did you say to her, Troy? She was so upset."

"I didn't mean for what I said to be for her. It just came out wrong. It appears I always say the wrong thing to her. My mouth just gets twisted and it comes out wrong," he said exasperated.

"And how was your swim?" Lady Matilda asked ever so innocently.

Just then Troy remembered it was his mother who told him what his father said about the river and he vaguely remembered going through the drawing room muttering about going to the river. He turned beat red.

"I apologize, Mother," he started.

"There is nothing to apologize for, dear. You just went to the river to cool off. The weather is still warm enough."

Penny looked from one to the other confused. She was sure she was missing something. Lady Matilda sat back and smiled through the rest of her dinner. Troy was red-faced the entire meal. Penny was very confused. As soon as he finished eating, Troy excused himself from the table.

"Before you have had dessert, dear?" questioned Lady Matilda.

"Yes, Mother, I have had quite enough," he looked at Penny. "Food that is just enough food."

"Alright dear, but please come to my chambers this evening and we will have that talk we are supposed to have."

Troy nodded on his way out of the dining room.

"Okay, Mother, what was that all about?" Penny asked aggravated.

"Really nothing, my dear. Troy is just beginning to learn some lessons. I think I will retire to my chambers," said Lady Matilda. She rose from the table and went to give Penny a kiss on the top of her head.

"I guess I will have dessert all to myself," she said and then thought better of it. She told the servant who had been serving the meal to send up two desserts to her room.

Cleavus meet with the leader of the gang, Doggon, at a pub in Leicestershire.

"I know she is in the castle but I don't exactly know where. They aren't hiding her. They are treating her like one of the family. But it is difficult to get into the castle. There are too many people going and coming all the time."

"I don't want to give any of that money back for not killing her. We did not complete the job because I was letting you guys have some fun before completion. I will never do that again. We must find a way into the castle to finish the job. I'll think on this. You are doing a good job, my boy. Keep looking for me. We will come up with some way to get her. Here is a little something on the side since you are doing such a good job." Doggon passed a small package over to Cleavus and left the pub.

Chapter 7

When Troy finally went to his mother's chambers, he was again in control of himself. He knocked on the door and heard "Enter."

"Good evening, Mother." He bent to kiss her on the forehead. "I do apologize for dinner. I was rude and did not mean to be."

"I know, my dear. You were embarrassed and I was terrible at teasing you." She poured them some tea. "You see I never saw this part of your father, so I am finding it quite enlightening watching you. You know you look just like your father. I can picture him going through what you are going through now. It is just part of life. I will not show my enjoyment so much anymore."

He sat down beside her and kissed her on the cheek. He laughed with her. They got down to talking about the ways of the season and some of his responsibilities. But she wanted him to remember that this was a good time for him to find a wife also. There would be enough chaperones around to protect Penny so he didn't need to be available all the time. He decided to ask his mother about what Matlock had mentioned to him about time of month.

"Mother, I heard a phrase today and am quite curious. It was 'that time of month'. What time of month and what does that mean between a woman and a man?"

"Oh dear, you are lacking, aren't you? This is one time I wish your father had that talk with you. The one about the birds and the bees."

"What?" Troy asked thoroughly confused.

"It is a saying to talk about how babies are made. I have a book downstairs and will get it for you. It will explain everything. I do feel this is outside my scope of teaching. I am sorry Troy, but I am quite uncomfortable answering these kinds of questions. The book will help you. For tonight, we will let this topic go. Just one word of advice, do not ever accuse a woman of it being 'that time of month' no matter how upset she gets with you and even if it is for no reason."

They talked for about an hour and then Lady Matilda said she was getting tired.

Troy went to his chambers and went onto the balcony. Bailey asked if there was anything he wanted before Bailey himself retired.

"How about a bourbon?" Troy said and continued to sit on the balcony.

He was enjoying the evening and thinking about all that had gone on that day. If this was love, how in the world would he figure it out. His parents never argued, at least not in front of him or Penny. Did his father know about the river because of his mother or some other women? How confusing this all was. Those words "that time of month" appear to be condemning so he would make sure never to say such a thing in front of a woman. As he was contemplating these thoughts, he saw a shadow down in the garden. It was Aspen, he was sure. She seemed to be deep in thought and then she sat down on a bench and put her head in her hands. Her shoulders were moving as if she were crying. He didn't want to disturb her, but he couldn't stand the thought of her crying. He went down and found her.

"It's you," she said looking up. The moonlight showed the wetness of her face and she turned to try to hide her face.

"I don't mean to intrude. I just wanted to apologize to you. I really didn't mean what I said this afternoon to include you. I was thinking of London and all the beaus Penny will be meeting. I can't stand the thought of her getting hurt just to find a husband. It appears that when I'm with you, I say everything I don't mean. I'm truly sorry."

She started crying again, even harder. Out of instinct, Troy pulled her into his arms and held her. He held her until her tears subsided.

"I'm sorry. I am making you all wet."

"That's okay. I'll cry," he said softly. "Let's sit down and talk a little. Can you tell me what's bothering you?"

"I can't tell anyone."

"Yes, you can. I'm here and I promise not to breath a word of what is said here tonight to anyone else." He lifted her chin with his finger.

She looked deep into his eyes. "It is just that I can't stand not knowing who I am or where I belong. I know I have a life out there somewhere, but I have no idea where."

She started crying again and he just held her. After a while, her sobbing subsided and she looked up at him. He couldn't stand it. He bent his head and kissed her on the lips and he felt her return his kiss. All of a sudden, she jumped up and hit him on the face with a really hard slap.

"How dare you," she turned around and ran into the manor and up to her room. She spent the rest of the night crying.

Troy sat for a while wondering what had happened while he rubbed his cheek. He knew he should not have kissed her. Oh, he was going to have to go back to the river if this kept up. Tonight, he decided to just suffer through it. He would have to apologize again. He just couldn't get it right with her. He went to his room and went to bed. He ended up dreaming of Aspen and that delicious kiss they shared.

Early the next morning, Matlock came to the door wanting to see Troy. They left together to go see the tenants on the west side. They were also complaining about some thieves. When they got there the tenants were all gathered together in front of the oldest tenant's cottage. They were talking and they were not happy. Troy dismounted and went to the tenants.

"What is going on?" he asked Senegal.

"They burned down the barn where we collect the harvest of wheat," one man answered.

"The whole barn burned and we lost the whole seasons crop," said Senegal.

"I understand how you feel," said Troy. "Don't worry about the lost crop. We will take care of you. Did anyone see anything before or after this happened?"

"Nah," Senegal replied. "We were all asleep in our cottages. Someone smelled smoke and raised the cry."

Matlock was standing beside Troy. "We need help catching the culprits who have been doing all this damage. They are getting away with too much. If someone knows anything or anyone sees anything, please come to us and help us catch these bandits."

Troy added, "They must be close by because it appears they are targeting just this district. I am offering a reward of one hundred pounds to anyone who can help us catch the band of thieves."

Matlock looked at Troy and said under his breath, "Are you sure about this, my lord?"

"I will take care of my tenants," he said to Matlock. He turned to the tenants and said, "Let me know what you need to keep your families in the manner they are used to. I don't want anyone to go hungry. Please come see me if you need anything. And anyone who can help us catch this band will get the reward."

All the men came up and shook Troy's hand.

"If I'm not at the manor, Matlock here will help you and I will inform my assistant to give Matlock anything you will need."

The men also shook Matlock's hand and disbursed from the group. Mr. Senegal was the last to come up to them.

"Thank you, me lord. I am very thankful we have you for our landlord. I knew your father and you are just like him, kind and generous."

"Thank you. Senegal. That means a lot to me." Troy shook his hand and they mounted their horses and went back to the manor.

When they returned to the manor house, Troy went into the dining room to see if anyone was still there. Penny was still sitting at the table.

"There you are brother."

"Yes," he said as he went to her and gave her a kiss on the top of her head. "Where is everyone?"

"Mother finished her breakfast and went to see Mrs. Trundle. For some reason, Aspen has insisted on eating in the kitchen with the help. She says that is her place in this household. Do you know anything about this, dear brother?"

"I'm not sure I had anything to do with that. I saw Aspen in the garden last night and she was crying so I went to comfort her. She confided in me which I promised not to repeat to anyone. So if you want to know more, you will have to ask her."

"I heard her in her room last night crying. This morning it looked like she cried all night. I will have to see what is wrong and why she is so unhappy. You don't have much luck with women, dear brother," she looked at him. "First something happened with Lady Lucy and now with Aspen. Please hurry up and find a wife instead of hurting them and making them want to cry."

"I know I haven't been the best towards women so far but dear sister, your turn is coming up soon. There is a lot more to relationships that you still do not know about. I am doing what I feel is proper. Yes, I have made mistakes, but not all are my fault."

Penny rose from the table and came to him. She bent down and gave him a kiss on the forehead. "You are still my favorite brother and the best man around here."

She smiled at him and left the room.

Troy ate his breakfast and then went to his office. He passed Donald Blake's office and asked him to come join him in his own office.

When Donald came in, Troy said, "Please, sit down. We have some things to discuss."

Donald took a chair across from Troy who was behind his desk.

"I haven't informed you yet but there have been some incidents among the tenants. The tenants to the south have had some cattle and sheep stolen. The ones they were going to sell to pay their rent. Then there was a woman we found bound to a tree by the rogues. Today I had to ride to the west because of another incident. They had all their harvest in their barn and someone burned down the barn, so they will not be able to pay their rent."

Mr. Blake looked thunderstruck, "My Lord, this is terrible. Where is the woman now? How are we going to handle these incidents?"

"That is what I want to talk to you about. The woman is staying with us. She had a traumatic occurrence and has lost her memory. I have put out a reward for one hundred pounds for anyone who can give us information to catch these rogues. Also, I have told the tenants not to worry about their rents this time and to come here for any help they need. They are to come to Matlock who will come to you. I don't want anyone to go hungry because of what others have done to them. We need to make sure a new barn is constructed for the tenants to the west. They are all hard-working men, women, and children. They should not suffer."

"I agree wholeheartedly with everything you have decided," said Mr. Blake. "I will help Matlock with whomever comes here looking for help. I'm glad you have amassed such a large bank account since you have taken over from your father. You have increased your wealth tenfold since you have been in charge. This will help the tenants tremendously and not really hurt your finances."

"One thing my father taught me well was how to invest our money to increase it. I'm very thankful to him for those lessons."

Mr. Blake stood up and said he was going back to his office to set aside the money needed for the tenants and the reward.

Troy stood up and shook his hand. "Thank you for all of your help, Donald."

Troy worked for a little while and then decided to go to his room and rest. He saw Aspen in the hallway, but she darted into her room when she saw him. He went into his room and tried to relax for a while. He found a book on his bedside table. He figured it was the one his mother wanted him to read. He sat and read it. He was very knowledgeable after that and was very thankful his mother told him to read the book.

The house was turning into a turmoil with the preparations for moving to London. One day Lady Matilda decided to rest in her chambers all day and did not come down for meals.

Troy looked at Penny across the table and said, "I have an idea about Miss Aspen."

He told her his plan and she clapped her hands in excitement. They both got up from the table and took their plates and silverware and went into the kitchen. They saw Aspen sitting at a table and sat down beside her.

"What is all this about?" she asked startled.

Troy looked at her. "You are as much family as we are. So if you insist on eating in the kitchen, then we will too."

"Oh, but…" she started.

"No buts," Penny said. "If you want to eat here, then we will also. If you want to join us in the dining room then we shall eat there."

Aspen looked at the two of them and said exasperated, "Fine! we will go to the dining room. I can't be responsible for you eating in the kitchen with the help. But I will still pursue what I feel is my duty and will keep a low doppelganger." She stood up with her plate and silverware and marched to the dining room with as much dignity she could muster.

Penny and Troy followed her laughing.

When they arrived in the dining room and sat back down, Penny looked at Aspen and said, "By the way, what is a doppel-whatever?"

Aspen replied, "It is a minor image, which means someone behind someone else."

"Where did you learn such a word?" asked Troy.

"I don't know," Aspen looked confused. "It just popped into my head. I have no idea where it came from."

After that, Aspen ate in the dining room with the family.

Cleavus met with Doggon again at the pub.

"I think I'm being followed," he said.

"We will have to make sure they do not find out about me. I will keep a look out when we leave tonight and watch to see if they start following me. Have you found out anything?'

"No. I saw the woman in the garden one night by herself. I thought of trying to kidnap her but then Lord of Bowling came out and joined her. I couldn't do anything."

"I understand. We don't want to be caught. Here is another little something for you. Keep up the good work." Doggon stood and left the pub.

Chapter 8

*T*roy *had a lot of work to do* in preparing for the move to London. He had to hire some wagons to take their necessities to London. The servants who were going were going with the wagons a couple of days ahead of the family. They would arrive at the London house and prepare it's opening so the family will have a decent place to stay upon their arrival. Troy was worried about the highwaymen so he also hired two large assemblages of guards, one to travel with the servants and one to travel with the family. Troy didn't want any problems with any of the bandits. He wanted everyone to arrive safely.

Troy was going to his room from his office one day. He saw Lady Matilda in the hallway.

"Mother, how are you doing?" he asked as he kissed her cheek.

"I am really doing fine, Troy. We are nearly packed and ready for the first to leave in about two weeks."

"I have all the wagons and guards ready to go whenever you say. But I am worried about you. Please take it easy and don't overdo it. Promise me?"

"Oh, my dearest son. Thank you for worrying about me," she patted him on the cheek. "I'm really in my element with all of this. It has been so long since we went to London for the season. I'm excited to see my old friends. But I promise I will not overdo anything. I will rest when needed."

"Thank you, Mother. I love you too much to lose you also." He bent down to give her another, longer, kiss on the cheek.

She smiled at him and walked away. He continued onto his room. He strode over to the balcony and sat out there for a while. He was watching the garden when he saw Aspen walking out in the garden again. This time in daylight. He decided to go and have a talk with her. It was ridiculous that she was hiding form him all the time. He went down and found her sitting on a bench among the roses.

"It is fitting to see you among the roses," he said to her. "You are as beautiful as a rose."

She was startled and turned to face him.

"I'm sorry I must return to my duties," she said getting up from the bench.

He stood in her way. "Please don't leave until you hear what I have to say. I want to apologize for the other night. I had no right to kiss you. You just looked so beautiful. I couldn't resist. But it was wrong and will not happen again. I do hope you will accept my apology."

"My Lord, I'm a servant in your home. I have no right to expect more than any other servant. I will keep my place in the hierarchy of household. Please don't expect anything more from me."

"But until we find out about you, you are one of our family. You are only helping my sister. You are not a servant."

"I'm sorry, my lord. For the whole time I'm a resident in your home, I will repay your kindness by serving wherever I am useful. Your sister appears to approve of my being her companion and I shall perform those duties to the best of my ability. If you will please excuse me, I do have some duties to attend to." She turned and walked away.

Troy was beside himself with worry about Aspen. She seemed so disheartened. He admitted to himself that he was in love with her. But the circumstance of her situation was interfering with his life. He decided to find someone in London to help investigate Aspen's background. The doctor thought it strange that she did not have any recollection of her past yet.

He could only figure that the trauma had to have been severe for her to still not remember anything about her past. Troy was certain that they would find out that Aspen was truly a lady and if she wasn't then it would not matter, he would court her no matter what her background turned out to be. He planned to talk to his mother about this and to make Aspen a lady within their family.

Troy was too distraught to go back to his room. He went to his office instead. Matlock was waiting for him.

"I have a report on Cleavus Ficher," he said. "The new employee whom we have been tracking."

"Come in and have a seat, Matlock. Continue with the report. I hope we have some good information to catch the gang of bandits."

"In a way, yes, my lord, we do. He was seen with a woman a few times but the other times he met with a gentleman in a pub in Leicester-shire several times. They would talk for a while and then the gentleman would hand Cleavus a small pouch and the gentleman would leave. No one approached either man. The gentleman was followed several times, but he would always ride his horse around in circles until they would lose him."

"I believe it is time to bring Cleavus in and question him. He must be one of them. Especially if they have been working under the cover of night, it would be easy for him to sneak out," Troy stated.

Matlock got up to leave. "Do you want him brought here?"

"No, bring him to the stables. There is a tack room in the back. We will do our questioning there. I will see you in about half an hour."

"Ah, my lord," replied Matlock. "I will see you then." He turned and left.

This was indeed good news. Finally, they have a lead and hopefully they will be able to let the sheriff know where to find the others. He would send for the sheriff as soon as the questioning was completed. He took out his book with the plans for the move to London. He wanted to go over the plans again to ensure nothing was left out.

He was looking over the books for a good ten minutes when a boy came running up to the office. He was out of breath and could hardly get out what he needed to say.

"Come quickly, me lord. There is a problem in the servants' quarters." The boy turned and ran back to where he came from.

Troy jumped up from his desk and ran after the boy. When he reached the servants' quarters, there was a congregation of men standing in the doorway and all outside trying to see in. Troy pushed his way in. He stopped at the doorway and looked at the agonizing picture within. Cleavus was hanging from a rafter. Sheets had been knotted together and flung over the rafter then tied around his neck. Matlock stood beneath him. He was as white as a ghost.

Troy ran forward. "Get him down from there. Is he still alive?"

They took Cleavus down. Matlock checked the body. "I am sorry, my lord. He is dead."

"Take his body out back and get the men outside disbursed. Have someone get the sheriff."

Troy sat down on one of the beds and watched the men take the body outside. When everything had been completed, Matlock returned to Troy.

"I'm sorry, my lord. We got to him too late."

"Do we know if it was suicide or did someone sneak in here and murder him?"

"I will ask around to see if anyone saw or heard anything. Is there anything else I can do for you right now, my lord? You do not look so well."

"I'm fine Matlock. Thank you. It was the shock of seeing the body," Troy said as he stood up from where he was sitting. "I'm going back to the manor house to wait for the sheriff. Please find out if anyone saw or heard anything and then join me when the sheriff arrives."

"Yes, my lord." Matlock turned and left.

Troy went back to the manor house but couldn't go back to the office. He went to the drawing room instead. He went straight to the cupboard and made himself a drink. He drank down the one and made another. He turned to go and sit in a chair by the fireplace when he noticed Aspen sitting on the settee.

"My apologizes, dear Lady Aspen. I have just had a very bad experience. One I hope never to see again."

She came over to him with concern in her eyes. "I do hope nothing is drastically wrong, my lord."

She touched his hand and her touch felt like fire on his skin. But he did not retreat from the touch. "It is a subject I can't talk about to a lady. I'm sorry, Lady Aspen, but it was quite dire. We are alerting the sheriff and I expect him within the next half hour."

"I do hope everything turns out for the best," she commented and took her hand back. She turned to go.

"Please stay, Lady Aspen. I would really like some company right now, just to talk about nothing at all. Just company."

"Very well, I can do that." She turned to take up the seat she had just vacated. "How are the plans for the trip coming?"

"I was just going over them again when I was called out to the servants' quarters. I do believe I have everything in order for the trip. Are you looking forward to the going to London?"

"Actually no. For some reason I'm feeling a dread of going. I can't explain it but this feeling of foreboding has come over me and gets stronger as the day draws nearer for our departure."

"Maybe what happened to you happened in London?"

"I wish I knew. It's not easy dealing with the feelings and not the memory of what happened."

"I can understand that. A feeling of dread with nothing to back it up can be very scary. If you do need any help, please let me know and I will help in any way possible. Even if it's a good shoulder to cry on," he smiled at her.

"Thank you, my lord." She smiled back at him. "I truly must go. I have duties to perform."

Troy took her hand and kissed it. "Please do not avoid me in the future. I mean you no harm."

"I know, my lord. You are full of kindness." She turned away and swiftly left the room.

Penny came into the room. "Again!" she exclaimed. "Why do you do that to women?"

"I didn't do anything to Aspen. She said she had duties to perform. Perhaps you work her too hard."

"At least I don't make her go running from a room anytime we are together."

Lady Matilda entered just then. "Children, you haven't argued since you were ten years old. Troy, what in the world are you arguing about?"

"Aspen," retorted Penny.

"What about Aspen?" demanded Lady Matilda.

"It appears every time Troy sees her, she goes running in the other direction."

"That is not true Penny and you know it," Troy was getting heated now with his sister.

Just then the butler brought the same boy who fetched Troy earlier to see the lord.

"Yes, what is it? Is the sheriff here?"

"Yes, my lord. The sheriff is waiting outside with Matlock and two other men." The boy was again out of breath.

"I have to go, Mother. I will talk to you later." He gave her a kiss on the forehead and left.

"Sit down, Penny and I will explain a few facts of life to you," Lady Matilda said as she took a seat herself. "What you are seeing is two people in love working out some differences. When two people fall in love, it's a surprise to their system because feelings and emotions start running rampant and tend to get out of hand. They do not realize they are in love until later."

"Is that why Aspen runs from Troy all the time?"

"I am afraid so. And Aspen has the added problem of not knowing who she is, so she is even more confused than normal. I have been observing the two. They are definitely in love with each other. I do believe Troy has realized the truth already but Aspen is still fighting it."

"Can we not help the situation along somewhat?"

"My dear, when it comes to love you just have to let it run its course. You have to have faith that it will all work out in the end. But we will see what we can do in London to help the situation."

"Oh, Mother. You are such a dear. Is this how it was with Father and you?"

"Pretty much. Of course, I didn't have the baggage that Aspen has. But when feelings start stirring within you and you are frustrated that nothing can be done with them, you become angry and usually take it out on the male. All of this happens without your knowing why. You have no idea what is going on. But you will see for yourself when the time comes."

"I'm not so sure about this love thing," Penny replied.

"Oh my dear, when it gets all worked out, and you get married, it is worth every second of it. It is glorious and hopefully you will have a long life together." Lady Matilda stared into the distance as if seeing the past. "But my dear, do not say anything about being in love to either Aspen or your brother. They must find their way by themselves."

"Alright, Mother. You're the expert anyway." Penny got up and went to kiss her mother. "You are the best mother ever. I love you." Penny turned and left the room.

Ah yes, thought Lady Matilda, *Indeed what it is to be young again.*

Doggon ran the flag and called a meeting in their secret meeting place. He wanted to let the others know about Cleavus.

"Cleavus has been killed," he told the others.

"How?" they wanted to know.

"I killed him. I made it look like suicide. I found out that he was talking to our enemies."

"Cleavus wouldn't have done that," one said.

"I have been meeting with him since he was in with Lord Bowling's people. I could tell he was getting soft against us. He started not looking me in the eye and always looking over his shoulder to see if anyone of them was there. I did it to protect us," Doggon said. The others started grumbling. "I will do it again if I find anyone trying to double cross us. I don't want to end up in jail. Do any of you?"

"No," they all agreed.

The meeting broke up and everyone went their own way.

Chapter 9

*T*roy went outside with the sheriff, Matlock, and two men. Troy told the sheriff how Cleavus' body was found. The two other men had witnessed someone sneaking around the castle compound. The sheriff questioned the two men then let them go. Troy then told the sheriff about his group of men investigating all that had been going on in the district. He assured the sheriff that when he had information, he was going to share it with him.

"Cleavus was clearly a plant in our camp to keep watch and report back to the leader. It was witnessed that Cleavus talked to someone in a pub in Leicestershire a few times and a small pouch was exchanged between the two men each time. Our only guess is that the leader was afraid we were on to Cleavus and eliminated him."

"I will need to talk to the men who had been following Cleavus. Then we can take the investigation from here. You are leaving soon for London, my lord?"

"Yes, we are leaving in about two weeks. I have added guards to both the servants' travel and our own. We will be safe on our journey."

"Good, I don't want anything happening to any of you. I think you can show me the men who conducted the trailing of the dead man. Then I will have some officers come and remove the body."

"I don't want anyone in the manor house to see the body. I want it kept away from their eyes. I don't plan on telling them about this event."

"Don't worry, my lord. We will be discreet. Matlock, are you ready to show me around?"

Troy shook hands with the sheriff and returned to the manor.

He once again went to the drawing room. This time he looked before going to the counter to get a drink. He missed seeing his mother sitting in the chair by the fireplace. After he drank one drink straight down, he poured another. He turned around and saw his mother watching him.

"Sorry Mother, but it has been a horrific day. I needed this to stiffen me up."

"I do hope it is not because of the argument with your sister."

"That didn't help matters any. I probably got upset with her because of the other problem. I will apologize to her."

"What has happened to make you so upset?"

"I will tell you but I don't want the girls to know. We found a man hanged in the servants' quarters today. We believe he was one of the gang of thieves that has been raking havoc on this district lately. We believe another member came in and murdered him."

"Oh, my dear. That really happened right here!?"

"Yes, and now I'm extremely thankful that I have secured the extra guards for our trip."

"I know you are quite capable of taking care of us. I'm so thankful you are here managing all of this."

"Managing what for us?" Penny asked as she and Aspen entered the room.

"Troy was just telling me about the security he has arranged for our trip. We will be very well taken care of," replied Lady Matilda.

"Thank you, Mother. And Penny, I want to apologize for my rush to anger before." He went over to give her a kiss on the cheek. "I'm truly sorry and didn't mean anything I may have said. It has been a trying day."

"I forgive you dear brother, and I apologize for my behavior. I honestly didn't mean the things I said."

"Well, now that the apologies are out of the way, maybe we can have a nice before dinner drink. May I have a sherry, Troy?" Lady Matilda relaxed back into her chair.

"Of course, Mother," Troy said heading to the cupboard. "Would either of you ladies like a sherry or other refreshment?" he asked.

"No thank you," Aspen and Penny answered together.

They each took a seat. Penny sat in the chair on the other side of the fireplace, leaving the settee for Aspen and Troy.

Troy brought over the drink for his mother. He looked around and decided to stand by the fireplace. Penny just sighed.

"So, tell us about your trying day, Troy," Penny said.

"It was just all the normal stuff. Making sure all the security for our trip is in place."

"That is not why the sheriff was here. Did something happen?"

"No, my dear sister," he stated. "I just wanted the sheriff to be aware of what has been going on in the district before we left on the trip. Our tenants deserve protection while we are away."

"What has been happening in the district with our tenants?" asked Penny.

"It is all taken care of. There is no need for you to worry your pretty little head over matters that don't concern you," Troy answered. He didn't realize at the time what he said or how he said it.

"Oh so now my pretty little head cannot comprehend the workings of an estate!" Penny exclaimed. "You are nothing but a pompous ass!" Penny took off out of the room.

Troy just looked at her as she rushed from the room. *Maybe she was right about me and women. I just can't seem to say the right things and I am surrounded by women. I am not sure I will make it through*, Troy thought.

Lady Matilda sat in her chair and just sighed. Dinner was announced as being ready.

"I think I should go and find Penny." Troy walked out of the room to go find Penny.

"Well, my dear," Lady Matilda said to Aspen. "Shall we go and enjoy our dinner, while they work things out?"

Troy found Penny sitting on a bench in the rose garden. She was crying. He came up and sat beside her and took her in his arms.

"I'm so sorry precious," he started. "I am a cad and can never say things the right way. Believe me, you really don't want to know some of the things that go on around here. The responsibility is great and sometimes it is overwhelming. I am not just responsible for you and Mother but everyone who lives here and all the tenants. I sometimes just get where I can't think straight anymore."

"But maybe I can help you a little and take some of the responsibility off your shoulders."

"Sweetheart, I love you for the offer. Let me tell you what has been happening around the estate and you will understand. Do not tell Mother I told you or she would have my head on a platter. It's just that I really want you to understand. Our tenants have had their cattle and sheep stolen and then some other tenants had their barn full of the harvest burnt down. Neither will be able to pay their rent this summer."

Penny looked up at Troy. "Oh Troy," she whispered. She turned pale.

"I have taken care of the tenants and are forgoing their rent this summer. But I'm responsible for all the lives of the tenants, men, women, and children. I had to take charge and react. I'm responsible for getting everyone and all our possessions to London safely. You, my dear, get to enjoy the ride. I will be on high alert the whole way until we arrive. Do you understand what I'm telling you? It is not that I think you can't handle things but that you don't have to because I'm the protector of the manor and surrounding district. It's a big responsibility and I inherited it from Father."

"I'm so sorry, Troy. I didn't understand all the stress you are under. I thought it was all keeping the books and keeping us in money."

"That is my part of the responsibility also. But Father did teach me well before he passed and I have been learning along the way.

"Oh Troy," Penny threw her arms around his neck, "I'm so sorry to be so selfish. Please forgive me."

"Of course I forgive you love, if you forgive me. You can help me tremendously. Learn what Mother does around the manor. It helps me that I don't have to worry about linens and food and such. Mother takes care of all the running of the manor. That is a huge help."

"I have been learning from Mother and I will be able to help you until I marry and then I will be able to help my husband. I do understand much more now. Thank you Troy for trusting me with this information. I understand so much more now that you have confided in me."

"Good, then let's go get something to eat."

Troy pulled Penny into his arms and gave her a big hug. They took hands and went into the house. It was funny, but Troy felt so much better having partially confided in Penny. He was still haunted by what he saw in the servants' quarters, but was extremely happy he didn't have to tell that part to Penny. It felt like a burden had been lifted from his shoulders. Maybe confiding in someone was a good thing.

Chapter 10

*T*he time finally came to make the move to London. The servants left two days earlier. Troy set up a scout to go between the two caravans if any trouble did arise. Everyone was up early and excitement was in the air. Troy was wearing gray breeches with knee high boots with a white linen shirt and a black waistcoat. Aspen saw Troy before he saw her. Her heart stopped for a few seconds when she saw how handsome he looked. She turned to go the other way. Troy saw Aspen in the hallway after all the luggage was taken to the wagons that were traveling with the coaches. He stopped Aspen from escaping from him.

"I just want to know how you are. I know you are very nervous about this trip. I just want to ensure you are okay."

"I'm fine, my lord. Please don't worry about me. You have enough to take care of on this trip," she replied.

"I do worry about you. I always will. You mean a lot to me."

"Please, my lord. I'm a lowly servant. You are the lord of the manor. It can never be."

"We will see about that. Just know that I'm always here for you."

He moved aside and let her go. Getting through to her will be a challenge. She passed him and went to help with the loading of the trunks of clothes. He watched her as she walked away. She looked so beautiful in her traveling dress. It was dark blue with white lace around the collar and cuffs of her long sleeves. Troy could see the outline of her body under the dress as she walked. He shook his head. Now was not the time for these thoughts. He went to his room to check and make sure he did not forget anything. He still wanted to check his office also. Bailey was in his room doing the same thing Troy had planned to do.

"It looks good, Bailey. You did an excellent job as usual."

"Thank you, my lord. I believe we have all the necessities."

"If we forgot anything, we will be able to purchase it in London, I'm sure. Go on down to the coach and I will be there shortly."

Bailey bowed and left the room. Troy was already wanting to return. He was excited about London but would miss the routine of home. He went to his office to make sure he had what he would need in London. He looked for Mr. Blake so he could go over the last-minute details.

"There you are Mr. Blake. I just want a short talk with you."

"Yes, my lord." Mr. Blake gave him his undivided attention.

"I will have a courier service send any correspondence I deem necessary and you can do the same. If anything really important happens, please let me know as soon as possible."

"I assure you I will, my lord. I will keep you well informed of what is going on here."

"Then I'm off to see the next person. I want to talk to Matlock before I go."

"Safe trip, my lord, and we will see you when you return."

They shook hands and Troy picked up a satchel he had left on his desk then left the room. He went outside to find Matlock.

"Matlock, take care. You know more than I do about the manor. I know you will do what is needed in an emergency. Please just keep me informed if anything major happens."

"I will my lord and God speed. I will look forward to seeing you back here at home."

They started shaking hands and ended up hugging each other. Troy left to get into the coach. Lady Matilda, Penny, Aspen, and Troy were traveling in one coach. Lady Matilda was dressed in a dark blue dress like

Aspen's but the lace was black and the blue was much darker. Penny of course was wearing a bright yellow traveling dress. She would never wear anything dark. She hated dark colors. Bailey and some of the other servants were traveling in the second coach. Troy had his horse attached to the back of their coach so he could sometimes ride. He did not like the thought of riding for a week in a coach. Bailey brought his horse also to ride along with Troy. The women were so excited to get on the road. They were talking incessantly. Troy brought some work with him in the satchel to keep him busy during the ride.

Troy busied himself with his work and listened to the women talking with one ear. Lady Matilda was talking about a dear friend of hers, Lady Judith Somners. Evidentially, they had been debutantes together and became fast friends. She had heard from Lady Judith and she wanted to be the first one to sponsor Penny. The girls "oooh"-ed and "ah"-ed while listening to Lady Matilda talk about the old days. Troy couldn't help but smile at the interchange between them. Penny had asked if Lady Matilda knew the names of any of the eligible beaus that she will be presented to.

"Lady Judith and I have corresponded back and forth through the years. She did mention a couple of names from last season. I'm not sure if they will return this season or if they are taken. Let's see, I believe there were two Beaumonts, from different families of course, I believe one is David and the other is Ethan. Then there is the Deveron family. They have two sons, Joseph and Edward."

Troy glanced at the girls across from him and saw the expression on Aspen's face. She turned absolutely white. He heard Lady Matilda mention the Deveron family. He would have to remember that name. If Aspen can't help him, maybe the investigator he would get would be able to help. But Aspen definitely reacted to that name. She had turned her face to look out the window to hide her reaction, but Troy saw it.

"And of course there are the Braxton's, their oldest son is named Timothy. I think that is all I can think of right now. But Lady Judith has a daughter about your age. Her name is Jewel. I do hope you will get along with her. That would be wonderful if my best friend's daughter became my daughter's best friend. No pressure, my dear, if it doesn't happen then it doesn't."

"We will see, Mother. Just because you and Lady Judith are best friends does not mean you raised your daughters the same."

"Back then they thought Judith and I were sisters. We were so much alike and inseparable. Oh, those were the days."

"Is that how you met Father?" piped up Troy.

"Yes, it is. In fact, he was best friends with Judith's husband, Lord Thomas Somners, the Earl of Somners. The two of them swept Judith and I off our feet. What a time it was! We laughed and cried so much that season. Your father and I were married the following May. Judith and Thomas were married in June. Then we had to devote our time to our responsibilities and we saw less and less of them. I just hope the best for the three of you."

Troy looked at Aspen when Lady Matilda said that. Aspen turned her head to look out the window. Troy sighed and went back to his paperwork.

They stopped at midday at an inn to get something to eat. They didn't stay long. The ladies were given a room to freshen up. They returned to the coach and Troy excused himself and said he wanted to ride for a while. He and Bailey took off before the others. Troy was hoping for a river to jump into. Sitting across from Aspen, smelling her scent, and covertly watching her was driving him mad. He decided he may have to ride his horse for the rest of the week. Riding his horse seemed to help just as much as a river. He rode the horse hard and then pulled up to rest him while they waited for the others to catch up. When the coach caught up to them, he rode the rest of the way beside the coach with the women.

Troy was in a good mood when they arrived at the inn. He had had his exercise and fresh air and it felt good. The women were tired and grouchy. They went to their rooms to freshen up and rest for a while. They returned after about two hours. They were hungry and ready for bed. Troy just laughed at them. Lady Matilda wanted to talk to the innkeeper before she retired for the night. Troy wanted to take a short walk. He asked the women if they would like to join him. Penny said "Yes," Lady Matilda said a resounding "No," and Aspen felt she must go where her lady went, so Troy set off with the two ladies. They didn't get far when Penny stopped.

"Oh, I think I have a stone in my shoe. You two go on, I will stay right here and try to get the stone out. Come this way back and get me. One of your guards can stay with me and the other can stay with you two to chaperone." Penny stopped and sat down on a large stone beside the path.

Troy always being the gentleman said, "No we will wait for you." He looked down at Aspen.

"I have to take off my shoe and it will take too long to take it off and put it back on. You go ahead."

"I can help you, my lady," said Aspen.

"No, Aspen. I am quite capable of taking off my shoe and putting it back on. I have been doing that by myself for at least sixteen years now."

Troy put out his arm for Aspen to take and started walking down the path.

"I am glad we are alone for a few minutes anyway," he said without stopping. "I noticed this morning when Mother was giving names of some people who might be in London for the season that you reacted to a certain name. I believe it was Deveron. I remember that there were two sons, Joseph and Edward. You turned white as a sheet when you heard their names. Please tell me what you remember."

"My lord, I'm sorry you saw that," she hesitated. "Alright, you know all my other secrets so I will tell you why I reacted so strongly to their name. When I first heard Lady Matilda mention those names, I saw a quick vision. It was one of stark terror. Someone I loved dearly was murdered by their hands when they had those other men kidnap me. They were holding me and someone, but I don't know who, was struck down by the two Deveron sons. All I saw was a crumpled figure on the floor. I don't even know if it was a woman or a man. All I know is that I loved them very much." She started to silently cry.

Troy stopped and held her. The guard stopped and turned around discreetly. Troy's head was at least a head and a half taller than hers. He wanted to kiss the top of her head. He wanted to soothe her in ways he knew were not proper, so he just held her and breathed in her scent until she was back in control of herself.

"I have not said anything to you or anyone else. I will tell you now. When we get to London, I will find out what happened to you and who you really are. I'm going to hire an investigator to look into what happened."

"My lord, that is too kind of you. That will be so expensive, I will never be able to repay you."

She looked up at him and he looked down at her. Their eyes locked. He wanted to kiss her so immensely, it hurt. But he was afraid of a repeat of the last time. He promised he would not kiss her again. Suddenly she put her arms up behind his neck and pulled his face down to hers. They kissed passionately and both were breathless when they parted. He held her tight then they parted.

"I am so sorry, Lady Aspen. I promised not to do that again. Please accept my apologies."

She turned beat red. "Please accept my apologies, I was the instigator of that kiss. It WILL not happen again."

She turned to go back and Troy had to catch up to her. *Now what did I do wrong?* he thought. They were silent all the way back to Penny and then all the way back to the Inn.

The next morning, they returned to the coach. Troy glanced at the inn receipt. He stopped and looked at it more closely. Twenty-five pillows! He went to the innkeeper and asked him about the invoice. The innkeeper explained Lady Matilda had asked to buy all the extra pillows he had. Troy went to the coach and opened the door. What he saw inside made him laugh. All three women took as many pillows as needed and surrounded themselves to make the ride much more comfortable.

"My dear, after yesterday there was no way I was getting into this coach until it was made more comfortable," said Lady Matilda loftily.

"I agree, Mother. I don't want any of you uncomfortable. However, I do wish you would have thought of that before we started the trip. It would not have been so expensive. We now have twenty-five extra pillows. Be sure we use them on the way back." He closed the coach door and mounted his horse.

"Are you not riding with us today?" asked Penny.

"No," Troy replied. "I'm enjoying the exercise I'm getting from riding my horse. I will ride alongside your coach. If you need anything, get my attention and I will attend to your needs."

They took off for London. The rest of the trip was almost the exact repeat as the first day. It took them little less than a week to reach London. They did not notice that there were people along the sidelines watching them. But there were so many guards there was no way they could get close enough to do any damage. They just rode along in silence the entire way, waiting and watching.

Chapter 11

*T*hey stopped in front of their home in London. It was a grand mansion in the western part of London. Aspen stood outside the townhouse and stared in amazement. She had never seen such a home as this or not that she could remember. The home was three stories high with a basement. Everyone started milling around her so she thought she should start moving also. Troy noticed her staring at the house. He was amused by her reaction. He had to turn his attention back to what was going on around him.

Lady Matilda grabbed hold of Penny and Aspen and took them into the townhouse. "Our rooms are on the second floor, girls. Come along and I will show you your rooms."

They followed Lady Matilda as they slowly looked around at the house. It was enormous. They found their rooms and each stayed there until their trunks were delivered. Servants came in to help them unpack and get settled.

Troy followed the last of the possessions from the wagons into the townhouse. He was as stunned as the girls had been at the magnificence of the house. He didn't know where to start. Everyone was moving around like they had been here forever. He didn't even know where his mother and the girls were. He had no idea where to find his room. Finally, he saw Bailey. He motioned Bailey over to him.

"Bailey, I'm lost. I have no idea where to go. Help me." For the first time in his life, he felt panicky.

"The bedrooms are on the second floor, my lord," said Bailey. "Please follow me."

Troy followed Bailey up a grand staircase. *How will I ever learn to maneuver around this house?* Troy thought. He saw Bailey turn into a room. He followed and stood in the doorway. He was stunned. The room was huge. The walls were cream colored. There was a huge closet to one side. Beyond that was a washroom. Straight in front of him stood two French doors curtained in white. He went over and opened the doors. He thought his balcony at the manor was big. This balcony was three times his balcony at home. He knew he would enjoy this. He went back into his room. There was a bed on the other side of the room. Beside the bed was another set of French doors curtained the same. He opened the doors and walked out onto the same balcony. He re-entered the room.

Between the two sets of French doors were a table and chairs. Beside the door leading to the closet were a settee and two chairs surrounding a fireplace. On the other side of the bed was a desk. Above the bed he just noticed was a huge picture of his father when he was very young. He stood and looked at the picture. It was as if he were looking in a mirror. He had no idea he looked so much like his father. Troy finally decided to try to find the other bedrooms.

He heard some talking from a room three doors down from his. He went there and found Lady Matilda, Penny and Aspen. He walked into the room.

"Well, I finally found civilization," he said walking in the doorway. "Whose room is this?"

"This is my room," answered Lady Matilda.

"Beautiful," said Troy.

The room was painted in a warm shade of blue. It was much like his room only larger. Above the bed was a portrait of his mother and father together. He was drawn to the picture. It was so enchanting. Their love was shining through their eyes as they looked at each other. He was mesmerized by the picture.

Lady Matilda followed his gaze. "It is my favorite picture of your father and me. It was painted shortly after our marriage. I will truly enjoy looking at this picture as often as possible."

"We must take it back with us to Battingham Castle," Troy said. "It belongs above the mantle of the fireplace in the drawing room."

Penny grabbed Troy's hand. "Come see my room," she said, pulling Troy along with her. "Come along Aspen."

They went across the hall to a room right across form their mother's. Again, it was much the same as Lady Matilda's and Troy's. Her room was painted in a soft rose color. It was beautiful.

"Wow," he exclaimed. "This is really beautiful. Are you sure you are in the right room? I thought yours was down in the basement." Troy said laughing.

Penny turned on him and started tickling him.

"Okay, okay, I give. This room suits you just fine." Then he grabbed her and hugged her.

They were laughing. Aspen enjoyed the interchange she was watching.

Penny turned around to Aspen. "We must go see Aspen's room," she said.

She grabbed Troy's hand with one of hers and Aspen's with the other. They went to the room right next to Penny's. It again was much the same only painted in a very pale lilac. Instead of two sets of French doors there was only one. But the rest of the room was the same.

"Very elegant," Troy said.

"Too elegant," Aspen replied. "I should have had the room in the basement."

"Why are you so down on yourself?" asked Penny. "You are acting so gloomily. Come on, we are in London. Be happy!"

"I'll try," said Aspen.

Penny took Aspen's hand. "Let's go explore the rest of the house."

She pulled Aspen with her out the door. Troy would have laughed but he was very worried about Aspen. He was going to have to find an investigator right away so we can find out who Aspen really is. He went back to his mother's room.

Lady Matilda looked at her son's face. "Come sit down with me. What's wrong?" she asked.

"I'm worried about Aspen. She seems very depressed." He didn't want to betray her confidence but he has always been able to talk to his mother. She has always been so insightful. She seemed to have the answer to everything. "I think I know how to help her but it will take some time. In the meantime, I worry about her depression."

"Yes, I have noticed her also. I must say, I was wrong about her faking the amnesia. She really is very sweet. I will try to spend more time with her. Maybe I can help her."

"You can probably do more than I can. I can never do or say the right thing with her. One moment we are fine and the next I do something wrong and she is angry with me. I don't even know what I'm doing wrong. Maybe it is that 'time of the month' thing. I never did say thank you for the book. I appreciate you letting me read about such things rather than talking about that subject. I don't think I could have listened to such things. I do have a much better understanding now."

"You're welcome. You are in love with her. That is part of why you can't do anything right. It's natural," Lady Matilda said.

"I don't know. I can't get her out of my mind. She is always there. And her scent. It drives me up a wall."

Lady Matilda chuckled. "Yes, you have been bitten by the love bug. I will tell you something. She is in love with you too. She is in a protection mode. She is having feelings for you and doesn't want to give in to them."

"I don't know, Mother. She is obsessed with the idea that she is a servant and we can never be. All I know is that I am feeling miserable. I can't figure out how to treat her. I want to help her so much but I feel I need to stay away before I do something else wrong."

"Patience, my dear. Keep doing what you are doing and you will win her." She patted his hand.

"Thank you, Mother. You as always are the one who knows best." He stood and went to her to give her a kiss on the top of her head. "I need to find Bailey. I have a chore I must complete before the day is out. I will see you at dinner tonight."

He walked out of the room and went in search of Bailey. He found him in his bedroom.

"Bailey, I need to have a talk with you. Please come and sit with me for a few minutes."

"Yes, my lord," Bailey said. He stopped what he was doing and sat down opposite Troy.

"I have to find an investigator. I have no idea where to start. Can you give me any advice on how to proceed with this?"

"I have not been to London for quite some time. I'm not sure. I can ask around."

"I need to find one immediately."

"Is it concerning the lady staying with us?"

"Yes, I want to help her get her memory back. I want to find her family even though I have very little information."

"Rumors get passed around very easily with the servant population, even outside of London. I have heard that if you want to hire someone to investigate something for you, your best chance is to hire a criminal. They know all the underground criminals and can find out information much easier than gentry trying to find the same information."

"And how, pray tell, do I find a criminal? I would not even know where to look."

"If you give me permission to work on getting you settled later, I can go and work on that detail for you. I might be able to have someone come to talk to you by this evening."

"By all means, please go and see what you can find out. I want this investigation started as soon as possible."

"Then, I shall go now and see what I can do for you, my lord." He stood, bowed to Troy, and left the room and townhouse.

Troy felt much better and decided to go explore the house himself. He met up with the girls after he had seen three parlors for receiving guests.

"How many people are going to come to see us?" he exclaimed.

Penny laughed at him. "If it's to woo me, we will need more than three parlors," she laughed.

He chased her around the settee in the third parlor. He finally caught her and hugged her.

"You are hilarious. What should I do with her Aspen? Should I tickle her like she did me this morning?"

He started tickling her and they squiggled so much around they both fell laughing onto the settee. Aspen couldn't help but giggle. All of a sudden, they heard a cough from the doorway. They all stopped in their tracks and turned towards the doorway. A tall woman, wearing a demure day dress of gold color stood there.

"I do not mean to intrude but I am trying to find someone who can lead me to Lady Matilda Bowling."

Troy jumped up, straightened his clothing, and went to the doorway to bow to the lady. "I am her son, Troy Bowling. I would be happy to fetch Lady Matilda for you. May I ask who is calling?"

She bowed her head to him in acceptance of his offer. "Please let her know that Lady Judith Somners is here to see her."

Troy bowed again and left to find his mother. In the meantime, Penny and Aspen came forward to greet their guest.

"Good day, Lady Judith. I am Lady Matilda's daughter, Penelope. This is Aspen, a guest staying with us." They both curtsied. "Please do come in and have a seat while we await Lady Matilda. My mother has told me much about you. I am very pleased to meet you and I am looking forward to meeting your daughter, Jewel."

"Thank you. You appear to be very well bred. I did not think Matilda would raise hooligans but was not sure upon entering."

Aspen looked at Penny and said, "I will try to find some refreshments in the kitchen. If you will excuse me, Lady Somners, Lady Penny." She curtsied and left the room.

Penny sat down across from Lady Judith. "I apologize for our behavior when you first saw us. It has been a long trip and my brother and I were just letting off a little steam. We really are quite well-behaved."

"Of course you are, you are my daughter," they both heard from the doorway and both turned to see Lady Matilda.

Lady Matilda and Lady Judith ran towards each other and hugged. They were about the same height. Troy stood in the doorway watching the two women. They finally parted, both wiping their eyes.

"I know I should have waited a day or two to see you and let you get settled, but I just couldn't wait. I apologize for the intrusion, Matilda."

"Please sit down Judith. Troy, you can have a seat also. These are my two children," Lady Matilda said proudly. "You will have to excuse us, Judith. We have just barely arrived. I will ring for some refreshments."

"Aspen has already gone to the kitchen to see about refreshments," said Penny.

"Such a dear child she is. It has been such a pleasure to have her stay with us," Lady Matilda answered.

"Whose family is she from? She looks so familiar." Lady Judith asked.

"We are not sure at the moment. Poor dear had a traumatic incident and has lost her memory. We are trying to help her regain her lost knowledge."

Troy stood up and said, "I think I will attempt to help Lady Aspen." He bowed to the ladies and left the room.

"I think I will help also," Penny curtsied and followed Troy. Once she got through the doorway, she took off running after Troy.

"You have done very well with your children, my dear," said Lady Judith.

"Thank you. They have been such a blessing since Troy Senior passed away."

"I am so truly sorry for your loss. Troy was such a dear. I loved him almost as much as Thomas. But you two were so much in love, no one could deter either of you.'

"The same for you and Thomas. Many gentlemen were very disappointed. They didn't have a chance with you once you met Thomas." Lady Matilda chuckled.

Lady Judith chuckled along. "The same for you and Troy. Ah, but those were the days."

"Yes, they were. At least I have twenty years of memories. I'm so lonely sometimes but Troy looks so much like his father and acts just like his father too. I get enjoyment watching him growing up. He can get into quite the situation sometimes."

"I'm sure. Jewel is such a blessing to me. I wanted many more children but could only have the one. I am thankful for that. I can't wait for you to meet her and to see Thomas again."

"I am looking forward to that. We will have a lot to talk about and a lot of time in which to do so. We shall be all set in a couple of days and then we can start arranging some activities."

"Why wait? Why could you all not come to our town house for a simple dinner tonight. Not part of the pre-season, just old friends getting together."

"That is wonderful of you. I will have to check with the others to see. I suppose we would be able to get cleaned up and meet you for dinner tonight."

"That will be wonderful. Let me get out of your hair so you can get ready and I will have to let Cook know there will be four more for dinner." Lady Judith stood just as the other three came back. Troy was carrying a tray. "Thank you, dear children, but I must run."

Lady Judith departed the premises.

Troy, Penny, and Aspen just stood there with their mouths open. Lady Matilda started laughing at them.

"You all look ridiculous," she said. "Set the tray down, Troy, over here by me. I will serve us all some tea."

Troy turned to Penny. "I swear I didn't do anything!" he said.

They all laughed, even Aspen.

"No, you didn't, Troy, "said Lady Matilda. "We have been asked to dinner at Judith's home to meet her daughter and husband this evening. It will not be part of the activities of the season or pre-season. It is just old friends getting together. I took it upon myself to accept for everyone, even you Aspen."

"Oh, but my lady, I can't possibly go. I am but a servant." Aspen objected.

"I am making a declaration here and now," Lady Matilda announced. "While in this house, you are our guest Aspen. It is ridiculous being a companion to Penny, get that silly idea out of your head. You, my dear, are a true lady. We shall hire some lady's maids for each of you. I'm sorry I didn't do that from the start You are our guest and I apologize for not making you feel so before now."

"What a wonderful idea, Mother," Penny said and went to kiss her mother on the cheek and turned to kiss Aspen.

Lady Matilda served the tea and tea sandwiches. "We will have to eat quickly and then get ready for tonight. I don't know about anyone else, but I feel really grimy."

They finished with their tea and Penny and Lady Matilda stood up to leave. Aspen looked at Troy and motioned for him to stay.

Chapter 12

When the first two had left, Aspen started, "I don't like the idea of being treated like a guest. I don't know what happened to me and I do not want to see someone who may have been part of what happened. It scares me to go among the public not knowing." Her eyes were wide with fright.

Troy took her hand and had her sit down. "I totally understand your feelings, but as our guest you would be expected to attend everything we attend." Troy got up and walked to the fireplace. There was a frown on his face. "I have a small idea that is growing in my mind. I can offer you protection in only one way that I can think of."

"And what one idea might that be?" Aspen questioned. She was not sure she would like his idea.

"We could pretend we are engaged." He held up his hand at her objections. "Let me finish before you berate me. It would be a way for me to be by your side and protect you at all times. We would have to act like you like me even when I do something wrong."

"You have never done anything wrong," she demurred.

"I don't know about that," he said rubbing his check. "I seem to remember several times I made you upset with me."

Aspen blushed. "It was not your fault. I was very confused and knew no other way to act. But I would really just prefer to stay as a servant."

Troy sat beside her on the settee. He took her hands in his.

"I understand how you feel," he said looking into her eyes. "My mother has told me how much you have come to mean to her. She already loves you as a daughter. It would hurt her terribly if you insist on staying as a servant."

"You and your family have been so kind to me. I came to you as a stranger and now you offer me as part of your family? I don't know what to say," she looked at him and saw the love in his eyes. "Alright, I will accept your offer."

"Then do you agree with me to be my betrothed?"

"Yes, I will accept your kind offer of your protection. I will play my part. Thank you for your offer." She bent over to him and pulled his head to hers. They kissed a passionate kiss. Troy melted.

"I do believe our kisses will have to be a little more chaste, especially in public. You know I love you. If I thought you would accept my offer, I would propose to you for real," he said holding her.

"And I would accept for real. For I have realized I love you too."

He couldn't believe his ears. He was ecstatic. He pulled away from her and looked down on her.

"Really?" he questioned.

"Really," she said.

He pulled her into his arms and gave her a resounding kiss. She melted into his arms.

"Then let's make this official," he said. He got down on one knee and said, "Aspen will you do me the honor of marrying me?"

"Yes, I will, with one condition. We don't make it official, official until we know who and what I am. If it turns out that I'm a maid or such, then I will have to refuse you."

"You are a lady through and through. I just know it." He knew he would be able to win her and change her mind about separation of stations if it turned out she was a servant. "But I feel we must go get ready for this evening. We must see Mother before we go to the Somners'. When you are

ready for this evening, come knock on my door. We will see Mother together."

He kissed her again, a chaste little kiss. They walked to their rooms
hand in hand. Troy was walking on the clouds. He stopped at her door and
waited until she closed the door behind her and then went to his room. He
went to the washroom. Bailey had left him some water in the basin. He
washed and changed into his evening clothes. He wore black knee-high
breeches over white stockings with a green waistcoat over a white linen
shirt with pleats at the cuffs. The green waistcoat brought out the green of
his eyes. He wore his buckled shoes. He didn't feel he had to mess with a
wig tonight. He was just ready when there came a soft knock at the door.

He opened the door to see Aspen in a beautiful low cut, short sleeved
gown of powder blue. The gown was empire waist and hung around her
body. She was wearing gloves on her hands and had a fan hanging from
her wrist. Her hair was done up with ringlets coming down the sides of
her face.

"You are breathtakingly beautiful and you are all mine," he said.

He bent down to give her a small kiss. He offered his arm and she took
it. They walked over to his mother's room and knocked on the door.

"Enter," said Lady Matilda.

Troy and Aspen entered the room. Troy went over to the chair Lady
Matilda was sitting in and bent down to give her a kiss. Aspen curtsied to her.

"We have something to discuss with you, Mother," Troy started. "I
have proposed to Aspen and she has accepted my proposal."

"Well it's about time," Lady Matilda stated. She stood up and walked
to Aspen. She gave Aspen a hug. "I couldn't be happier with Troy's choice
of a wife. I'm very happy for both of you. Now we definitely need two
lady's maids."

"That is not necessary for me, my lady. I will be fine taking care of
myself."

"Nonsense," replied Lady Matilda. "You will be part of this family and
will start having all the amenities that go with the title."

"But my lady, what if I am truly a lowly servant? You do not know any more than I do what my lot in life really is. You cannot disgrace the family by allowing your son to marry a lowly servant. I only agreed to pretend to become engaged due to Troy concocting this way to protect me against the unknowns in London.'

"You did accept my proposal, did you not?" Troy countered. "I even got down on one knee, Mother."

"I accepted on the condition of what we find when we find out who I really am."

Lady Matilda took Aspen's hands. "My dear, no matter about the station of your life before, what is important is the love that two people share. Do you love my son?"

Aspen lowered her eyes, "Yes my lady, with all my heart."

"Then there will be no talk of what ifs. It is what it is."

She gave Aspen a big hug just as the door opened and Penny waltzed in. Penny was dressed in a gray evening gown with lace around the low-cut neckline and the sleeves that belled out from her elbows. Her hair was swept up like Aspen's and held together with a pearl comb. She also had on hand gloves and a fan hanging from her wrist. Lady Matilda was wearing the black gown of a widow. She had her hair swept up and a fan hanging from her wrist.

"What's going on?" asked Penny.

"May I introduce your future sister-in-law," Troy said, bowing to all the women in the room.

"Oh my goodness!" shouted Penny. She ran to Aspen and hugged her. "I'm so happy. Congratulations, Troy." She kissed him on the cheek. "You have both made me so happy." She clapped her hands. "When's the wedding?"

"Too fast, my dear," said Lady Matilda, "Let us get used to the engagement. We will keep it to just intimate friends at this time. We don't want to rush anything."

"If it was up to me," said Troy, "The wedding would have been yesterday." He took Aspen's hand and kissed it. She blushed.

"Are we ready to go?" asked Lady Matilda. "I took the presumption to order a carriage for this evening. I noticed you were tied up, Troy. I hope you don't mind."

They all headed toward the front door. The carriage was awaiting them. They had an interesting drive to the Somners' townhouse. All were looking around London. When they arrived, a livery man came to open the carriage door for them to exit. When they approached the front door, the butler opened it before they were completely there. Their capes were taken by a maid by the door and the butler escorted them to the parlor.

Thomas saw Lady Matilda and came to her to kiss her on both cheeks. "My dear Matilda, how are you? You look marvelous. I am so sorry to hear about Troy. I'm sorry we have been remiss in our duty to come and visit with you."

"Thank you, Thomas for those kind words. I am doing fine," said Lady Matilda. "I would like to present my son, Troy Junior, my daughter Penelope, and my new soon to be daughter-in-law Aspen."

"You didn't tell me this afternoon that your son was engaged," exclaimed Lady Judith.

"That is because it just happened. Although I have been waiting for it for quite some time." She smiled at Aspen.

"Well, I would like to introduce my daughter Jewel," said Lady Judith.

Jewel was dressed in a beautiful gown of pastel pink, again very low cut. The sleeves came to the elbows like Penny's gown. Her hair was a pale blonde and very beautiful. Her eyes were blue. She had her hair swept up and gathered with feathers of different pastel colors. She was tall like both her mother and Father.

"I'm pleased to meet you, Lady Matilda," Jewel said in a soft voice. "And I am pleased to meet your family. My mother has told me so much about you and your antics when you were our age."

"Let's all sit down," Lord Somners said. "May I get anyone something to drink?"

"I would not mind a bourbon and water," Troy answered. "Would you like a sherry, Mother?"

"Yes, please," she answered. Troy went over to help Lord Thomas with the drinks. "Oh, this house brings back many memories as does our townhouse."

"I felt the same thing when I went to see you this afternoon," Lady Judith said. "You bring back the greatest memories. We will be able to talk every day and still not remember all we have been through."

Troy went over to stand beside Aspen where she was siting.

Thomas distributed the sherry to the ladies and held his glass up. "A toast to the newly engaged couple."

Everyone, even Penny, Aspen, and Jewel, raised their glasses since the girls were drinking lemonade.

"I would like to comment on the engagement," Lady Matilda started. "Right now, we are keeping the announcement to include only family and intimate friends."

"We totally understand," Lady Judith said. "But to the newly engaged from us."

The three older adults started talking amongst themselves. Jewel turned to Troy, Aspen and Penny.

"I hope you had a good trip to London," she said.

"It was uneventful," Penny replied. "It was exciting being our first trip to London."

"So you have always lived in the country outside of Leicestershire, is it?

"Yes," Troy interjected. "We live in the Castle Battingham."

"Have you only lived in London?" Penny asked.

"Yes, this has been the only home I have ever known. My father is a banker. Where do you live Aspen?"

Troy answered for Aspen, "Aspen is staying with us as our guest. That is how we have gotten to know her."

He patted her on the shoulder and left his hand there possessively. She put her hand on his and rested it there.

"What is your occupation, Troy?" Jewel asked. "I hope you do not mind me calling you Troy, do you?"

"No my lady, I do not mind you calling me Troy. I am the lord of the Manor at Battingham. I have approximately five hundred acres of land to tend. I have tenants living throughout the land and I tend to the affairs of the castle. It is quite a handful to take care of."

"Please, call me Jewel. It sounds like you are quite busy. And you Penelope, what occupies your time?"

"Please, call me Penny. I keep busy with the household. Mother has been teaching me how to run the manor house so Troy can concentrate on his responsibilities. I do like to read books when I'm not busy with my responsibilities."

"What kind of books do you like to read?" Jewel asked.

She and Penny got off to talking about different authors they each like. Troy and Aspen listened.

About fifteen minutes later, dinner was announced. The all retired to the dining room. Thomas offered his arm to both ladies, Troy offered his arm to Aspen and the girls walked in together. Dinner was a delight with a first course of cold soup followed by roast beef with vegetables and a dessert of Yorkshire pudding. Troy and Thomas stayed in the dining room while the women and girls retired to a different parlor. This parlor had French doors leading to the garden.

When Troy came back, he asked Aspen if she would enjoy a stroll in the garden. The girls said they would go also. Troy offered Aspen his arm and the went to the garden with Penny and Jewel following. The walk felt good after so many days on the road. Of course, Troy was hoping the girls would get lost so he could spend some alone time with Aspen. That did not happen, so he just enjoyed the walk and to be in Aspen's presence. They stayed about another hour and then returned to their own townhouse. By that time everyone was tired and wanted to go to bed. It had been a long day.

Chapter 13

B *ailey was waiting for Troy as he entered his room.* Bailey had his room all organized.

"Good evening, my lord," he stated. "If you would like to take a stroll in the south garden by the roses, you might find something interesting."

"I think I just might do that. Can you point me in the right direction, Bailey? I'm still lost in this house. And can you make me a bourbon and water?"

Bailey told him which parlor to enter to get to the south garden and then which path to take once he got there. Troy was actually able to find it pretty easily and found a bench to sit upon. He was nursing his drink when a man approached.

"Are you Lord Bowling?" he asked.

"Yes, I am. May I have your name?"

"That can come later if we agree on terms. Your man, Bailey, said yous was needing some work done to help a lady?'

"That is correct."

"Can yous tell me a little bit to see if I's the one to help you?"

"Come sit down with me so we can talk together." The man moved over to sit beside Troy. "There is a lady I rescued out by Leicestershire. She had been abducted by a group of bandits or highwaymen or whatever you want to call them. We believe she was abducted from somewhere in London. She has no memory of before she was abducted. We call her Aspen because she says the name sounds and feels familiar to her. Also, the name of the Deveron brothers Joseph and Edward were familiar to her. She actually turned pale when she heard their names. She said she had a small vision when she heard those names. Someone was holding her and the brothers struck down someone she loved when that person tried to rescue her. She said they killed the person but she is not sure the person was a male or female. She only saw a person crumpled on the ground. That is all I know for now. Do you think you can help me? I will pay handsomely for being able to help her remember who she is."

"She doesn't know if Aspen is her real name or the name of someone else?"

"No, she does not."

"And she has no memory of the actual abduction so she has no idea who did it or where it happened?"

"No, the doctor caring for her believes that some type of trauma caused her memory to be blocked. She had no bumps or anything on her head to cause her to lose her memory. The only hint is the vision she had of the Deveron brothers. And she had that vision on our way here to London. My guess is that the abduction happened here in London."

"I can try to gather some information that might help the lady remember. I will work for you but since there is not much information, it will cost you."

"I don't care about the cost. I want the lady to know who she is."

"Ah. I will see what I can do. I will meet you back here in about one week. My name is Slick." The man stood up and left Troy alone.

Troy sat for a while nursing his drink then went into the house and to his room. Bailey was waiting for him.

"He is going to try to find out some information. Thank you, Bailey, I will see you get a bonus for all the help you have given me." Bailey bowed to him and left the room.

The next morning. Troy looked out into the hallway before he went to his mother's room and knocked on the door. "Enter," he heard, so he went into his mother's room. She was seated outside on the balcony. She was still dressed in her night clothes with a wrap around her. She was enjoying a morning cup of tea.

"Come join me, dear," she said when she saw him. "There are some biscuits with some marmalade along with the tea."

"Thank you, Mother," he said, bending to kiss her forehead. "I believe I will just have some tea." He sat down at the table with her and helped himself to the tea. "Have you heard from the girls yet this morning?"

"Not yet, but I expect to any time now. I thought I heard some stirrings. So what do you think of the Somners?"

"I think they are a very nice family and a good distraction for you. I believe you will have a great time here in London."

"They are such dear friends. Yes, I believe I will enjoy our time here."

Just then the girls came in laughing and almost skipping. Aspen was dressed in a day dress of deep rose red color. The color brought out her blonde hair and darker complexion. The dress had short sleeves and was just as low-cut as last night. That was the fashion right now. Troy was enjoying it on Aspen Penny had a day dress of yellow which brought out her pale hair. She looked like the sunshine. Her sleeves were also short like Aspen's. Both were wearing their hair up with ringlets on top of their heads.

"Good morning, Mother," Penny said, bending to kiss her mother's forehead. She then ran over to Troy and gave him a kiss on the cheek.

"What are the two of you laughing about?" asked Troy.

"Nothing, dear brother," answered Penny. "Just some girl stuff."

"Lady Judith will be sending over two lady's maids for us today. When they arrive, we will decide which will go with each girl." Lady Matilda put down her cup of tea. "What are everyone's plans for today?"

"Lady Jewel is coming over to take Aspen and I on an open carriage ride. We are to bring our parasols," answered Penny.

"I suggest you ride your horse alongside their carriage, Troy, to deter any young men from trying to engage the girls in conversation," said Lady Matilda. "It is not proper for gentlemen to speak to girls who have not been presented at the debutante ball."

"But what about the soirees before the ball?" asked Aspen.

They all looked at her.

"How do you know about soirees?" asked Lady Matilda.

"I don't know, but I know they are meetings or parties at someone's home. Sometimes words just pop into my head. I have no idea where from. They must be from my memory."

"Well, to answer your question," said Lady Matilda, "In a group of people, you are allowed to talk to a gentleman, but not alone. For instance, if you, Aspen, and Troy were with Penny and a gentleman approached her, she can talk to him in public. He cannot corner Penny by herself. That is not done in polite society. Lady Judith and I are getting together today to plan a few soirees for you girls. You and Aspen will also have to keep yourselves available to chaperone these events."

"I will do my duty, Mother. Just let me know. Aspen and I will be at your disposal. Is it alright if I take Aspen down for a stroll in the garden? Or is that forbidden even for an engaged couple."

"An engaged couple is allowed some time alone together," Lady Matilda answered.

Troy jumped up and took Aspen by the hand. He pulled her out of the room and they heard Lady Matilda and Penny laughing.

"Finally, we get to be alone for a while," he said, giving his arm to Aspen.

She took his arm and smiled at him. His heart melted. He walked her to the rose garden he had been in last night. When they came to the bench, he turned to her and held her. He bent down and gave her a chaste kiss on the lips. He put his hands up to her hair.

"I have been waiting so long to be alone with you. I want to just take in your scent and the feel of you. You have no idea what you do to me," he said, kissing her again a little more passionately.

"And you have no idea what you do to me," she commented back. She put her hands up to his face. "I love your eyes and your nose and that mouth is so sensuous. I can hardly stand it. I want to feel you too," and she lifted her head for his kiss again.

They kissed a few more times and then sat on the bench. He put his arms around her and held her. She was so content.

"Are you okay with our responsibilities for the season?" he asked.

"As long as you are with me, yes, I am okay with it," she answered.

Penny came out just then. "Lady Judith sent a message. She is on her way over with the two lady's maids. I think Mother and Lady Judith will be spending most of their time together while we are here in London."

Troy had risen so Penny could sit on the bench with Aspen.

"I agree with you," Troy answered. "And it appears you are becoming fast friends with Jewel."

"We are and I'm very happy to have someone help direct me. Mother never really explained all the rules to me. I had no idea. You're lucky to have Aspen. You are already taken. You don't have to be put on parade."

"Is this how you think of it?" Aspen asked.

"Sometimes. Oh, I'm hoping to fall desperately in love with someone. But it scares me also because I don't really know what to expect. From what Mother told me about her and Father and then you two, I'm not sure I want to fall in love at all."

"My dear," Troy answered. "It's really the best thing in the world to find the one you love. Yes, until you are both in this together it is difficult. But when you both realize how much in love you are, it's beautiful."

Aspen took Penny's hands in hers. "The only advice I have for you is to sit back and enjoy it. Have fun. When it happens, it will be because it is meant to be. Just let it happen."

Penny gave Aspen a hug. "I am so glad you are going to be my sister-in-law. I will leave the two of you alone now." She stood and ran off towards the townhouse.

Troy and Aspen laughed after her. They looked at each other. "I guess we have to go in and get ready for the rush of the day," Troy said. He pulled her into his arms and kissed her deeply. "Please don't forget about me."

"I won't," she replied breathlessly. "And don't you forget about me."

"I can't. You are in my mind every moment of every day." She smiled up at him and took his arm as they walked into the townhouse.

Chapter 14

*L*ady Judith arrived and all were waiting in the front parlor. They were introduced to the two lady's maids. Lady Matilda talked to each maid and determined who would go where. Then Lady Matilda and Lady Judith went into the second parlor and started talking about all the parties coming up in the next month and a half. They each had their calendars to mark the dates and create new ones. The two girls took their maids to their rooms and sat and talked with them for a while. Just before it was time for Jewel to come with the open carriage, they all met in the front parlor again. Troy had been becoming more familiar with the townhouse. He was finally learning his way around.

They were drinking tea when Jewel arrived. She joined them for some tea before their carriage ride. She was dressed in an enchanting dress in a blue-green color. It was flat in the front and back with wide side hoops. The sleeves came to her elbow with lace around the end. Penny jumped up and hugged her. She pulled away with her arms still around her.

"Oh, I love your dress," she said.

"It's one of the newest fashions to hit London. Isn't it adorable?" said Jewel turning around. She sat and accepted a cup of tea. They talked small talk for a short time, then got ready to go.

Aspen went over to Troy and took his hand. "I do hope you understand, but I think I will stay here in my room this afternoon. I have a slight headache and would like to lay down and rest."

He looked at her concerned, "Are you going to be okay?" he asked. "I can stay with you."

"Of course you can't stay with me. You must escort Lady Penelope and Lady Jewel on their ride. I will be fine and I will be here when you return."

"Alright, but I will come check on you as soon as I return. Please take care." He took her hand and kissed it. He turned to Penny and Jewel, "Aspen has a slight headache and wants to rest this afternoon. Are we ready to leave?"

The three of them headed for the door.

"You could sit in the open carriage with us instead of riding your horse," Lady Jewel commented.

"Thank you, my lady. I appreciate the offer but I would much rather ride my horse. He needs the exercise anyway." He bowed to the two ladies and mounted his horse.

They went towards St. James. The girls were just talking away. When they reached St. James, there were many carriages being driven very slowly with mostly women within while men were riding on horseback, nodding and lifting their hats to the women. It was quite the show. Penny was thrilled at seeing so many men and most of them nodded towards their carriage. She demurely hid behind her fan but her eyes were twinkling. Troy was so happy he did not have to be one of those men trying to woo the women.

As he rode, he kept thinking about Aspen. He hoped she was alright and just nervous about being in public. There was one man who made an attempt to stop the carriage with Penny and Jewel inside. Troy maneuvered his horse to block the gentleman. He bowed to Troy and moved on. An hour of riding around St. James and they had had enough. The girls wanted to return to the Somners' townhouse, so Troy escorted them there and then went to his own townhouse. He had told Penny to send a messenger when she was ready to come home.

As soon as he returned home, he went to Aspen's room. He knocked and heard an "Enter" and opened the door. Aspen was sitting on the balcony. Her lady's maid was working around the room so Troy knew it was alright for him to enter. Her scent enveloped him when he entered the room. He went to her and bent to give her a chaste kiss on the lips.

"How are you feeling, my dear?' he asked.

"Much better now that you are here."

She started pouring him some tea. He sat down beside her.

"Maybe when you are done, we can take a stroll in the garden. The fresh air may do you some good."

"I think I would like that. How did your ride go?"

"Fine, but the whole experience of finding a mate is totally different here in London." He took her hand. "I like the direct approach much better." He smiled into her eyes.

"So do I. The other is such a parade, just as Penny suspected."

Troy was a little surprised at her response but put it down as coming from her conversations with Penny.

"Are you ready for our stroll?" he asked, pulling her up into his arms. He held her for a moment and said into her hair, "I hope you know how much I honestly love you."

He backed up and she smiled up at him, took his hand in hers and turned to go out of the room. They went to the garden and just strolled around looking at all the beautiful flowers.

"They will be in bloom for a long time," she commented.

Again, he was surprised at her. He stopped and looked at her. "You seem different after your rest this afternoon. Are you sure you are all right?" he asked tentatively.

"Yes, I'm fine. I love you with all my heart. Nothing will ever change that."

They had stopped and turned to each other. She put her hands around his neck and he bent down to kiss her. It was a passionate kiss with almost a desperation to it. He sensed something was going to happen but he wasn't sure what. He wanted to hold her forever and never let her go. They continued walking and holding hands. Neither said a word, just enjoyed their time together. It was finally time to go in and get ready for dinner. He walked her back to her room.

"I'll be back to escort you to dinner as soon as I'm ready."

"I'll be waiting for you," and she closed the door.

He stopped at his mother's room and knocked on the door. "Enter" was heard so he opened her door. She was seated on a chair by the fireplace.

He went to her and kissed her forehead. "How are you feeling, Mother?"

"Wonderful. Judith and I had such a lovely time together today. How was your drive through St. James?"

"Interesting," Troy replied. "I am so very thankful all I am is a chaperone."

Lady Matilda laughed. "You won't always have to go. I will go sometimes myself."

"I'm happy to hear that. I have a question for you. Have you noticed a change in Aspen?"

"Not really, although she seems calmer than before. I haven't really seen that much of her since we have been here."

"True, you have been very busy with Lady Judith."

"Is there something bothering you, dear?"

"I feel that something is different and that something unpleasant might be coming, but I have no idea what it is."

"Maybe you are afraid of her regaining her memory. Maybe she belongs to a very different life. Have you thought of that? Maybe she is already married. She might be getting her memory back and doesn't know how to tell you."

"I want her to get her memory back and I want to be there with her to help meld her two lives together. If she was married, someone would be looking for her. I don't think that's a problem. Are you about ready for dinner?"

"Yes, I will be down shortly."

Troy left to get Aspen. When he knocked, she came to door and opened it.

"Just on time," she smiled at him and it was her old smile so he felt relieved.

He gave her his arm and they walked to the dining room. Lady Matilda joined them shortly after. They talked all during dinner about the upcoming soirees and parties and when they would hold some of their own. Aspen was quite attentive at dinner and joined in the conversation. After dinner, Lady Matilda retired to her room. Troy received word that Penny was ready to come home. He went to get the Clarence carriage and left to get Penny. He kissed Aspen softly on the lips before leaving. Penny was all excited when she returned home. She went to see their mother and tell her all about it. Troy was going to stop in to see if Aspen was still up but went to his room first. Bailey was there and told him there was someone waiting for him in the garden. Troy made himself a drink and headed for the garden.

He sat at the same bench and Slick came out to join him.

"That was fast work," commented Troy.

"Wait 'til you hear to decide whether I am fast or not," he replied. Troy nodded for him to continue. "There was a woman taken by a group of criminals from the area around Leicester. The woman is of royal blood but from the wrong side."

"What do you mean the wrong side?" Troy was confused.

"Do you remember any history lessons of Great Britain?"

"Vaguely," Troy replied.

"There was a daughter of one of King George III's brother who married a king of Denmark. The king liked to sleep around and had slept with a maid of his wife's who happened to be from Great Britain. When the king's wife found out her maid was pregnant, the queen sent the maid back to her mother in Leicester."

"I don't understand what any of this has to do with the woman I found." Troy was very confused.

"The young girl has been said to have been abducted to try to get blackmail money. Her name was Aspen. But the real plot was that she would not return home. The girl and her sister had come to London with an uncle to be part of the season last, so she was abducted in London. I don't know for sure if it is the woman you know. I will have to look a little deeper with the information I have. I just wanted you to know. The rumor is the dear king was a little mad also. The girl's sister is not the nicest person around and is friends with the Deveron brothers."

"I will have to think about all of this. If Aspen is actually the illegitimate daughter of a king, what kind of life did she have? How was she brought up? We have to find out about the sister and the uncle. You have done well Slick and will be well rewarded, but we will have to find out for sure this is the right family." Troy took an envelope out of his pocket and handed it to Slick. "This for the work you have already done. Please keep digging to find out what I need to help the lady."

Slick took the envelope and took off back into the darkness.

Troy stayed for a while in the garden. He nursed his drink and thought about what Slick had told him. It fit, even the timeline. Could Aspen be the illegitimate daughter of a mad king? What problems might this present? He was going to have to proceed very carefully.

He walked back to his room. As he passed by Aspen's room, he thought he heard some crying. He knocked softly. The crying turned to a muffled sound.

He said softly as he could, "Aspen, it's me. Please open up."

After a few minutes, the door opened slowly. He went into the room and Aspen had indeed been crying. Troy took her in his arms and held her. He led her to the bed and laid her down. He got in on the other side of the bed and took her in his arms. He held her and let her cry. He held her for a very long time.

"Do you want to share with me what is wrong?" he asked.

"No," she answered weakly. "Just hold me, please."

She sounded so desperate. He held her close and they both fell asleep.

Troy was dreaming he was holding Aspen and could feel her body. He started rubbing her body with his hands. He heard her groan and woke up. He wasn't dreaming. He sat straight up in bed. What was he doing? His memory came back to him. He had been soothing Aspen and had fallen asleep. By his jumping up, he woke her.

"What's the matter?" she whispered.

"I need to leave right now," he said. But first he kissed her a deep kiss. "I love you. We will talk in the morning."

She pulled him to her and gave him another deep kiss. He groaned and quietly got out of bed and went to the door. He looked out into the hallway and didn't see anyone so he tiptoed to his room. He had just gotten to his door when he heard someone coming up the stairs. He quickly opened the door and went into his room. Was he out of his mind? If they had been caught, all would have been ruined and they all would go back to Leicestershire in disgrace. He was going to have to be more careful in the future. He undressed and got into bed and went back to sleep. He needed some sleep to deal with Aspen in the morning.

Chapter 15

*H*e woke early and dressed in tan breeches over white stockings with a brown waistcoat over a white linen shirt. He went to Aspen's door and knocked loudly. Her lady's maid came to the door.

"Would you please tell Lady Aspen that I am requesting her in my quarters for breakfast this morning. Whenever she is ready is fine with me," Troy said.

He went back to his room and left the door open. Bailey came in a little later.

"Could you order me some breakfast up here, please and bring it out to the balcony?" he asked.

"Yes, my lord," he bowed and left the room.

He sat on the balcony and contemplated the events of last night. He was really worried about Aspen but he had faith in himself that he would be able to help her. He loved her more and more each day. He never thought he could feel this way about another human being. He knew she returned his love. He sat there thinking of all he had learned last night. Bailey returned with a tray of tea with biscuits. Aspen entered the room shortly after. She looked so tired. He got up and went to her. He took her in his arms and kissed her. Then he took her by the hand and led her onto the balcony. She looked so beautiful in a flowered day dress with short sleeves and her hair piled high on her head.

"I am wondering if we can get married right away. I don't know if I can wait much longer. You are so beautiful."

She blushed. "I don't know if that is possible. I feel we have been pushing it a little the way we have been kissing."

"I know and I will have to start behaving myself." He took her hand and held it. "Can you talk to me this morning and tell me what the problem is?"

"I don't really know, my lord. I feel so out of sorts. I have been seeing more and more of little visions but cannot put anything together. It is so frustrating."

"Can you tell me some of the visions? Maybe I can help."

"I keep seeing this house in the country and this older woman. But I can't place her or the house. I feel happy though. There is also an older gentleman. He makes me very happy."

She was confirming the story he had heard last night. He was becoming sure she was the daughter of the King of Denmark. But it was still too early to say anything to her. He was about to make some sort of comment when they heard Penny at the door.

"Good morning Troy and Aspen. Do you have room for one more at your table?"

"Of course we do," said Aspen. "Please come and join us." Aspen took her hand back.

Penny was wearing a day gown of golden silk. It made her hair appear highlighted. Penny took the seat on the other side of Troy. She had some cards in her hand.

"We have been invited to a party at the Somners tomorrow night. Jewel wants to go for a carriage ride again today. Will you be able to escort us, Troy? I do hope you can come with us today, Aspen."

"I would be honored to escort you again and Lady Aspen is definitely going with us today. I might even ride in the carriage with you instead of on my horse."

"That will be wonderful. I will let Jewel know to pick us up about one o'clock. I can't wait. Here are your invitations to the party tomorrow night." She handed each Troy and Aspen their invitations. "I'm going to go talk to Mother again. I will see you two later." Penny bounced out of the room.

"I think I will go back to my room and rest a while. I will see you downstairs in the parlor a little later," she said.

He stood up and bowed to her as she left. He was going to have to start thinking of her feelings and not just his own. He was going to have to be more of a gentleman towards her. It was going to be so hard. But for proprietary's sake, he would have to do it. Troy was in the parlor with Lady Matilda when Penny and Aspen entered. It had been quiet for a while, but Penny's high energy bounced around the walls. She was becoming impatient for the events to start. She wanted to start being part of the society and the parties.

Lady Matilda was awaiting Lady Judith. They were going to go over some of the scheduled soirees and parties. Lady Judith was informing Lady Matilda of the personalities of some of the gentry who will be attending the events. Lady Matilda was out of touch with what has been going on in London. Finally, Lady Judith arrived with Jewel. The young people all went to get into the barouche-sociable. They started towards St. James.

Troy sat with Aspen on the one side and Ladies Penny and Jewel sat opposite them. Ladies Penny and Jewel started talking together about their favorite topics. Troy and Lady Aspen sat quietly. Troy was holding her hand. They just relaxed together and Aspen felt very safe so she just relaxed back into the barouche. Again, when they reached St. James, there were other barouches and some gentlemen on horses. Nods were given to them and returned but no untoward advances were made today. After about an hour of this, they left and returned home. Lady Jewel and Lady Judith were invited to stay for dinner. Lady Judith declined, stating she still had her husband to attend to. Lady Jewel decided to leave with her mother. The others went into the dining room for their meal. After the meal was finished, Troy asked Aspen if she would like to take a stroll in the garden. They left hand in hand.

They walked over to the bench in the rose garden.

"Ah, this is my favorite place in the garden," Troy said after seating Aspen on the bench.

"I agree, but only because we are always together when I come here. If I come on my own, I have memories of the two of us. It makes me feel very happy."

Troy sat next to her and put his arms around her. He gave her a little chaste kiss which stirred both of them.

"I do apologize. I should show much more restraint. I just can't seem to get enough of you. I love you with all my heart."

"Don't apologize. I feel the same way and I should put up more blockers for you but I can't because I am so in love with you. I feel the same as you but society says we must wait at least six months for us to even announce our engagement."

"I know and we are supposed to wait two years for marriage. I will definitely not be able to wait that long. When do you want to get married?" Troy asked her.

"I don't know. I haven't given much thought to the end result. There is much to think about and prepare."

"Would you like to get married in London or wait until we return to the country?"

"Troy, may I call you Troy?"

"Of course you can. We are way past the stifling 'lord' and 'lady'. We are much more intimate and can now address each other by our given names."

Lady Aspen turned her head away from Troy. He placed a finger under her chin and turned her head back to him. He looked deep into her beautiful eyes.

"What did I say wrong this time? Please tell me."

"I don't know my given name. I don't know anything and it is wearing on me. I can't help it but I get so depressed. I thought by now I would know all that I have forgotten. But it is taking its time coming back to me." There were tears in her eyes.

Troy pulled her to him. "I can't stand to see you so sad. I have hired an investigator."

She perked up. "You have?" she sounded happy.

"Yes, and although he has found some information, he is investigating more to find out details to ensure the information he has uncovered is about you and not someone else."

"What information has he uncovered?"

"He has found out a rumor of a woman or girl by the name of Aspen being abducted at the end of the London season last. But he has no details as to whom it was so we cannot say whether it was you or not. But the name is correct so I do believe it is you."

"But he found out there was someone named Aspen who was abducted. It has to be me. How many women or girls named Aspen are abducted in London?"

"Probably more women are abducted than we realize. I'm not sure how popular the name Aspen is here in London. Would you do something for me?" he asked.

"I want to say anything but knowing you, as I am starting to know you very well, I hesitate until I know what your thoughts are."

"My only thoughts are of you and helping you in any way possible. I want you to relax, sit back, let all the bad thoughts go, and enjoy this time we have together. I want to see you happy and carefree for now. We will get to where you want to be. But for now, we are in a situation we can't change at the present, so come into my arms and relax. Let my love surround you and cloak you in feelings of joy and safety."

"I'll try. I promise." She bent forward to kiss him. They kissed a deep passionate kiss. "I love you," she said and laid her head on his shoulder.

They stayed like this for a little while. Finally, they started back inside. They found Lady Matilda and Lady Penny in the front parlor.

"There you are children, I thought we had lost you to the stars outside," Lady Matilda commented.

"Almost, Mother," Troy responded laughing. "It is a beautiful night out and it was made more beautiful with the company I was with."

Aspen blushed, "You are too kind, my lord."

"Come sit with me," Penny said to Aspen while patting the seat next to her on the settee. "I haven't talked with you for quite some time."

Aspen went to sit next to Penny. They started talking. Troy went over and sat opposite his mother. Before he sat, he inquired if anyone wanted anything. Lady Matilda wanted a sherry and he poured himself a drink. They had a pleasant evening together until it was time to retire. They all walked up to their rooms. Troy offered his arm to Aspen and walked her to her room. He bent and gave her a chaste kiss on the lips. Then watched her enter her room and close the door. He turned and went to his room very lonely. Lady Matilda was in her doorway watching them. She felt sad for them but knew it would be a happy ending.

When everyone woke up the next morning, they gathered in Lady Matilda's room. Excitement was in the air. Penny was so excited to finally get things going with meeting others in society. The anticipation has been almost too much for her to bear. The excitement was filtering over to Aspen. She was excited to be going to a party with Troy. She knew his attention would be split watching her and Penny. He took his responsibilities to heart and wanted to do what was required of him. She loved him all the more for that. Lady Matilda was also excited to be back in the London society. It had been so long since she was involved in this type of excitement.

Penny asked her mother to come and look at her dresses to help pick out the perfect one. Penny then told Aspen she would help her find the perfect dress. They also discussed finding a seamstress to come and make them some ball gowns for the season. They would have to start preparing for the balls. Troy rolled his eyes with the discussion. Lady Matilda chuckled. This went on for most of the day. The women rested in the afternoon to be ready for the evening.

Troy just wandered around. He never did look over the entire house. He went to the basement to see what was there. The kitchen was downstairs and the servants were working at whatever they were assigned to do. Troy found Marple.

"I found you!" he stated. He picked her up and twirled her around. "Now I can pester you again."

Marple laughed and slapped at him. He went on to explore the rest of the basement. He found a wine cellar that was very well stocked. He checked the inventory. Then he moved on to see what else was there. There were no dungeons, he was a little disappointed. His imagination could go wild in a place like this. There were several rooms with different set ups, some were storage rooms and some had tables and chairs for meetings. Interesting and good to know.

Troy went back to the first floor. He knew about the three parlors and the dining room but there was more he had not seen. He went towards the back of the house. He came to some huge doors and opened the one side. On the other side was an enormous ball room. He stepped inside and looked around. *Wow,* he thought. *I never saw anything like this.* He was very surprised his parents had such a house and never used it. From what he has heard, once his parents married, they moved to the country and stayed there for the twenty years of their marriage. His father had inherited this house when his parents passed away. Maybe London was not their thing in life. But his mother had come alive being in this element. He should ask his mother about this when he had a chance. It made him curious as to why they stayed away from London. He decided he had seen enough. He went to his room and got ready for the evening.

There were eyes watching them and trying to find a way to damage the Bowling family. They were not done with them as of yet.

Chapter 16

*T*roy dressed in his black breeches over white stockings with a blue waistcoat over a ruffled white linen shirt. He had some wigs the same color of his as his own hair. He picked one of those and put it on. He hated wigs and wore them only when he absolutely had to. He slipped on his buckle shoes and went to the door. He went down to the parlor to see if the ladies were ready yet. Lady Matilda was there dressed in a black silk dress. It was long sleeved and was waist length bodice with a flowing skirt. She looked very beautiful. Her hair was swept up in a reliable arrangement. Troy bent over to kiss her on the forehead.

"You look beautiful, Mother. I can understand why Father married you."

"You are so kind, Troy. You are so much like your father. It sometimes takes my breath away when I see you."

"Would you like a sherry before we go, Mother?"

"Yes, my dear. I think I would enjoy that."

Troy made the drinks and handed the sherry to his mother. "I was exploring the house this afternoon and found the ballroom. I was very impressed but it conjured up some questions I have about why you and Father never returned here and to London."

"I don't really know, dear. We just never had the desire to leave the country. We were so happy there and were enjoying our lives and raising our children."

"I understand that. I miss the country and the quiet. It is a whirlwind here in London. They want you to be doing something all the time."

Just then the girls came waltzing in. They had their arms joined and were laughing and giggling. Troy was so happy to see them both in this mood. Aspen looked absolutely beautiful in a cream-colored gown. It was empire waist, short sleeved, very low cut, and draped around her figure very noticeably. She was wearing her gloves and had her fan attached. Penny was dressed in a flowing red dress with a very low neckline. There was lace draped around her shoulders and some on the skirt of the dress. Both girls had their hair swept up loosely and attached with combs at the back of their heads. They were too excited to sit down. Troy had ordered a carriage for seven o'clock. He was standing by the fireplace and Aspen walked over to him.

"I hope you approve, my lord," she said as she twirled around in front of him.

"Very much so, Lady Aspen. Mother, when is the earliest we can get married?" Troy asked.

Lady Matilda and Penny laughed.

"Patience, my dear. I will let you know when it is proper to start making the wedding plans."

The butler announced the carriage had arrived. The ladies each put their wraps on. Troy offered his arm to Aspen and they all walked out and entered the carriage. It was a really short drive over to the Somners' townhouse. They arrived amidst many other carriages. Finally, their carriage pulled up in front of the entrance. The footman opened the door and they all exited and went up to the door.

The house looked magnificent. They walked in together. Aspen was on Troy's arm. Lady Judith came and took Lady Matilda's arm. Penny went to where Jewel was surrounded by younger people. The room was set up with groups of chairs all around the room. Troy looked for a place for Aspen to sit and where he could stand to keep an eye on her and Penny. He spotted some vacant chairs in the corner. He had just gotten Aspen settled when a couple came up to them.

"Good evening," said the gentleman. "We have not had the pleasure to meet you before. I am Robert Glasswell, the Marquess of Heath and this is my fiancée Lady Eloise."

Troy bowed to the couple. "It is nice to meet you. I am Lord Bowling, Earl of Battingham and this is Lady Aspen, also my fiancée."

Lord Robert returned the bow to Troy and Aspen and Lady Eloise curtsied. There were some other chairs next to Aspen.

"Do you mind if we sit and get acquainted?"

"By all means, please. I would sit but I must keep an eye on my sister also."

"And who might your sister be?" asked Lord Robert.

"My mother is Lady Matilda Bowling and my sister is Lady Penelope," Troy answered. "We are newly arrived from Leicestershire. Lady Aspen has been staying as our guest."

"Yes, I am familiar with that area. We are both from the north. We are from the northwestern border between Scotland and England."

"I'm sorry, I'm not familiar with the area you are from. I have not traveled much except in my district. This is even my first time to London."

"This is my second visit and Lady Eloise has never been here before."

"Then we share something Lady Eloise," Troy said as he nodded to her."

They started talking small talk while Troy kept looking Penny's way. The group surrounding Jewel and Penny was growing with more boys than girls. Troy could see some ladies in the room giving them disgruntled looks. But Troy could see Penny and Jewel were laughing and having a good time. He even watched his mother. She and Lady Judith were by the opposite wall with some other ladies that were possibly from the same debutante group. They were talking away. Lady Matilda was having such a good time, Troy was afraid she forgot about Penny but he did see her glance over to Penny a few times.

Penny was meeting so many people her head was spinning. There were a couple of gentlemen who interested her. One was an earl. He was the Earl of Braxton. Penny thought he was just gorgeous. But she played the role she was supposed to and didn't let anyone too close. The other gentleman didn't have a title, his name was Brady Worrell. He kept looking at her over a drink in his hand. He was so handsome she almost swooned when he talked to her. He was asking her if this was her first time in London.

"Yes, we are just newly arrived and this is my first time in the city of London," she answered demurely.

He bowed to her and said, "I do hope we will be seeing much more of you."

Jewel piped up, "She is one of the debutantes this year, along with myself."

Penny turned and looked at Jewel. She was not sure that information should have been given out at this time. But Jewel was so much more knowledgeable than she was herself. She just turned back around and gave the gentleman a smile and then put her fan up. Troy saw the gesture and was not too happy with it, but no harm seemed to come from it so he let it go.

They were finally told that refreshments were being served in the dining room. Troy offered Aspen his arm and they walked along with the crowd towards the dining room. The food was set up buffet-style with a servant serving the dishes picked by each patron. Troy helped Aspen and they went back and found a place to sit while they ate. Penny was being escorted back by a single gentleman. Troy stood up, placed his plate on the chair, and told Aspen he would be right back.

Troy went over to Penny. "My Lady Penelope, please come and sit by Lady Aspen and myself. There are plenty of seats available over here."

He guided her over to the seat beside Aspen. The gentleman followed. Troy was not too happy.

Penny made the introductions. "Troy please meet the Earl of Braxton, Lord Timothy Braxton. Your lord, I wish to introduce my brother, Lord Bowling the Earl of Battingham and his fiancée Lady Aspen."

Timothy bowed to both Troy and Aspen.

Troy relented a little with the boy, "Would you like to join us while we eat, my lord?" The smile on Timothy's face was brighter than the lights in the room.

"It would be my pleasure, my lord," he replied as he sat next to Penny.

"Tell me a little about yourself, my lord," Troy stated. He was thinking he would be making conversation and learn about the boy.

"I am the son of the Earl of Braxton. I am the oldest of seven children and will inherit the title when my father passes which I hope will be many years from now. I have been attending Cambridge University and studying business. I reside in London during the time I attend the university and then spend time at home with my family."

"Is your family here with you in London now?" asked Troy.

"They will be here by the start of the season," replied Timothy.

They talked some small talk for a little while, then Penny spotted Jewel and they were off. Troy and Aspen meet a few more people and after a couple more hours the party was starting to break up. Troy sent for their carriage then he went for Lady Matilda and Penny. He went to Aspen and offered her his arm. She took it smiling, but she looked very tired. They arrived home after midnight. Lady Matilda and Penny went to their rooms. Troy pulled Aspen towards the gardens.

"I would like a little alone time with you since I have been in your company all evening and have not been able to hold you or barely touch you."

She smiled up at him. "I am tired but would love to spend some time with just the two of us," she said as they went to their favorite spot in the garden.

They got to the bench and Troy pulled her into his arms. She clung to him. He bent down and they kissed a long and passionate kiss. He didn't feel much better afterwards.

"I don't know why I do this to myself. It's killing me."

"I feel the same way. Oh, I want you so much. These feelings are getting way too intense. We really must find a better way."

"Short of not seeing each other until the wedding, I know of no way. Just being close to you drives me wild."

They sat down on the bench and he held her. They sat for a while and then Troy decided it was time to take her to her room. He walked her to her room and gave her a chaste kiss and pushed her into her room and watched her close the door. He turned and went to his room. He sat up for a long time trying to calm down. It wasn't working. He finally went to bed just to dream of Aspen.

Chapter 17

The next morning, Penny burst into Troy's bedroom, not expecting him to still be a sleep.

"Troy," she started and then stopped.

"What?" he called from the bed.

"Oh Troy, I am so sorry," Penny said and started leaving.

"Well since you woke me up, don't leave me here alone." He reached for his robe and wrapped it around himself. He looked out on the balcony and saw a tray of coffee, tea and biscuits. "Thank you, Bailey," he called. He walked out to the balcony. "Come on out Penny. I am decent for the moment."

Penny came bouncing out. She was dressed in a white cotton day dress with short sleeves and an empire waist. There were some embroidered flowers around the waist of the dress.

"I just wanted you to see all the invitations we received already this morning."

"That is why you got me up at this ungodly hour?" Troy asked.

"It's not an ungodly hour," Penny retorted. "It's after nine o'clock already. You never sleep this late. Are you not feeling well?"

"No, I didn't sleep well last night."

"That must be catching. Aspen was still in bed also. She said the same thing. I hope you two are not coming down with any illness. This pre-season has just started for me and I want to be a part of it completely."

"Penny, it is not just you," Troy tried to say softly. He didn't want to upset her. "Even Mother was tired last night. I love you and want you to have the best season ever had in the history of seasons but please think of the rest of us also. I will talk to Mother and work something out so you can attend most of the parties."

"I don't want to be selfish, Troy. But I also want the best season."

"I'm so sorry, sweetheart. I am just being very cranky this morning. I'm in a bad mood from not getting enough sleep. I'm taking it out on you. I don't want to spoil your time. Do you forgive me?"

"Of course I do. You are still my favorite brother."

"Wake me up like this a few more times and I might not be. I'll let your other brother be the favorite." He joked with her.

"I love you Troy and you will always be my favorite." She got up and kissed Troy on the cheek. Then she turned and skipped out of the room.

He was beginning to feel old. He got up and got dressed. He decided to wear black breeches that came to mid-thigh with white stockings under. He wore a black waistcoat with a white linen shirt beneath. He put his riding boots on. He went in search of Aspen. He found her in her room. He left the door open when he entered. She was sitting on her balcony but was not dressed as of yet.

"I'm sorry, darling, I'm not moving all that fast today. I'm still tired."

"I understand. I didn't sleep well either last night. I don't know what to do. Why can't we just marry and have done with this? Why must we suffer? But of course, I'm being the selfish one now. I just know we would be better off if we could just get married."

"We are not the first in this situation and we won't be the last. No one has died from having to wait to get married and neither will we. We will make it through." She put her hand on his cheek. "We must be patient, but I love you for being so impatient. Let's have fun and enjoy the season. It's a good thing you never had a season before. You would have been married before I came along."

"Never, you are the only one I could fall in love with. No one else would have been able to take my heart. Only you." He kissed her a chaste little kiss.

"I suppose I should get ready to go downstairs and try to be human today. You kept me up too late last night." She spanked his hand. "I dreamt about you most of the night and didn't get much sleep."

"The same with me. I dreamt about you all night. I will leave you to get dressed." He stood and bent down to kiss her a chaste kiss on the cheek this time and left the room closing the door after him.

He met his mother in the hallway. He bent to kiss her on the cheek. "How are you, Mother?"

"Not as young as I used to be. I think all that time in the country has spoiled me. I miss my routine. But I am having fun catching up with all my friends."

"I saw you with a group of women last night and wondered if they were part of the debutantes from your time as one."

"You are being very astute. I also saw you head off one of your sister's follies last night to save her reputation. That was really well done. It shows my faith in you is justified. Thank you, Troy."

"You are welcome, Mother. What are the plans for today?"

"Come down to the parlor and we will discuss the issue."

Troy followed her to the parlor. She picked her chair and he picked the one opposite her.

"I have Penny sorting through the invitations and writing down all the names and addresses. She also has to distinguish which night the invitations are for. That should keep her busy for a while."

"Good thinking, Mother. She needs to be toned down."

"I felt it would be a good exercise in patience for her, plus diligence. Anyway, it appears we are invited to the Wentworth's tonight. Abigail is a dear friend of mine. She is having a soiree tonight. It will be another long night so I hope you get a nap in before tonight. You look terrible, Troy."

"Let's just say dreams are not always the best for trying to get some sleep. Aspen and I are trying very hard to be good, but it is getting harder and harder."

"Patience, my dear. It will pay off in the long run. Although I am thinking of allowing you to have your wedding towards the end of the season. Maybe it will help to have an end in sight. Plus, you two can be busy with the wedding plans."

"That sounds great, Mother. I'm sure Aspen will approve of the information. I will talk to her when she comes down from her nap. She was having dreams also."

"I know it hasn't been easy on the two of you. If we were in the country it really would have been much simpler. You would have been permitted to have been married by now. London society is so much stricter. By the way, I believe Bailey is talking to someone out in the garden, you may have an interest in. He appears very unsavory. Please do try to get rid of him quickly."

"Why didn't you tell me that right away?" he asked as he stood up and moved quickly out of the room. He went to the rose garden and to the bench. Slick was there talking to Bailey.

"There you are, my lord. Slick came to see you and I told him you were still resting."

"Thanks to Penny I'm up before I wanted to be. You may leave for now. I will be up in my room shortly." Bailey bowed and left. "Have you found out more information for me?"

"Yes, me lord. I have more information. I also want to say you are very generous. I appreciate that. Anyway, I found out the name of the family involved. It appears the maid never married so the children have her name, which is Whitley. The king had insisted the maid return after giving birth and she became pregnant a second time. After that the queen refused to let the maid return. She had two daughters, Leslie and Aspen. The mother of the queen raised both girls with the help of her brother, Charles. The younger sister is devious and wanted the older sister out of the way because of an inheritance offered by the queen's mother. Both were to inherit but the younger sister wanted it all for herself. Evidently the grandmother wouldn't last much longer."

"Are you sure the older girl's name is Leslie and not Aspen?"

"No, me lord, I am not sure. Anyway, the younger daughter had the older girl abducted by the band of highwaymen and were told to do what they wanted with her. They told the grandmother that the older sister had run off to get married. Before she finally passed on, the brother took up care of the sister. However, the sister didn't want the old man interfering in her life so they have had him somewhere in London all doped up since the abduction. The grandmother finally passed away alone."

"Do you know where he could be?"

"No, me lord, but I could do some more digging and find out."

"Please continue on with your investigation and let me know where the uncle is being held. I want to secure his safety. Thank you again, Slick. You have done me a big favor. It appears the girl in our home is the sister who was abducted. I'm thankful I was able to save her. I would like to find out who the bandits are and apprehend them plus the sister. If you can help me with this, I will be forever thankful. I didn't expect you so I don't have another payment with me right now."

"That is alright, me lord. You were more than generous last time so for now we are even. I will let you know what I find out."

Slick stood and was gone before Troy could acknowledge him. *I think it might be time to let Aspen and Lady Matilda know what is going on.* Troy walked back to the parlor. Lady Matilda was there alone.

"Did you remove the rogue?" she asked.

"Yes, Mother, he is gone. But I must talk to you in private. Can we retire to my room?"

"Of course, Troy."

He offered his arm and they went to his room. He didn't even trust his balcony so he sat his mother in a chair by the fireplace. He asked Bailey to get them some tea. He sat opposite her and told her everything he had learned.

"But Troy, how do we know she is the girl that was abducted?"

"The timeline of when I found her fits, right after the season ended in London. Then she has been having some visions of a place in the country with an older woman and gentleman. Then the name. I don't know who else it could be. But she is the daughter of a maid and I'm sure she will give me a hard time about marrying me. Besides that, her father is said to have died a mad man. I know her and she will be afraid of having children with me not just marrying me. I have to tell her what I have found out but I really don't want to. At least not until we are married."

"You do have a dilemma," she answered. "The only thing I can say, Troy, is that you will have to try to win her over before you tell her. What are you doing about the situation?"

"I am having Slick find her uncle and I plan to rescue him and return him to his rightful home. I just hope it's not too late. Second of all I am having Slick find out who the bandits are and will have them arrested along with the sister. I will regain all of Aspen's inheritance and return it to her. Those are my plans. Let's see how they work out."

"Those are very noble plans. Don't get yourself hurt or worse killed in the process. You have much to live for. You also have a lot to think about and a lot of emotional things to work out. I feel for you. Yours is not the normal problems of a man and a woman. Yours is much more complicated. Leave it to you to fall in love with someone who has all these problems hanging around her. However, I love her also as my own daughter and am proud of you for saving and helping her. God speed to you and the best of luck. If there is something I can do to help you, please let me know. I will help in any way possible."

Troy went to kiss his mother on the cheek. "Thank you, Mother. Having your approval means a lot to me. I was afraid you would tell me to find someone else and that I cannot do. My heart has been given to Aspen and no one else will do."

"I understand. Now I must go to see to Penny and to help her if need be. I will drive with the girls this afternoon so you can get some much-needed rest. Be ready for this evening."

She left the room and went to Penny's room. He was relieved she was with him in his adventures.

Chapter 18

Troy went in search of Aspen. He went to her room and knocked on the door. He entered upon hearing the ascent, leaving the door open as he entered. He stopped short. Aspen was sitting on the balcony a vision of loveliness. She was dressed in a day dress of powder blue with an empire waist and short sleeves. Her hair had been brushed, but not put up as yet. It flowed around her as a halo and hung long down her back. She looked up at him with those yellow-gold eyes of hers and his heart melted. He went to her and pulled her into his arms. He kissed her deeply. She swooned into his embrace. He finally realized what he was doing and pulled away.

"I'm sorry, my love. I couldn't help myself. You are a vision of loveliness and I was beyond any help to stop from kissing you."

"No apology necessary. It is not your fault. I love you so much that I react to your simplest touch."

"How about we go down to the garden and take a stroll. I have several things to talk to you about." He offered her his arm and they went to the garden. They strolled around for a while and ended up in their favorite spot.

"I am curious. What is it you have to tell me?"

"First of all, Mother has said we can set a wedding date for around the end of the season. I would like to get your opinion as to what type of wedding you would like and when you would like to get married."

"I would like to get married as soon as possible. The season starts in about two weeks. We can make the wedding for four months from now. I believe Lady Matilda would approve of that. I would like a very small, intimate wedding. Just family and very close friends," said Aspen.

"That sounds just the way I would like it. We will start planning it right away. I also want to ask you some intimate questions." He pulled her into his arms and held her. "How many children do you think you want? Where do you want to live, here or the country? Will being the countess of the Battingham Castle be okay for you? Of course, my mother will be there to help. Will you mind living with my mother?"

She put a finger to his lips. "As long as I am loved by you, all is fine with me. And I want as many children as you. I love you and will love and honor you the rest of my days."

"Do you promise to love me all the days of your life? Do you promise me never to leave me, no matter what?"

"I promise," she said and he kissed her deeply.

When they parted, he held her to him and hoped she would keep her promise when she found out the truth of her parentage. He didn't want to let her go.

"Mother is riding with the girls this afternoon so we have most of the afternoon to be together. There is a soiree this evening and we are required to attend. If you would like to rest, I will let you go after a bit but for now I would like to hold you a while longer."

"That is fine with me. I am very comfortable in your arms. I love you so."

Troy lost himself in the goldenness of her eyes. He felt like he was swimming in a golden pool. He finally took a deep sigh and just held her. They sat quietly for a long time just enjoying being together. Finally, Troy asked her if she was hungry.

"A little," she replied.

They stood and started strolling back to the house. It was wonderful to have this time to themselves and not to be bothered by the hustle and bustle of keeping up with Penny. They found a servant and asked for a light lunch to be brought to the table just outside the doors leading back into the house. They wanted to stay out and enjoy the fresh air. Just as the food arrived, they heard Penny and Lady Matilda return to the house. They asked the servant to send a request for the two ladies to join them. Penny came bounding in. She took a chair and was followed by Lady Matilda. Troy stood up and kissed both on the cheek.

"We have ordered a light lunch and there is plenty for all of us."

Lady Matilda sat down. "Thank you, Troy and Aspen. This is lovely.

"How was your drive around St. James today?" inquired Troy.

"It was thrilling now that I know some of those we passed. I am so excited for tonight. How about you, Aspen? Are you excited?"

"Yes, my dear," she said patting Penny's hand. "It can be quite exciting going to a soiree. Lady Matilda knows more than I and can probably say how a soiree will be conducted."

"Well things have changed since I was your age. When we had a soiree, it was a time to talk about politics and such but literature is also discussed and new books that have come out. Talk of new ideas and trends and dances and whatever else someone might want to talk about."

"I'm not sure politics is a subject that should be discussed in the presence of women," Troy commented.

"And pray tell, why not?" asked Aspen surprised. "Is it that us women don't have a mind to comprehend the complexities of what is going on around us?"

Troy took her hand. "No, my dear," he said smiling. "What I meant is that men tend to get overheated by remarks made from others of the opposite view point. I quite like hearing the opinion of women." He bent and gave her a chaste kiss.

Penny looked at them with adoring eyes. "I do hope I find someone who can love me as much as the two of you are in love."

"You are finely learning to say things correctly and not upset the delicacies of the female mind," said Lady Matilda chuckling. "Have you discussed with Aspen the subject of your wedding?"

"Yes, we have not set the definite date but we have planned a date four months from now. We would like to have a very small and intimate wedding. Just family and very close friends."

"It will be your wedding and it will be the way you want it. May I make a suggestion, Aspen and Troy? Since you want a small and intimate wedding, why not have it here in the garden? We could set up a nice dinner for after the ceremony."

"Oh, that sounds perfect, Lady Matilda," Aspen exclaimed. "We could have it by our favorite spot by the rose garden," she realized what she said and blushed.

"That sounds perfect to me," Troy laughed and bent to give her another chaste kiss.

"How exciting," Penny joined in. "A wedding to end the season. This will indeed be a perfect year."

Lady Matilda stood, "I believe it is time for us all to get some rest to prepare for this evening. Come along Penny." She turned and went into the house.

Penny followed but came and gave Aspen a kiss on the cheek. Then she went running after Lady Matilda.

Troy looked at Aspen. "I think you need to get some rest. Come, I will walk you to your room so you can get undisturbed rest."

"Alright, my love," she stood and took his hand. But she pulled back a little. "The wedding sounds like it will be perfect and just what I would ask for on the best day of my life."

Troy pulled her to him and kissed her intensely. "My thoughts exactly. Now we better get you up to your room so you can rest."

"You make that a little difficult, my lord. But now I have sweet dreams to look forward to."

They walked into the house and up to her room. Troy hugged her and pushed her into her doorway and watched her close the door. *Soon,* he thought, *I will be taking you to my room and there will be no closed doors between us.* He could hardly wait for the four months to pass.

Troy spent the afternoon going over some correspondence which had arrived from Mr. Blake. It appeared that everything was quiet in Leicester-shire. Matlock and Blake had things under control. It was a relief that he didn't have to worry about things back home. He worked on the finances and got everything all caught up. It was time for him to dress for the evening. He dressed in his black breeches over his white stockings covered by his black waistcoat and a frilly silk ruffled shirt. He put on his buckled shoes and carried his wig. He would only put it on at the last minute. Last time for the party, he just about took the wig off in the middle of the party. He went looking for the ladies. They were all in the front parlor.

"Good evening, my ladies," he said and bowed to them.

Lady Matilda was dressed in her silk black dress with white lace around the bodice and at the end of her long sleeves. She had finally changed out of the black lace. Troy was happy to see this. Penny was dressed in the fashionable dress of light blue silk empire waist and bil-lowed out slightly from the waist. It was short sleeved and looked adorable on her. But his eye went to Aspen. She was wearing a dress much like Penny's but in a gold color. The color brought out the color of her eyes and the gleam of her hair. She was undoubtedly the most beautiful person in the room. He was sure she would be the most beautiful at the soiree also and she was his.

"A sherry, Mother? Would anyone else like anything?"

Lady Matilda nodded yes and the other two ladies shook their heads no. Troy handed Lady Matilda her sherry and went to stand behind Aspen. They chatted small talk until the carriage was announced. They arrived along with the throng of others. They went into the house. The parlor was arranged more open than had been at the Somners' party last night. Penny made a beeline towards Jewel and her group. Lady Matilda went to Lady Wentworth and that group. Troy and Aspen made their way to a corner to sit. Some of the people they had met last night came by to chat and some new people introduced themselves. There were some gentlemen who had come over to be introduced to the lady. Troy was polite but sent them on their way. Aspen was laughing and having a good time. Troy was scowling. Soon the room was filling up and people were taking seats around the room. The discussions began with literature. To Troy, the evening was boring but he was trying hard to listen as he held Aspen's hand. Aspen seemed to be thoroughly enjoying the evening. The subject did turn to politics. As Troy predicted it did get heated and someone had to break in and change the subject before a fight broke out. But mostly the evening was uneventful. They went to share in the refreshments and went back and sat for a while longer.

They stayed until just after midnight and then made their goodbyes. They got home and everyone went to their rooms. Troy walked Aspen to her room and gave her a chaste kiss on the lips. She went into her room and shut the door. When Troy got to his room, Bailey was waiting for him.

"The gentleman is waiting for you in the garden, my lord."

"That was awful fast," Troy commented.

He went to his safe, took out another envelope, and put it in the inside pocket of his waistcoat. He then went to the garden to his and Aspen's favorite spot. He sat on the bench and Slick came out and sat next to him.

"That was very quick work," Troy stated.

"Well, I am not sure about that," Slick replied. "I found someone who knows of an old gentleman being kept at a certain house in London. But we are not sure it is the uncle of the girl staying with you. It is difficult to determine who the gentleman is. I have a couple of men working with me and we are trying to make sure who the gentleman is. My question to you is what do you want us to do if the gentleman turns out to be the one we are looking for?"

"What do you suggest? I would like to be informed before any attempt is made to rescue the gentleman. However, I understand the circumstances of waiting, we could lose our chance of rescue or we could get there too late for a rescue."

"Ah, me lord. I would like to wait for the situation to become clear. We really won't know what to do until we have all our proof in place. I do have one question. What do you want us to do with the gentleman if we are successful in our rescue attempt?"

"Bring him here. I will have something ready to take care of him. Bring him around to the back of the townhouse, hopefully under the disguise of night, so we will be able to sneak him into the townhouse. The fewer who know of this the better, so I will leave the plan to your discretion. I would like to be there to help but I also have no men to help back me up. I must rely on you and your knowledge of London and the ways of London. I'm largely at a disadvantage here. I'm out of my element."

"Ah, me lord. I understand. It is a privilege helping you, me lord. I will take care of things and handle it in the manner you want. I will try to get word to you before anything happens so you can be in on the rescue."

Troy took the envelope out of his pocket and handed it to Slick.

"No, me lord. You have already paid me handsomely."

"As you said, you have men working for you. You will need money to pay them. Please take this and do what you have to do. The other money was for you. I want to pay you for any expenses you might incur. Again, I can't tell you how much this means to me."

"Thank you, me lord. I will be in touch." This time when he stood, he bowed to Troy and then took off.

Troy went back to his room and was glad Bailey was still there. "Bailey, I have a situation again. I need your help."

"Yes, my lord. How can I help you?"

"I haven't kept you up with the information I have gotten from Slick." Troy went on to fill in the blanks of what Slick had found out. "If the gentleman in the London house is Aspen's uncle and if he is ill, we will need somewhere to keep him and I want him out of prying eyes. I was in the basement the other day and saw some rooms that looked like meeting rooms. Maybe one of them can be converted into a room to take care of someone who is sick. Also, we will either need to find another door for entrance or make everyone leave the area when we bring him in. Not only that, we will need a doctor to examine him and will probably make several trips and this all has to be unseen."

"I understand what you are saying, my lord. Let me look around to-morrow and see what I can find. I will work on setting this all up as quickly as possible. Is there anything else you will need before retiring?"

"No Bailey, that will be all. I can finish the rest. Thank you again."

Bailey bowed and left.

The eyes were still watching. From the group only one could be left to watch the house. One person alone would not be able to disarm one person and grab another without an alarm being sounded, so they watched and waited.

Chapter 19

The days settled into a routine of events. However, the week of the party being held by the Bowlings finally arrived. Penny, Aspen, Lady Matilda, and Troy had been busy writing out invitations for the party so they could go out today. The party was on Friday and today was Monday. Lady Matilda asked Troy to be chaperone all week so she could concentrate on preparations for the party. All parlors were going to be used and the dining room for refreshments. Lady Matilda had all the servants bustling to get things done. As this was one of the last events before the start of the season and all the balls, Lady Matilda wanted everything to be perfect and special. She had a few ideas she wanted to try at the party to make their party the best of the year.

Troy was kept busy chaperoning Penny and trying to pay attention to Aspen. He was so glad to see the day arrive for their party. This meant he either had to stay out of the way or help where needed. He didn't mind either and did a little of both. Both girls were so excited but went to their rooms early to rest and then prepare for the evening. Lady Matilda seemed to gather more energy the more she supervised the work. She was really in her environment.

Troy finally went up to his room to rest a little and then get ready. In the back of his mind, he was wondering why he had not heard from Slick. Bailey had come through again. He had found another door and had prepared a secret room to bring Aspen's uncle. Troy was thankful she still had not regained her memory and was having a good time with all these events. It made it easier on him and he was able to enjoy her company. They had been able to control themselves a little better now that they were in a type of routine.

Bailey was waiting for him with news that Slick was here to see him. However, the garden was amassed with servants setting up for tonight so Bailey had taken Slick to the secret room. Troy left to go talk with Slick and find out what has been going on. He found the room from Bailey's directions. It indeed was off the beaten path. He found Slick sitting and waiting for him.

"Good evening, Slick. I have been wondering about you," Troy said.

"It has been hard to keep up with what has been going on," Slick countered.

"Tell me what has been going on."

"We went to that house here in London and checked on the old gentleman. He was in bad shape, me lord. They have been giving him all kinds of drugs. Mostly the kind to keep him quiet. Since he is in such bad shape the guards was loose with watching him. We were able to get in and out easy like. We tried to find someone who knew who he was. We was finally able to find a woman who had helped them at the beginning. She confirmed who he was and we now know he is the girl's uncle, so we set up a plan to go in and get him. We set it for last night. We went and he weren't there."

"What do you mean he wasn't there? Did he pass?"

"Well that is what I'm trying to tell you, me lord. We went and he weren't there. We didn't know ourselves what had happened. We had someone watch the house, but they didn't see nothing. We found the woman again and she said he was taken to Leicester to his old home. How they got him out we don't know but they did. So now what, me lord?"

Troy thought for a few minutes. "How are you with traveling outside of London?"

"I have a man works for me that knows a lot of the area outside London. He could help me. What do you want us to do?"

"Battingham Castle is in Leicestershire. That is my property. I have a man that works there by the name of Matlock. I want you to go see him. I will write a letter and have you take it to him. I think if you work with my men, we will be able to save her uncle. We just might be able to catch the whole gang. Let me go up and start writing the letter. Return tomorrow night and I will hand off the letter to you to give to Matlock. He is a good man and will help you with this situation plus I have plenty of men who can help."

"I will see you tomorrow night, me lord." Slick left the room and the building.

Troy went to his room and started the letter. He didn't have much time and wanted to make sure he told Matlock all he would need to know. He knew he could finish the letter tomorrow, but it was on his mind now. He kept working until it was past time to be ready. He made himself stop and hurriedly got dressed. He was not even sure he was properly dressed when he went out the door to go to the parlor. He saw Bailey and asked if he had everything on correctly before descending the stairway. Bailey gave him the once over and said he looked just fine. Troy entered the parlor to see all three pairs of eyes looking at him. *Oh no,* he thought. *I must have something on wrong.* He bowed to the ladies.

"Is everything alright?" he asked. "Am I on backwards or something?"

They all laughed.

"No, my dear," replied Lady Matilda. "We were just wondering if you were going to join us. Our guests will be arriving any minute."

"I apologize. I was working on some correspondence from Mr. Blake and lost track of time. I literally threw my clothes on."

"That's why your wig is all askew," laughed Penny.

Troy put his hands up to straighten his wig to find it was sitting correctly on his head. Penny and Aspen laughed so hard. They were still laughing when the first guests arrived, which were the Somners. From then on, the flow of people was nonstop. Troy offered Aspen his arm so they could walk around and talk to different groups of people. Lady Matilda had done an excellent job of decorating their townhouse for tonight's party. She had candles everywhere. When they did a tour of the garden, they were amazed at the display. It was absolutely beautiful.

"Oh, Troy. Look at it. Lady Matilda outdid herself. It is so beautiful."

"Almost as beautiful as you, my precious." He told her. She blushed. "And that blush makes you even more remarkable."

She smiled up at him. They continued walking around and finally stopped to accept some drinks. Troy accepted a bourbon. He drank the first one straight down and went looking for another.

"I was not aware you were into drink so much, my lord," Aspen said concerned.

"It has been a horrific day. I don't usually drink like this and you know it," he said sharply.

"Yes, my lord. I will say nothing more about it."

He looked at her acutely. "Am I saying things wrong again?"

"No, my lord. You are quite fine."

That really got him a little heated. Now was not the time to have a discussion like this. He was not sure if she was upset with him or he was upset with her. He didn't know if he was too sharp with her to begin with or she was out of sorts. He decided to drop the whole thing and just do his duty tonight. He had so much on his mind it was hard for him to concentrate. He just wanted the evening to be over so he could complete the correspondence to Matlock. They continued to walk for a while and then Troy found a seat for Aspen to sit. He stood behind her.

The evening seemed to pass quicker than the others had. Troy and Aspen took several more tours around the three parlors. Soon it was time for the refreshments. Lady Matilda definitely outdid herself. In the middle of the tables, she had an ice sculpture made of a swan with the punch for the dinner flowing over it into glasses below. It was an absolutely fantastic idea. The guests cooed for the rest of the night. Troy saw Lady Matilda go to her group of friends and she was all smiles. Penny and Jewel were surrounded by admirers all night. No one seemed to do anything inappropriate towards them so everything was fine. Being the hosts of the party, they could not leave at midnight. They had to stay until the last guest left. It was four o'clock in the morning before they were able to go to their rooms. The servants took care of extinguishing all the candles. Lady Matilda told the servants to go to bed and worry about the cleanup in the morning. The ice sculpture was taken out to the garden so it could overflow out there. Troy was very tired. He didn't have any time to rest yesterday. He walked Aspen to her door and gave her a chaste kiss on the lips then pushed her towards the door and watched it close as usual. He didn't notice the perturbed look on her face. He decided to just go to bed and leave the letter for in the morning.

He didn't wake up until after ten o'clock in the morning. He heard a soft knock on his door. He pulled his robe on and went to the door. Aspen was standing outside looking beautiful as always in a pale blue day dress that showed off her figure. He started having stirrings and was afraid to let her in. He was afraid he would devour her. She saw his hesitation and started turning away. He saw there were tears in her eyes. He grabbed her arm and pulled her towards him. He gave her a chaste kiss and told her to come in but leave the door open. He led her to the balcony and sat her down.

"What is the matter, my love?"

"Nothing, my lord," she said as she started wiping her eyes.

"Tears do not say nothing," he replied. He gently pulled her into his arms. "Please tell me."

"It appears that I no longer please you, my lord," she said in a quiet voice.

"What do you mean, you don't please me? I love you dearly."

"You have just been so, so…I don't know I can't think of the word."

"Well when I saw you at the door, I was afraid I would drag you in here and devour you. Are you upset because I hesitated? I didn't want to ruin your honor which for a moment I was prepared to do."

"Oh, I thought after last night, you would not want me anymore."

"I apologize for last night. I had some things on my mind and was only half at the party. I didn't mean to slight you."

"I guess there are still things we have to learn about each other."

"There definitely are. Let me go and get some clothes on. I will ring for breakfast and we will sit and talk."

She nodded. Troy went to ring the bell and Bailey appeared immediately. Troy asked him to have some breakfast sent up for Aspen and himself then went into his wash room behind the closet. While he was in getting cleaned up and dressed, Aspen walked around his room. She walked over to the writing desk and saw the letter he was writing to Matlock. She was thinking it was the letter to Mr. Blake and picked it up to look at it. She saw her name and started reading the letter. Troy came out just as she finished reading the letter. His heart dropped. She turned to him.

"Why have you not told me any of this? You know who I am?" she accused him.

"Aspen, let's go sit and talk. Let me explain.'

"Explain what? That you have been hiding information from me? That you lied to me by withholding information that would help me know who I am? How could you, Troy? You profess to love me and then do this to me."

"Do what to you?" Penny asked from the doorway.

Troy and Aspen both turned and said at the same time, "Not now Penny!"

Penny turned and ran from the room.

"Come sit down and I will explain," Troy said frustrated.

"How can I believe anything you say when I find out the information you have known for how long?"

"Please just come and sit down. I am begging you. I don't want to say anything wrong, so let's sit down and calmly talk. I do love you with all my heart."

Aspen walked over to the chair on the balcony and sat down. She wouldn't let him touch her.

"I only found out recently and was waiting for proof as to who you are. In the meantime, I found out that your uncle was in dire need of help and I was working on helping him. So I had my mind going in so many directions I couldn't think what to say to you until I had the whole story."

"Do you have the whole story now?" She asked.

"Let me start at the beginning. I found out that the investigators in London are mostly criminals. I didn't know how to find one so Bailey helped me." He went on to tell her about Slick and all the information he had found out. He left out the information about her being the daughter of a servant and was supposedly illegitimate. Troy was afraid to leave anything out or she would find out later and really hate him. But he wanted this bit verified before telling her. So he told her everything else and about her uncle.

"So what are you going to do?" she asked.

"I am sending Slick and a friend of his to Matlock. I'm going to have Matlock assess the situation and take care of your uncle as soon as they can. We are hoping the band of criminals that took you are also the ones taking care of your uncle. If we can save him and catch the band of thieves, we will be able to put all of this behind you. We can be married and live happily ever after."

Chapter 20

*A*spen sat for a long time not saying anything. As Troy had been talking, everything was coming back to her. Her grandmother, the house they lived in, the happy times growing up, never knowing her real mother or father, and her sister who always seemed to hate her. Even as they were growing up her sister was always jealous of her and the attention she received. It all came rushing back to her. It made her head hurt.

"I must go and lay down. I don't feel very well."

"Let me help you. I will help you walk to your room and help you into bed."

"No, I need some time alone. Please give me some time to digest everything." She stood and walked to her room.

Troy was devasted. He stood and walked to his mother's room. He knocked and entered upon receiving permission. Penny and Lady Matilda were on the balcony. Troy bent to kiss each on the forehead. He looked as bad as he felt. He couldn't chit chat about the party last night with the ladies which is what they were mentioning. Finally, he excused himself and went back to his room. He still had responsibilities so he sat down to finish his letter to Matlock. When he finished, he asked Bailey to give the letter to Slick tonight. He still had to save Aspen's uncle. He still had to act as chaperone for Penny. He still had to be the head of the household for his mother and sister. He was just hoping he still had a fiancée. When it was time to chaperone Penny and Jewel around St. James, he went but his heart wasn't in it. Aspen had been in her room all day. As he rode his horse next to the barouche-sociable with the ladies, people were stopping them constantly telling them what a grand party it was last night. Penny was enjoying it very much. Next week, the balls would begin. Then it would really be hard keeping an eye on her. He was so looking forward to dancing with and holding Aspen. He was looking forward to her enjoying the time together and getting married right before the end of the season. He felt so sorry for himself but he especially felt sorry for Aspen.

What he didn't know was that as soon as Troy and Penny left that day, Lady Matilda went to Aspen's room to talk to her. Lady Matilda knocked on the door and heard a muffled, "Go away, please." Lady Matilda opened the door anyway. There was no impropriety here. It was her house.

"Lady Aspen, I wish to talk to you. Please come and sit with me."

Aspen jumped out of bed. "I am so sorry, Lady Matilda. I didn't know it was you."

"No, you thought it was Troy."

"Yes, I did and I'm just not ready to talk to him."

"Tell me what you are thinking and feeling. I want to help you."

"I feel so betrayed by Troy. Why didn't he tell me what he had found out when he learned it? Didn't he trust me? Did he want me to stay in the dark as to who I am? How can I trust him in the future? What am I going to do now that I remember everything? I cannot continue on with this charade. I'm just so miserable."

"I understand, my dear. But Troy loves you and wants to protect you. He is terrified of losing you."

"Then why did he lie to me by not telling me what he found out?"

"I never said he was correct in his decisions. I said he loves you and wants to protect you."

"That was not protecting me. That was keeping me in the dark. I had no idea who I was or where I belonged. He gave me a place to belong, but it was a false place."

"Do you really believe that? Then maybe you didn't truly love him."

"How can you say that? I loved him with all my heart and trusted him to take care of me."

"Are you listening to yourself? You trusted him to take care of you. Right or wrong, he did the best he could for you because of his love for you. Can you fault him for that?"

"I don't know. I'm getting so confused."

"Maybe you should talk it out with him. He was only doing what he felt was best for you at the time. He loves you too much. He didn't want to see you hurt. It's killing him inside thinking he did this to you. By rights if he had told you from the beginning, you probably would have reacted the same way. He would have lost you. It would have destroyed him."

"I'm beginning to see what you mean. But I do have to process all that has just come back to me."

"Let Troy help you. You owe it to him. He loves you completely and would do anything for you."

Aspen smiled for the first time. "Alright, I'll stop feeling sorry for myself and will talk with him."

"Good and for the record, my pet, I love you as much as he does and I'm really looking forward to you becoming my daughter. I could care less if you are the Queen of England or a lowly maid. You are a true lady. You have won our hearts and we feel happy to have you. We love you, dear." Lady Matilda stood up and came over to Aspen and kissed her on the cheek. She then turned and left the room.

Aspen put her head in her hands and started crying.

Troy was so thankful the ride was over. Jewel took Penny home with Troy riding beside them. They waved good bye to Jewel and entered the townhouse. Troy went into the parlor to get himself a drink. Lady Matilda was sitting in there and so was Aspen. They were talking small talk. Troy went over and poured himself a drink. "Would you like a sherry, Mother?" he asked.

"Yes, I believe I would like one," she replied.

"I think I would like one myself, my lord," Aspen said.

Troy made the two sherries and handed them to the two women. "You are looking especially beautiful this evening, Aspen," he said.

"Thank you, my lord," she replied. Troy went over to the cabinet and made himself a drink. "I was thinking it would be a good night for a stroll in the garden, if you would like to accompany me, my lord."

He turned to look at her. "It would be my pleasure, my lady," he said and downed his drink. He walked over to her and offered her his arm. She stood and took his arm and they strolled out to the garden.

"It is such a beautiful night," she said. They walked to their favorite place and sat down. "I am so sorry I upset you, my lord."

"I understand how you feel, but I genuinely was not trying to keep anything from you. I was simply trying to find out more information before telling you just bits and pieces."

"I know you were trying to protect me and I really do appreciate it. It was such a shock reading about it in a letter."

"You should never have seen the letter. I should have put it away."

"I should not have been snooping around your room. I apologize for that."

"So where does this leave us? I still love you with all my heart. I'm just feeling like I honestly let you down and I am so sorry."

"I don't feel like you let me down. It was just a shock reading all that and it coming back to me full force. I can't believe my sister did that and my poor uncle, do you really think you can save him?"

"He has been drugged for almost a year. I do hope there has not been too much damage done. However, we will help him just as fast as we can. I have a doctor standing by to help him. I will do everything I can for him."

"Thank you, my lord. I am genuinely appreciative of all you have done and are doing for me and my family. I'm sorry to hear that my grandmother passed while I was in the dark."

"You really should have been told this and should never had read it in a letter. I am so sorry to do that to you. It hurts me gravely that you found out that way."

She took his hand. "It is done and cannot be changed. We must move on from this."

"But move on to where. Do you still love me?"

"With all my heart. However, I would like to start over. Now that I know who I am, I am seeing things differently. Please give me some time."

He took her in his arms and kissed her deeply. Then he just held her. She relaxed into his arms and let him hold her.

The next week was a flourish of getting ready for the season. The ladies were busy with the seamstress. Troy was wondering if he should install larger closets for the ladies. There was the usual ride around St. James every day. More and more people were showing up and it was getting quite crowded. Troy and Aspen were spending time alone together and working through their problems. Troy was anxiously awaiting word from Battingham Castle.

He finally received correspondence from Matlock. They were able to rescue Charles and they brought him to Battingham for protection and care. He was not in very good shape, but the doctor was hoping for a full recovery. Aspen's uncle was still sleeping from whatever drug they had given him. They had rescued him two days before. He was very thin and frail. Troy didn't know if he should mention it to Aspen as of yet. There was nothing she could do right now. Her uncle needed the care he was receiving at Battingham. Matlock also made mention of someone of the Gentry had been helping the culprits. The sheriff was looking into it. He went in search of her. He found her in the library looking at the books.

"There you are sweetheart. Are you interested in reading a book? I thought you were up to your eyeballs in fabric."

Aspen laughed. He loved the sound of her laugh. "I am taking a break from all the choices of colors and styles. My mind was getting confused between green, gold, yellow, and all the rest."

Troy chuckled and took her in his arms. "I will love you in any color. However, my favorite is gold. That brings out the color of your eyes, which I adore, and it highlights the color of your hair, which I also adore. Along with your mouth," which he kissed, "and your nose," which he tweaked with his finger.

"Alright, so you really like my face."

"And much more," he replied.

She blushed and turned towards the books. She started picking them up and reading the title of the books. "These are really old books."

"They are from my father and his father before him and back I don't even know how far."

"Ah, but you know where you are from. I don't. My grandmother and uncle would never discuss anything with me. I do know that my grandmother was the mother of the Queen of Denmark and that her husband who died, was very dear to her. I know she had a lot of children and some grandchildren. She went to see them often but they never came to where we lived. I loved her so much. She was like a mother to me and my uncle was like a father to me. Have you heard anything as of yet concerning my uncle?"

"I just heard today. They have rescued him and the doctor is taking care of him. They don't know yet whether he will make it, but the doctor will do all within his power to help him."

Aspen sat down. "I don't want to lose him too. It will be too much." She started crying.

Troy took her in his arms and held her. "I have faith in the doctor. He is good. That is why I would like to keep him at Battingham. I trust this doctor more than any other."

"I trust your judgement, Troy. I will take a wait and see position. Please let me know if you get word that he is getting worse. I would like to see him before he passes, if it comes to that. I pray it does not."

"I will keep you informed, my love." Troy let her go.

"I think I will retreat to my room for a little rest."

Troy bowed to her and let her go.

Chapter 21

*I*nvitations were coming in fast. Lady Matilda and Lady Judith were busy going through all the invitations and setting the date of their balls. They were huddled in the front parlor. They had placed a table in the middle of the room with a chair for both so they could look at the calendar and the invitations. They were working diligently when Troy entered the parlor.

"Lady Judith, might I be able to talk you and Jewel into joining us at dinner tonight?" Troy asked.

"Oh, dear. Is it that late already?"

"It is close. I will send down word for two more at dinner and will have a message sent to Lord Thomas if you like."

"Lady Matilda, you have raised the perfect gentleman. Thank you, Troy. I accept for Jewel and myself. Are you sure you and Aspen are a sure thing? I would love you for my Jewel."

Troy laughed. "I am sorry Lady Judith, you will just have to hope Jewel picks someone as sweet as me. My heart is completely gone to Aspen."

"Did I hear my name?" Aspen said as she entered the parlor with Penney and Jewel.

"Your fiancé was just ensuring us that he is totally in love with you, my dear," answered Lady Matilda.

Aspen went up to Troy and put her hand on his arm. "I was thinking a stroll in the garden is in order before dinner."

"Let me do a couple of things and I will take you on that stroll," he said. He had learned not to give her even a chaste kiss in public. "I will return shortly."

The girls sat down on the settee and Aspen sat in the chair.

"When is the first ball?" asked Penny.

"A week from today," answered Lady Judith. "I believe we have enough time to be ready by then. It will be the debutante ball. You both know how it will go? Lady Matilda has picked a night next month for the ball here and I picked the month after for ours."

"We have both been instructed as to the debutante ball, Mother. Any new surprises for the ball as you did for the party you held?" asked Jewel. "People are still raving about it. It was so stunning and exceptional."

"Thank you, Jewel. I read about it in a newspaper from the United States. It was presented at a hotel. I asked one of our pastry chefs if he could duplicate it and he did a terrific job I am so glad people enjoyed it. But no, I think I used up my bright ideas, so the ball will be just the usual ball."

Troy returned. "You are all set to stay for dinner, Lady Judith and Lady Jewel. And I'm all set to take the love of my life to the garden for a stroll before dinner."

Aspen stood and went to take his arm. He couldn't resist and gave her a peck on the cheek. She blushed and they left.

They strolled around the gardens slowly. They enjoyed the beauty surrounding them and the time of just being together. They found their way to the rose garden, as usual, and sat for a while. They just held hands and didn't say a word. They were becoming closer again. Troy was happy and wanted to keep it that way. They were becoming very comfortable in each other's presence. He was beginning to understand the engagement period. First, it was frenzied with the feelings going haywire. Now they were in the stage of companionship. He was still looking forward to after the wedding, but he was becoming much more patient. Especially since he could spend this time with her. They decided it was time for dinner so they went back to the house. The evening was delightful with good friends.

The rest of the week was still a whirlwind with the seamstress putting the finishing touches on all the gowns and getting all the invitations straight and recorded on the calendar. Anyone who wanted to know what was happening on which night just had to look at the calendar. Finally, the night arrived. Everyone had rested in the afternoon and started preparing for the ball. Penny was so excited. Her first ball. She was so excited but also very nervous. What if no one signed her dance card? What if she became a wallflower against the wall? She wished women could be the ones asking for the dances instead of waiting to be asked. Penny chose a white gown made of silk covered in sheer muslin. It was indeed low cut and had a full skirt with a wired hoop petticoat beneath the dress. She wore a necklace of amber and diamonds. She had matching earrings and bracelet. Her hair was swept up and attached with a comb made of amber with diamond dust to make it sparkle. Penny also attached her dance card around her wrist along with her fan.

Lady Matilda was dressed in a black silk gown with the wired hoop petticoat beneath. She wore a diamond necklace Troy Senior had given her. She was wearing a diamond tiara in her swept-up hair.

Aspen decided to start with the gold dress she had made. It was low cut with golden ruffles around the neckline. The ruffles made the neckline tantalizing. The skirt was full with the wired hoop petticoat beneath. She had no jewelry to wear. She did have her hair swept up gently to the top of her head in a bun. She was almost finished dressing when there was a soft knock on the door. When she said "Enter," Troy came into the room holding a box. He handed it to her and said it was for her first ball as his fiancée. She opened the box and was shocked to see a diamond necklace along with diamond earrings, a bracelet and a tiara,

"Oh, Troy. This is too much," she said.

He took the necklace and placed it around her neck. It dipped down to settle in her cleavage. He kissed her neck.

"It fits the person wearing it, beautiful," he said. "I will let you finish and will wait for you outside the door to escort you downstairs.

She stood up and put her arms around his neck. She pulled his face down to hers.

"I do love you," she said and gave him a deep kiss.

Troy groaned and pulled away. He turned and left the room.

When they entered the parlor downstairs, Troy stopped and said "I will be the envy of every man there tonight. I will have the most beautiful three women at the ball in my presence." He went over to Lady Matilda and kissed her on the forehead and then went to Penny and did the same. "You are making it hard on me tonight sister. I am going to have to get a gun to keep the boys away from you."

She hit him with her fan and laughed. The carriage was announced and they were off to the Langford's tonight.

Troy, Aspen, and Lady Matilda were escorted to the ball room and announced. Penny went to the room with the other debutantes. Troy and the ladies paid their dues to the Langford's standing in the reception line. The ballroom was lined with chairs all around the room. At the right side of the room was a little stage. The orchestra was positioned on the stage. They were playing soft music as the guests arrived. Servants were walking around with trays of drinks and refreshments. Troy took Aspen with Lady Matilda and seated them with the other mothers of the debutantes. He then went to find Penny. He would be escorting her as her name was called opening her debutante season.

Guests continued to arrive. When the Somners arrived, Jewel went to be with Penny. Lady Matilda and Lady Judith sat at the end where the women watch their daughters. Lord Thomas was to escort Jewel. He went to find the debutantes.

The debutantes started to be announced. As each girl was announced, they stood in the center of the dance floor. After they were all announced, gentlemen started asking them to dance. Lord Timothy reached Penny first and asked for her hand. Jewel was asked by Lord John Devonshire. The first dance was only for the debutantes. After which, all the gentlemen raced to the floor to write on the dance cards for later dances. Penny's dance card filled up immediately. Lord Timothy was able to get four dances with her that night. Troy took over his duty to stand by Aspen. He got her some refreshments during the first dance. He asked her to dance and they danced several dances in a row.

"I am so grateful to you and Penny for teaching me these dances," he whispered in her ear.

After a while, Troy noticed a gentleman come up to Lord Thomas and start talking. He also noticed that Lord Thomas was introducing Lady Judith and Lady Matilda to the gentleman. Troy presumed it was the way of balls. The gentleman didn't appear to have a wife with him. Troy wanted to keep an eye on this man. Troy bowed to Aspen again and asked for the dance with her. They took the floor with the other young people. This way he could keep Aspen entertained. They danced several more dances and then took a stroll out to the garden. Troy was surprised to see some couples running past them.

"What behavior is this?" he asked more to himself.

"You are in London, my lord. Not all are gentlemen like you or ladies like myself. I am sorry to say some have loose morals."

"I will have to keep a closer eye on Penny."

"Penny's upbringing has been impeccable. I don't believe you will have to worry about her."

"But I for one know what the frenzied feelings are like. They are easy to give way to. I am just so happy I was able to control mine barely," he said kissing her chastely.

"Penny was taught the same restraint. I don't believe she will have any problems."

He bent and gave her another chaste kiss on the lips. "I am so honored to have you by my side for the rest of my life."

She smiled up at him. "And I you," she replied.

They turned and went back to the ballroom. Penny was still dancing. Lady Matilda was engrossed in a conversation with the gentleman. She was laughing at something he had said. He felt a stirring of emotions he was not familiar with. He thought he might be jealous of his mother laughing with someone who was not his father. He didn't want her to forget his father and have fun with another man. Maybe he was going to have to chaperone his mother also. The dancing stopped for a while and dinner was laid out in the dining room. People went and made up their plates then went back to the ballroom and the gardens to sit and eat. Aspen wanted to sit in the garden but Troy wanted to keep his eye on Penny and his mother.

Penny had several boys trying to sit next to her. Jewel was a few chairs down from Penny and had the same problem. Evidently, they were the bells of the ball. Troy was glad to see his sister having so much fun. His mother was still talking to the gentleman. Troy was still not happy about this. When he mentioned it to Aspen, she laughed at him.

"Your mother is still very young and beautiful. Men lose their wives just as women lose their husbands. There is no reason they cannot get together and live a very happy life."

"I don't want her forgetting my father," Troy said.

"Troy, my love, your father was taken away too early. Your mother still has a lot of life in her. She will never forget her first love and will always love him even in death, but she is entitled to live a full life even with him gone. She can love again. It will never be like her first love but she still has a lot of love in her to give. You should want her to be happy again and not just missing your father all the time."

"When did you get so wise?"

"My grandmother lost her first husband. She was always so kind and happy, but there were times I saw her sitting and staring into space as if she was seeing her husband again and wanting him back."

"I never thought of mother that way. I don't know that I can change my mind about seeing her with another man."

"It will take time, my dear. Give it time." She patted his hand.

The music began again and the dancers went to the floor. The ball lasted until four o'clock in the morning. Everyone was exhausted by the time they left.

Penny took her slippers off in the carriage. "Oh, my poor aching feet. I don't know if I will ever be able to walk again. "

They all laughed at her.

"Maybe you shouldn't attend any more balls," Troy offered.

"Are you kidding, brother? This was the best night of my life. I had a ball at the ball."

They all laughed again. When they arrived home, they all fell into bed and went to sleep.

They were unaware of eyes watching their townhouse. People were watching and learning their habits of coming and going in the household. Looking for ways to enter without being noticed. Looking to do wrong to the Bowling family.

Chapter 22

*T*he household was slow in getting up the next morning, but they didn't have time to wake up properly. Around eleven o'clock the doorbell started ringing. It was a good thing most of the household was up and dressed by then. Penny started having suitors come to visit. Troy went down to the parlor to sit with suitors and wait for Penny. Penny entered the room in a flowered day dress. It was an A-line dress with an empire waist. Her hair was swept up in a bun with ringlets around her face. Lord Timothy Braxton was the first to arrive and then five more arrived after.

While waiting for Penny, Troy asked Timothy about his parents and if they made it to London safely. Lord Timothy answered that yes, they had arrived safely and were set up in their townhouse. His parents would be presenting a ball the following week.

"I look forward to meeting them," Troy said.

"I am anxious for you to meet with them, my lord. I believe you and my father will have much to talk about. He has a district to watch over as you do."

That is when Penny entered the room. Timothy only had eyes for Penny. Small talk was stunted due to Timothy getting tongue-tied around Penny. Troy was kind of enjoying it. He wasn't the only one who couldn't say anything right to the woman he had fallen in love with.

Timothy seemed quite upset when so many other suitors showed up. It was really funny to watch six young men vie for Penny's attention all at the same time. Penny was eating it up. Aspen came in and joined them after a bit. All the boys jumped up and bowed to her. She sat beside Troy. They held hands and just sat back and enjoyed the show. Lady Matilda entered shortly after. All the boys jumped up and bowed to her. She nodded back and went to sit down. Refreshments were brought soon and all the boys were trying to be the first to offer Penny a plate of food. She chose the one from Lord Timothy. He seemed very pleased. Troy had to hide a grin on his face several times watching the boys clamor after Penny for her attention. Soon, they all departed and the house became quiet again. They were still sitting in the parlor.

"I noticed you also had some attention last night, Mother," Troy said.

"Yes, I did," she answered. "Someone who Lord Thomas knows came to the ball last night. We had a very nice conversation. I quite enjoyed it."

Just then the doorbell rang again. The butler came in and introduced Lord Robert Gatsby was here to see Lady Matilda. Troy's eyebrow came up as he looked at her.

"Please show Lord Robert in, Henry," Lady Matilda said.

The gentleman from last night walked in. He was tall dark and handsome. He had dark hair with green eyes. He was much taller than Lady Matilda. He looked to be a few years older than she also. Lady Matilda stood as did Troy. Lord Robert went over to Lady Matilda and bowed to her and took her hand and kissed it.

"I do hope I am not intruding, Lady Matilda," Lord Robert said.

"Not at all, Lord Robert. May I introduce my son Lord Bowling, his fiancée Lady Aspen, and my daughter Lady Penelope."

Lord Robert bowed to the ladies and shook hands with Troy.

"Please have a seat, Lord Robert."

"Thank you, my lady. I do hope you don't mind my coming to see you today but you were so enchanting last night, I just couldn't stay away."

"Would you like a drink, Lord Robert?" Troy asked. He said he would. "Mother, would you like a sherry?" she answered yes. "Aspen and Penny can I get you anything?"

They both answered a lemonade. Troy poured the drinks and handed them out. Lady Matilda and Lord Robert started talking as if no one else was in the room. Troy listened attentively. Penny soon made her excuses to leave the room. The four of them sat around talking for about an hour. Then Lady Matilda asked Lord Robert if he would like to stroll in the garden. He accepted. Troy asked if he and Aspen could join them.

"I do believe Lord Robert and I are of age where we do not need a chaperone, Troy."

Troy gave in to her apprehensively and said, "Yes, my lady."

He stayed in the parlor until they returned. Aspen made her escape and went up to her room. When they returned, Lord Robert took his leave.

Troy looked at his mother. "Explain Mother."

"Troy, dear, may I have another sherry, please?"

Troy got her a sherry and sat down beside her. "I am waiting, Mother."

"My dear, you have no idea how it feels to have another man look at you at my age. Please don't be so condescending. I love your father still, but I'm nevertheless young and can still have some emotions of my own. It is not unheard of to marry again after you become a widow."

"Marriage already? You just met him!"

"Troy, really!" exclaimed Lady Matilda. "It is my life, not yours. I don't know if we would ever get married but let me enjoy life a little. It's hard always being the third person out. Everyone else has a husband or wife. I have no one. It gets lonely sometimes. I am not saying I will remarry but let me enjoy the attention for a little while. Lord Robert is a widower also. There is nothing wrong with us becoming friends."

Troy got up and walked around the room. "I know, Mother. It's just that I am thinking of Father."

"He's gone, Troy. I must go on. He would never deny me finding someone else to share the rest of my life with, since it can't be with him. I'm human, Troy, with feelings. But we are getting way ahead of ourselves. For now, let me enjoy just a little bit of attention."

"Yes, Mother. I can do that." He left the parlor and went to his room.

The rest of the week was uneventful. The Bowling townhouse was filled with young people. Troy was rather enjoying giving the young suitors the evil eye of the big brother. Lord Robert came to visit Lady Matilda almost every day. Troy was still struggling with his feelings about that, but he was warming towards Lord Robert. He was a really decent man and was good for Lady Matilda. So, he grudgingly accepted the situation as it was.

Time for the second ball came around. Troy was waiting in the parlor for the ladies. Aspen was the first to enter. She was dressed in a green gown with an overlay of sheer gold. The combination was striking as she walked. She was wearing a wire hoop petticoat beneath. She was wearing her diamond jewelry and looked spectacular. Penny came in shortly after and was wearing a pale blue silk gown with the wire hoop petticoat beneath. She was also wearing diamond jewelry this evening. Lady Matilda finally made her entrance. She was dressed in her usual black silk dress but was exceptionally beautiful this evening. Troy could see the self-confidence and happiness beaming through from within her. He was finally able to see the affect Lord Robert was having on her. He finally felt happy for her. The carriage was announced and they took off for the Braxton townhouse.

They were escorted into the ballroom when they arrived and were announced to the room. They went through the reception line. Lord Timothy Braxton bowed to the group and introduced his parents, Lord Oliver and Lady Tabitha Braxton. Lord Oliver bowed to the ladies and shook Troy's hand.

"Young Timothy has told me about you. I look forward to having a discussion with you this evening, my lord," he said to Troy.

"Likewise," Troy returned as they went into the room.

Troy found a chair for Lady Aspen to sit and he stood beside her. The room filled up and the dance began. Troy asked for Lady Aspen's first dance again. They twirled around the room to a waltz. When they were finished, they took a seat again. Lady Aspen was smiling up to Troy when she noticed someone behind him. Her face went white and Troy turned to see what she saw. A beautiful woman was standing behind him. She was tall and stately dressed in a very daring dress of dark blue chiffon. It was very low cut, more than was socially acceptable, and was straight to the floor showing every curve of her body. Her makeup was done with a heavy hand. It took away from her beauty.

Aspen stood and took Troy's arm. "Lord Bowling, may I introduce my sister, Leslie," she said in a stilted voice.

Troy turned and bowed to Leslie. "My lady," he said as he bowed to her.

"A pleasure, I'm sure," she responded. "Sister, I heard you were in London. It is good to see you again."

"I am not quite sure I can say the same," returned Aspen. "We do have much to talk about. How would you like to take a stroll in the garden? I don't believe I would like to say what I have to say here in the ballroom."

Troy took Aspen's arm and escorted her to the garden expecting Leslie to follow. She did. They found a place where they could talk. Aspen turned on her sister and slapped her face. Troy was taken aback with the viciousness of the act.

Leslie rubbed her cheek. "You will pay for that, sister."

"And you will pay for what you did to me and to Uncle Charles. How dare you show up and act as if nothing had happened between us?"

"Well, well, the spitfire is awakened. It won't last long. I have plans for our reunion. Just be made aware, you do not know all the truth about our family. Dear grandmother liked to keep you in the dark about our births. I found out our dirty little secrets. But you were always shielded from the truth."

"What are you talking about? What truth?" Aspen asked.

"About our mother and father, dear sister. Grandmother was not any relation to us and neither was Charles. We are the bastard children of the

King of Denmark and his wife's servant. Yes, we have royal blood in our veins, but it is the blood of a mad king. His wife sent the servant to her mother and her mother raised us. Why we will never know. She is dead and gone as all of them are now."

Aspen turned even more pale. "This cannot be true," she said as she found a bench to sit down.

"It is dear, sister. We are bastards." Leslie turned away laughing and walked away. She had hurt Aspen just as she had intended.

Troy was shocked by the encounter. He took Aspen in his arms. He held her as she started shaking.

"This is not true. It can't be. Why wouldn't grandmother tell me?" She hid her face in Troy's shoulder and cried.

"I am so sorry about this," Troy said as he held her. "I see how evil your sister is. I can't believe she is your sister or any relation to you. You are an angel and thank God are nothing like your sister."

"But we are of the same blood. She was always so jealous of me. I have never known why she has hated me so."

"We may never know. I forbid you to see her again."

Aspen turned on Troy. "You have no right to forbid me to do anything. I can't stay here. I'm leaving."

She turned and ran away from him. He ran after her but couldn't catch her. He finally caught up with her at the front door.

"Let me make arrangements and I will take you back. We will talk."

She calmed down a little and agreed. He took her arm and steered her towards Lady Matilda. He spoke to his mother quietly then turned to take Aspen back to the townhouse. She was quiet on the way back.

Chapter 23

When they arrived, Troy made arrangements to send the carriage back for Lady Matilda and Lady Penny. He turned and ran after Aspen who was already in the house. Aspen was already going up the staircase to her room. Troy walked behind her up to the landing. He went into her room with her and took her into his arms. She started crying and he held her for a while. She was finally able to calm down.

"Let me get your lady's maid to help get you more comfortable and then we can talk."

"I don't want to see anyone, even a maid. You can help me with the buttons I cannot reach."

Troy knew he shouldn't, but his heart was breaking watching her so he assisted her. He was amazed at how much clothing was under the dress.

"You have to wear all this underneath? I never knew."

She almost smiled. "Yes, this is all necessary to be a lady."

She was able to get undressed and put a night gown on. She undid her hair and it flowed around her shoulders. Troy took her in his arms and kissed her deeply. Before they knew it, most of his clothes had disappeared. They went to the bed. He kissed her and his hand started moving gently over her body. She groaned which set him on fire. He could hardly control himself, but he finally pulled away and started breathing hard. He wanted her so urgently but he knew he had to stop this.

"Please," she said. "I need you now."

"I can't. I know we will both regret this as soon as it's over. I can't do that to you. I love you too much. Let's get up and talk, please?" he asked.

She got out of bed and got a wrap to cover up with. He took his clothes and her hand. He then went to the door and looked out. No one was in the hallway so he ran with her to his room.

"I don't want to leave you alone for a second so come in and let me get decent and I will have Bailey get us some brandy."

"Alright," she answered and went towards the balcony.

Troy finished getting undressed and put on his robe. He joined her on the balcony.

"Bailey is bringing some brandy for us. How are you, my love?" he asked.

"I apologize for putting you in a terrible situation, Troy."

"I understand your need for comfort and that seemed to be the way to attain it." He took her in his arms. "You truly tried my stamina, my dear. I was almost not able to stop. I want you so much, I am on the brink of getting what my heart most desires. Just a couple more weeks and we will be able to do what we want to do most."

"Was my sister just telling me a story to upset me or was she telling me the truth?"

"I don't know for sure. I haven't had time to investigate those rumors. Right now, that is all they are is rumors."

"My uncle would know. Have you heard how he is doing? Can I talk with him? Maybe there are some documents at the house in Leicester."

"That is possible."

"Surely the queen would not give up two daughters if they were hers. I can't comprehend all of this. It has to be true. It fits better than us being a byproduct of a union between the king and queen."

"My dear, we don't have facts only rumors. Let's work on finding the facts and then take it from there."

"But if I am the daughter of the servant, and illegitimate at that, how can I ever hold my head up in polite society again? Your mother told me it would make no difference, but it would. Your entire family would suffer because of me. That is no way to repay all of you for such kindness towards me."

"Let's not get ahead of ourselves, please. Besides you are not responsible for what your parents did."

"Grandmother never told me about our parents. Why would she keep it a secret? My sister has to be right."

He held her again. "I know you have a lot of thoughts and emotions going around right now but try to think positive."

There was a cough behind them. Bailey had a tray with the brandies and a brandy decanter.

"Place it here on the table, Bailey and leave the door open when you leave."

"As you wish, my lord," Bailey said on his way out.

Troy picked up the two glasses and handed one to Aspen. "This should help to calm you down. Then maybe we can put this aside until we have more facts." He watched her take a few sips then she drank the rest of the glass. "Would you care for another?" he asked.

She nodded. She sipped the next glass but soon started falling asleep. He walked her to her room and helped her into bed. He had left the door open as he took care of her. As soon as she was settled, he went back to his room. Lady Matilda came to his room as soon as she arrived back home.

"What was the emergency?" she asked.

Troy told her about Aspen's sister and the conversation that took place. "It was quite an ugly show. Aspen is very upset."

"Indeed, I would be too with a sister like that. Oh dear, as if the two of you don't have enough problems. I would think the sister has to be watched. She can do a lot of damage to one as sensitive as Aspen."

"I know. She has already sown her seeds of discord. I just don't understand how the two can be sisters. Leslie is horrible. I do not even see how she is permitted around polite society."

"Ah, but not all society is polite. Unfortunately, there are the unsavory people who intermingle with the well-bred." Lady Matilda stood up and went and kissed Troy on the top of his head. "Let me know if there is anything you will need, my dear."

"I will, Mother."

Aspen was much better the next morning. Nothing was said about her encounter the evening before. The usual suitors came by the next morning. However, Lord Timothy Braxton brought his father with him. Troy was surprised to see him. He asked to speak to Troy and Lady Matilda nodded for him to go. Lady Aspen and Troy took him out to the garden.

"I do hope you don't mind my fiancée joining us?"

"Not at all," answered Lord Braxton. They sat at the table just outside the door. "Your fiancée is very beautiful."

"Thank you, my lord. May I offer refreshments? Tea or a little stronger?"

"Tea would be fine. I save the stronger for later in the day."

"What might I be able to help you with, my lord?"

"Please just call me Oliver and if you don't mind, I will call you, Troy.

"That suits me just fine, Oliver."

"I was sorry to hear you had an emergency last night and had to leave the ball so quickly. I was looking forward to a talk with you then. I know you can tell that young Timothy is smitten with your sister. I am hoping to sound you out on the matter. She is a very lovely girl and I think it might be advantageous to have our families come together. My property is in the south of England by the English Channel. I import a lot due to having warehouses and such on the channel."

"That is very good to know, Oliver. However, in our family we do not interfere with the love life of our members."

Aspen started choking. Both men turned to see if she was alright. She started laughing and apologized. "I'm so sorry, my lord. But Troy here just spent last week stewing over his mother having a beau even though she has been a widow for the last five years."

They all laughed at that.

"Alright, Aspen, you got me on that one," Troy said and felt so happy to see her laughing again.

"What I am trying to say sir, is that I'm not against an alliance with your family, however it is strictly up to my sister Penny as to whom she chooses. Mostly whom she falls in love with."

"I fully understand, Troy, and commend you on your decision. It is so much better to marry for love than any other way. It makes for a much happier life for all."

They sat talking small talk for a while. The young people started coming out to the garden. Troy, Aspen, and Oliver stood to let the young people enjoy the garden.

"I do believe it is time for me to take my leave. It was a pleasure to meet both of you. I look forward to seeing you at the future balls." He bowed and left them.

"I think we need to stroll around the garden to keep an eye on the young ones. Do you have any idea how old that makes me feel? You know we are just as young as they are, really."

"Yes, my lord. Keep telling yourself that and you might make yourself believe it," Aspen giggled.

"You come here," and he pulled her into his arms forgetting where they were. He was in the mist of giving her a deep kiss when they heard someone.

"Who needs to be chaperoned around here?" they heard Penny laugh.

Troy groaned and Aspen blushed. They continued walking and watching the youngsters. Finally, the beaus took their leave. Troy wanted to sit down with Penny and have a talk. Aspen went to her room to rest.

"I just want to inquire if you have a lead on who you might want to pick as a husband in the future, of course."

"I think I am falling in love with young Timothy. He is so funny and so smart. He is so handsome and dresses so smartly. He makes my heart flutter whenever I see him and when we dance, I want him to hold me forever."

"Yes, my dear sister. You have been smitten, but do not rush the decision. Enjoy it as long as you can. I will let you in on a little secret. He is smitten with you also." He gave her a kiss on her cheek. "I'm happy for you."

She jumped up and hugged him around the neck, then went skipping off. No care in the world, as it should be.

The days started flying by. They had more and more invitations to balls all over London. They attended the ones they could without becoming overly exhausted. They held their own ball and it was a smash. They were attending three or four balls a week. Almost every other night was a ball. Penny was thoroughly enjoying herself. She still had a large following but she started saving more dances for Timothy. Occasionally, Aspen would take a night off and stay at the townhouse but for the most part she would come to the balls. Troy and Aspen started dancing more and having a good time.

The plans for their wedding were coming along. Lady Matilda was a big help to Aspen. Her wedding dress just needed the final touches to it and the garden was being made into a wonderland. Troy was becoming more and more excited. It appeared Aspen was too. But she also was beginning to be more and more nervous. She wasn't sure she was doing the right thing for Troy. She still didn't know for sure if she was the daughter of a servant but was pretty sure she was illegitimate. She didn't want to ruin his life by marrying him. She was so torn. She loved him with all her heart. Her uncle was still not out of the woods according to the doctor, but was making progress. That was a good and encouraging sign.

Lady Matilda stopped her one morning in the hallway. She tried to avoid Lady Matilda but Lady Matilda grabbed her arm and guided her into her suite. "I've been wanting to talk to you, my dear. Please sit down and have a cup of tea with me."

"Yes, my lady. I would like to join you. What is it you would like to say to me? I've gotten to know you quite well and know you have something on your mind."

"Troy told me what your sister told you. I want to reinforce with you that no matter what we find out about your parentage, it makes no difference. We love you as part of this family and will be over joyed when you finally become one of us. If you think it will make a difference to myself or Penny, you are sadly mistaken. We will still be part of society no matter what your station in life was. You would not be a black mark on this family. You are a lady from the top of your head to the bottom of your feet. There is no way you are not a lady. Which is much more than I can say for your sister. Did you not ever wonder why you were brought up to be a lady and your sister evidently was not?"

"No, my lady, I never wondered why. I wish Grandmother had confided in me. But if I am the daughter of a servant and the king, then people will surely turn against you, Penny, and Troy. I can't do that to any of you. I love you too much."

"If you love us as you say, please don't hurt us by not marrying Troy and becoming part of this family. I only ask you to look into your own heart and know where you belong. You can't forget the royal blood that does flow within your veins. If anyone in society turns their backs on us, they weren't worth knowing in the first place."

Aspen got up and hugged Lady Matilda. "Thank you, you have helped me so much. I do love you, Penny, and Troy with my whole being. I will stay and marry Troy. Thank you so much for your support."

Lady Matilda was progressing well in her relationship with Lord Robert. Aspen was worried about hurting that relationship and Penny's pending engagement to Lord Timothy. Aspen wished she could talk to her uncle. She made the decision to stay and she would honor her promise to Lady Matilda.

Chapter 24

*T*wo nights before their wedding, Troy and Aspen went to their last ball as a single couple. Aspen was ravishing in a gold dress with the wire hoop petticoat, very low cut and wearing her diamond necklace, earrings, bracelet, and tiara. She was wearing a wrap of spun gold around her shoulders. Penny was dressed in a yellow gown covered with a sheet muslin of gold. She again wore her amber and diamond jewelry. Lady Matilda surprised everyone by wearing a light blue gown with the wire hoop petticoat and her diamond jewelry.

Troy was taken aback. "Mother, you look most ravishing tonight."

"Thank you, Troy. I have decided to come out of mourning. It's time." She gave him a side long gaze.

"The decision is entirely yours, Mother." He went to her and kissed his cheek.

She smiled at him. *Yes, Aspen has been good for him,* she thought. Troy and Lady Matilda had a drink before the carriage arrived. When it arrived, they all stood to go to the door.

"Where are we bound to tonight, Mother?" Troy asked. "I can't keep up anymore."

"Tonight, we are going to the Somners'. There is a lot to do tomorrow so we will not be staying quite as late." She gave Troy and Aspen a smile.

They arrived at the Somners' townhouse and were escorted to the reception line. Lady Judith hugged Lady Matilda when she saw her.

"I felt it was time," she stated.

"I totally agree. Thomas won't have to worry about me. I might give him a year of grieving," retorted Lady Judith.

Thomas laughed. "I doubt she will mourn me that long."

Lady Judith hit him on the arm with her fan. They all laughed.

Troy walked Aspen to a chair and got them some refreshments. "Mother is having such fun. I'm so glad we came to London."

"Yes, she is very happy," Aspen said. "I'm very happy for her. She deserves all the happiness she is feeling. She is a very special person. She is so kind and generous."

"She has been a good mother to Penny and I." He took Aspen's hand. "I'm sure you will be just as kind, generous and loving." He gave her a chaste kiss on the lips before too many people started arriving. Troy looked for Penny and saw her with a group of young people. "Yes, it looks as if we have had a good season in London. One we will all look back on kindly, especially me."

"I will also look back on it fondly, for the rest of my life," she smiled up at him.

Someone stopped in front of them and they both looked up. Lady Lucy was standing in front of them with several men hanging onto her.

"Good evening, my lord," she said and curtsied.

Troy stood. "Good evening, Lady Lucy," he said and bowed to her. He turned towards Aspen and said, "May I introduce my fiancée, Lady Aspen."

"Lady indeed, I heard otherwise. Really, my lord," and she turned away from them and strode off.

Troy was livid. He turned to Aspen who had paled.

"Don't give her any mind, my dear. Let me tell you a story about Lady Lucy and you will see what kind of lady she is." He went on to tell her what happened before he had met her.

It didn't make her feel much better. But she relaxed into Troy's arm he had placed around her. Penny had disappeared with young Lord Braxton and Troy decided it would be a good idea for him and Aspen to stroll the garden looking for the two of them. They strolled leisurely and came upon the couple just as Lord Braxton was getting up from his knees. Troy stopped and gave him a look. Penny surprised Troy by throwing her arms around him.

"We are both engaged, dear brother," she said laughing. "I have accepted his proposal of marriage."

"I thought it customary to ask first for permission to propose." Troy said. Aspen went to Penny and gave her a hug and kiss on the cheek. "You two ladies stay here while I have a talk with young Lord Braxton."

"Troy, no. Don't ruin this for me," Penny said.

"We will only be a minute." He took Timothy's arm and escorted him off little distance.

Penny started to cry. Aspen not knowing what Troy was going to do tried to soothe Penny.

Troy stopped Timothy a short distance away. "Welcome to the family," he said and shook Timothy's hand. "I believe you were supposed to ask me for permission but I'm happy to say I would have given it to you. So welcome."

Timothy almost fainted from relief. "Thank you, my lord. I'm happy to become part of the family. I'm sincerely in love with your sister and will take the best of care of her."

"I have no doubt about that. Good luck making it through the betrothal period. It's not easy. If you ever need advice, come see me."

"Thank you, my lord." Timothy ran back to Penny all smiles.

Aspen was smiling when she saw that.

Troy came up to them. "I will allow you two one small kiss. But for now, that will have to be it."

They kissed and ran off hand in hand.

"What did you say to him?" Aspen asked.

"I told him he really should have asked permission first but then welcomed him to the family. I had to scare him a little."

She hit his arm with her fan. When they returned to the ballroom. Lady Matilda was hugging Penny and Lord Braxton. Then he saw them go to his parents. They all started hugging and kissing. Lastly Penny went to Jewel and the group of young people. Jewel was just as happy because it appeared she was also proposed to by Lord John Devonshire and had accepted. The group was in high spirits tonight.

Aspen and Troy danced almost every dance that night. They were having so much fun. After they partook in the dinner, they went for a stroll in the garden. Troy was relieved that his role as chaperone was almost at an end. Very little was required of him. They strode to a secluded spot in the garden. He took her in his arms and kissed her deeply. She melted against his body and stayed there.

"Just a couple of more days and nights and you will be mine," he said breathlessly.

He was bending down to kiss her again when he was struck on the head from behind. At the same moment, a hand was put over her mouth to stifle her scream. She was then picked up and carried off.

Troy laid there for quite some time. People had seen him lying there and assumed he was drunk. Finally, Lady Matilda and Lord Robert had gone for a stroll and saw him. Lady Matilda screamed and ran to him. There was blood coming from his head. Lord Robert went to get help. Lady Matilda stayed with him. Some men came and took Troy into the house. They took him the back way to a room on the first floor. Lord Thomas sent for the doctor and the sheriff. Troy took several more hours to wake up. No one could find Aspen. No one knew what had happened. Everyone was waiting for Troy to wake up.

When he woke up, he asked for Aspen immediately. Lady Matilda had to tell him that she had disappeared. He tried to jump up but his head was spinning so he had to lay back down. The sheriff came in to ask him questions. Troy told him that he was kissing Lady Aspen when he got hit from behind. He didn't see anyone or anything. He wanted to know what happened to Aspen. Penny was there with Troy and Lady Matilda. They were the only ones with the doctor and the sheriff. Lord Braxton, his family, Thomas and Lord Robert were waiting outside the room. Lady Matilda told the sheriff about Leslie Whitley.

"Lady Lucy may have had something to do with it or may have knowledge," Troy said. "She stopped to talk to me tonight and made a disparaging comment about Aspen being a lady. If she was part of this, I swear I will see her hang."

"Troy, please," said Lady Matilda. "I know you are hurting physically and emotionally, but they are our neighbors. Please do not talk about them that way."

"You don't truly know her, Mother, or what she is really capable of. If they harm one hair on her head, I will kill them myself."

"Lord Bowling, please let us handle this matter. We need you to stay back and let us do our job," the sheriff joined in.

"Mother, I want to go home now."

"You can't, my dear. You can't even walk." She was desperate. "Stay here and rest tonight. We'll take you home tomorrow. I'm sure Lord Thomas and Lady Judith would insist you stay."

"I highly recommend you staying the night. I'm giving you some medicine to relax you and help you rest tonight."

"NO!" he shouted. "I don't want any medicine. I want to go home." He again tried to get up but couldn't do it. He fell back onto the bed. "I want to go home, please help me."

Lady Matilda started crying. She didn't know what to do for the first time in her life. She had always been patient and could think clearly but now she was beside herself. She was helpless. She left the room and went in search of Lord Robert. He was there waiting for her.

"I don't know what to do, Robert. I'm lost." She started crying and he held her until she could calm down.

"Tell me what is happening? Maybe I can help."

"Troy wants to go home but he can't even walk. The doctor wants to give him medicine but he refuses. Troy is threatening the people he thinks are involved in the kidnapping of Aspen. I just don't know what to do."

"I can take him home very discretely with the help of some good strong boys like young Lord Braxton here."

"Yes Lord Robert, I will help and I will gather some of my friends."

"Then go now." Lord Robert turned back to Lady Matilda. "Where is your daughter?"

"She is still in with Troy," she said.

"Let me go get her to help you, my dear."

"No. I should go get her." She said turning towards the door. She re-entered the room. Troy was still trying to get up. "Troy, dear. Lord Robert is getting some boys together and we will get you home tonight. The doctor can come along and give you some medicine for your headache. You need some rest to be able to help the sheriff tomorrow. The shape you are in tonight, you will not be able to do anything. The longer you wait to get some rest the longer you will be down."

"But Aspen," he started. He groaned. "I can't stand it. I have to go find her. Tomorrow will be too late."

"I know how you feel, my dear. I know. But you can't do anything tonight."

Chapter 25

The doctor made sure Troy stayed asleep for a long time. Lord Robert and the boys got Troy home and into his bed. Before the doctor arrived, Troy insisted on talking to Bailey. He wanted to talk to Bailey alone.

"Bailey, I am in desperate need of your help right now. Find Slick, get him to find out what happened to Aspen. I can't lose her, Bailey. I just can't lose her. Please help me."

"I will do my best. I have never let you down before and I won't now, my lord."

Troy felt so much better. If he couldn't be out there, he had friends who would help him. He finally relaxed and let his mother help to make him feel better. Lady Matilda and Penny sat with him for several days while he slept and got better. He finally woke up three days later and said no more medicine. He wanted to get up but was too weak to do so. He sat up in bed and ate the soup Lady Matilda had insisted he eat to get back his strength. He asked to see Bailey when he finished his soup. Lady Matilda said she would call for him. She left the room and Troy tried to get out of bed. He made it to the chair and had managed to grab his robe and put it on before he sat down.

Lady Matilda came back into the room. "Troy!" she exclaimed as she entered the room. "What do you think you are doing?"

"Sitting up, Mother."

"We can't find Bailey. He has been gone since the other night when you sent him off. Troy you really must rest, my dear. I'm worried about you."

"I know, Mother. I know you care about me and Aspen. But also realize that I will never be better until I find her."

"I know, my dear. I really do understand. I'm worried about you and her. I'm beside myself with worry."

"Then help me get better so I can find her. I have wasted so much time already."

"Well, I always thought you had a hard head but now I find out you don't. Either that or they found out and brought a big stick to hit you with. Alright, Troy I will help you get your strength back.

"Thank you, Mother."

Penny came into the room just then. "Troy! What are you doing?" she exclaimed.

Troy groaned. "Mother, you explain to her? The two of you are making my head hurt."

"Come along, Penny, I need a cup of tea to settle down. Let's go down to the parlor."

Troy sat for a while and then tried to get up. He took a few steps and had to sit down again. He waited a few minutes and tried again. He took a few more steps. He pushed himself back and forth until he was able to walk across the room and back. *Progress,* he thought. His head was beginning to clear the more exercise he was getting. His progress was slow but it was progress. He kept it up all day and almost felt like himself. He was still weak and had a slight headache but would not stop.

He sat down to write a letter to Matlock. He explained what happened to Aspen and himself. He informed him about sending Bailey for Slick but has not heard back from Bailey and it had been three days since Bailey left. Troy wanted to know the condition of Aspen's uncle. He wanted to know if her uncle would be able to help him find Aspen. He also wanted to know if there were any available men who could come to London to help with the search for Aspen. He knew he was asking a lot, but he was desperate at this point in time. Troy rang for a servant and said he wanted the letter taken to Battingham Castle as soon as possible. The servant bowed and said it would be done

Penny came up to his room to sit with him for a while. She came in and gave him a kiss on the cheek. "I'm so sorry, Troy. I wish there was more I could do. I love you and I love Aspen. She is terrific."

Troy was becoming his old self again. "It's alright, Penny. I love you too."

"Is there anything I can do for you now, Troy?"

"No, my dear. I just want to get my strength back and find Aspen. Go see your fiancée. I thought I heard the doorbell ring."

"Oh, that was Lord Robert. Timmy is coming over later. "We are attending another ball tomorrow night."

"Mother will be pleased," he said.

"I just feel like I should not be having any fun while all this is going on," she said.

"Nonsense," he replied. "Enjoy this time and have fun. Get to know your soon to be husband." He gave her a kiss on the cheek.

He decided to lay back down for a while. There really wasn't much he could do until he talked to Bailey and Slick. So he decided to catch up on some more rest. He fell asleep but slept fitfully. He kept dreaming Aspen was calling to him. Wanting to know where he was. Why was he not helping her? Where are you? He kept asking her but she wouldn't answer him. He awoke sweating and was all tangled in his bed covers. He got up and poured himself a bourbon. He downed the first one and poured another. He sat out on the balcony and sipped the second one.

His mind went back to the times he was out here with Aspen. He could feel her in his arms and taste her kisses. Oh, how he ached for her. Yesterday would have been their wedding day. He would have finally been able to claim her as his wife. The irony of the situation. He sat here not knowing where she might be or when she might be back. He finished the second drink and poured a third. He downed it and went to bed. This time he slept.

He slept late the next morning. There still was no word from Bailey when he did get up. Lady Matilda had a servant ask him to join her for breakfast. He dressed and went to see his mother.

"Good morning, Mother. I hope you slept well last night."

"I did but when I went to bed I saw a light on in your room. I take it you were up late."

"I was, but I have had a lot of sleep the last few days."

"Yes, I know you have. I wanted to ask you to do me a big favor, Troy. Would you please chaperone Penny this evening? I feel a little under the weather today and would like to stay home tonight."

"I really would prefer not to, Mother. I'm really not up to going to a ball tonight."

"Well, I could tell Penny she can't go without a chaperone. I'm not sure how she will take it."

"If it is anything like how she used to act when she didn't get her way, I'm not sure I would want to be around to see it."

"Unless you change your mind, my dear. I promise I will get rid of this bug and go next time."

"Alright, Mother. I will go this time. You go next time."

"Thank you, my dear. You really are a very good son."

Troy went back to his room to await word from Bailey. He was getting concerned that he had not heard from him as of yet. He sat down with the correspondence he had received from Mr. Blake. He worked on it all afternoon. It was finally time to get ready for the ball. He had no idea whose ball it was and had no interest to know. He went down to wait for Penny. When she entered the room, his heart broke. He was so used to seeing Aspen with her. She looked beautiful as always. She was wearing a green silk gown which had an empire waist and fell straight to the floor. She wore her amber and diamond jewelry.

"Thank you, Troy for helping us this evening," Penny said giving him a peck on the cheek. "It means a lot to me."

He tickled her under the chin and made her smile. "I told Mother I didn't want to see you throw one of your temper tantrums tonight. That is why I'm going." She hit him with her fan. Just then the doorbell rang. "Our carriage awaits."

Then Timothy walked in.

"I didn't have a chance to tell you, brother. Timmy is taking us tonight."

They all went out and got into the carriage. Troy really felt like the third man out. Now he understood how his mother had felt all those times. Troy kept an eye on Timothy and Penny but kept a low profile. He stayed mostly in the corner and was bored all night. He didn't want to think about the last ball he had been to. Some of the girls noticed him and were giggling behind their fans. He wasn't sure they knew he should have been here with his wife or if they were just flirting with him. He never went through any part of the season with anyone but Aspen. He didn't take any refreshments and dinner. Finally, Penny and Timothy had done enough dancing and were ready to return home.

Troy got ready for bed and laid down. He kept seeing Aspen as she looked the last night at that fateful ball. He went across the hall to her room. All her things were there. Her wedding dress was on the bed waiting for her. He laid on her bed and cried like a baby. His heart was completely shattered. He fell asleep holding her pillow in his arms, but he had sweet dreams of her that night.

He awoke the next morning disoriented. He got up and went to his room. Bailey was there waiting for him.

"Where have you been? I have been worried that you too were waylaid."

"I'm sorry, my lord. I looked for Slick that night and the whole next day. No one had seen him for weeks. I then figured he was still at Battingham Castle so I went there. He was still there with Matlock. Matlock had received your letter before I left and wanted me to bring your answer. I also brought Slick and four other men along. Slick is waiting for you downstairs in the garden. Here is your reply from Matlock. Aspen's uncle is on the mend and doing well."

"Thank you, Bailey. You are the best groomsman any one could have."

He went to find Slick. He found him by the rose garden. He shook hands with Slick and they sat down on the bench.

"I'm that sorry to hear about your troubles, me lord. How can I help you?"

"A week ago at the ball, I was hit over the head and Aspen was abducted. I need you to find out where she is and this time I definitely want to be there for the rescue. No buts. It has been a week so I don't know how deeply they have covered their tracks. They have had time to really hide her. I have faith in you to help me."

"I hate to say this, me lord, but what if they did away with her? It's a possibility. Are you prepared for that answer?"

"Never, Slick. I can't think like that."

"Maybe while I look you should prepare yourself for either answer I can bring you."

"No, Slick. Only bring the answer of where I can find her." Troy walked away. He would not listen to any more of that type of talk. He would never believe she was gone.

Troy strolled around the garden. For some reason, he became much calmer. He put it down to the thought that Slick was finally looking for her. He had done a great job in the past. He had faith that Slick would do an impressive job this time. He had only to wait and he would have her back with him. If anything had happened to her, he knew he would know in his heart. He knew she was somewhere and he would find her. He ended up at the table outside the doors leading to the garden. He caught a servant and had them send messages to Lady Matilda and Penny and to ask them to join him for breakfast here, then he sent word to the kitchen to send up some food and tea for everyone. When the food and drink arrived, he sat and poured some tea.

Soon Lady Matilda arrived. He stood and went to her and kissed her on the cheek.

"Good morning, Mother," he said cheerfully. "I hope you slept well."

"Yes, my dear. I slept very well last night. How about you?" she said as she sat down.

"I'm feeling my old self this morning. I think I'm on the mend and doing well. When is Lord Robert coming? I would like to get to know him better."

Penny walked in looking as lovely as ever. She has taken to wearing mostly yellow which made her look like sunshine. Troy walked over to her and kissed her on the forehead.

"And how are you this morning? You look lovely, like you are full of sunshine. The cloudy skies of London give way to your beauty."

"I am well brother, and I must say you are looking well yourself."

"Thank you Penny and when is Lord Braxton expected today?"

Lady Matilda spoke up first. "You are scaring me Troy. You don't have thoughts of doing away with yourself due to Aspen being gone, do you?"

"Absolutely not, Mother. The thought never entered my mind. Do you know that when two hearts are joined, you can feel the other without them being there? If something bad happens, you can feel it. Well, I don't know where Aspen is. I have no idea where she can be found, but I know she is out there somewhere and we will be able to find her. Bailey has returned and Slick is out looking for her. I have faith he will uncover the information needed to rescue Aspen."

"That is good news, Troy," Penny answered. "And Timmy is expected around eleven."

"I do believe you picked a good man from a very good family. I will spend time getting to know his family. I will probably ask to visit them this week."

"Thank you, Troy. I really appreciate you making the effort to know my fiancé and his family. How I love the word fiancé and how I love being engaged to Timmy. He is so wonderful."

Troy and Lady Matilda laughed.

"We will see how the engagement goes, my dear," replied Lady Matilda. She was so very pleased with the outcome of the season. She only wished Aspen were found quickly so Troy could be genuinely happy.

"You have a long wait, dear sister. It will be fun to sit back and watch how your engagement works. I know it is a hard period to go through, but the end result is worth it."

The doorbell rang.

"That will be Lord Robert," Lady Matilda announced. "He said he would be around early this morning."

The servant brought him to their table. Troy stood and shook his hand. Lord Robert stopped by Lady Matilda and gave her a kiss on the forehead.

"Good morning, my dear. You look especially lovely this morning. Good morning, Lady Penny," he said as he bowed to her. "And good morning, Lord Bowling. You are looking very well this morning. I do hope there is good news concerning Lady Aspen."

"Only that I finally have men out looking for her. Would you care to partake in our breakfast?"

"Thank you, my lord. I would like some tea if I might," he said as he sat with the others. Lady Matilda served him some tea.

"I want to thank you for your help the other night. I apologize that I was in such a fitful mood. It was not fair to you to have to deal with a deranged man."

"You have nothing to apologize for, my lord. You were hurt physically and emotionally. I'm very glad to see you much improved. Your mother and sister were beside themselves with worry of you. I'm only happy I could be of assistance."

"Thank you, sir. Please call me Troy. I feel we are becoming family." Troy looked at Matilda and smiled. She smiled back a bright shiny smile.

"I agree Troy and I'm Robert."

They went on to talk small talk about the weather and how the ball went last night. Hoping the bug Lady Matilda contracted was gone. They finished their meal and went into the parlor. It wasn't long and the doorbell rang again. Lord Timothy joined them in the parlor. He went straight to Penny and gave her a peck on the cheek.

"I'm going to start calling you sunshine. You look ravishing this morning." Penny blushed. He then turned and bowed to Lady Matilda. "Good morning, Lady Matilda. You also look lovely this morning. I can tell where Penny gets her beauty."

"Thank you, Lord Timothy. You are so very kind." He then turned to Troy and Lord Robert and bowed.

"Good morning, gentleman. I hope you are both doing well."

"Yes," Robert and Troy said together.

"Have a seat, Lord Timothy. We are just sitting around, as a family should, enjoying each other's company. It's a leisurely day after the ball last night."

"Yes, it was a nice ball. I do hope you all will be able to attend our ball next week. Mother and Father are looking forward to seeing you all again. Lord Bowling, I would like to say I'm glad to see you recovered from your injuries."

"Thank you. Let's do away with the 'lord' and 'sir' stuff. I was telling Robert earlier, I'm Troy and would like to call you Timothy."

"Thank you, my l... I mean Troy. That would be very nice."

"We are all becoming family anyway, why be so formal?" Troy stood and excused himself and said he had some work to finish in his room.

He walked out of the room and up to his bedroom. He talked a little to Bailey and then went to the balcony. He saw Robert and Lady Matilda walking in the garden. They were holding hands and talking as they walked. Then they stopped and he was kissing her. It was such an intimate moment. He imagined Penny and Timothy spending some alone time in the parlor. They were allowed some private time together now that they were betrothed. His heart started hurting and he turned away. He walked back in the room and sat at his desk to work. He had to keep his mind busy so he wouldn't fall apart again. He worked for several hours on his correspondence back to Mr. Blake. He also started correspondence to Matlock keeping him updated about Aspen. He wanted updates on the progress of Charles. He was thinking of taking a quick trip to Battingham Castle, but the season would be over in a couple of months. Then he would be able to return and take up his life hopefully with Aspen. He did want to stay here and wait for news.

Chapter 26

*I*t was finally time for lunch. Troy went downstairs to the parlor. It was empty. He went to the cupboard and poured himself a drink. Then went to sit by the fireplace. He was deep in thought when Lady Matilda and Robert entered the room. Troy started to get up, but Lady Matilda bade him to stay sitting.

"Robert will get me a sherry, dear. You can stay seated."

"So, when is the wedding going to be?" Troy asked.

"Troy, I haven't been asked yet," Lady Matilda actually blushed.

Both men looked at her and laughed. "While I have you two here, I would like to ask your permission to propose to your mother, Troy."

"Should I think about it, Mother?" he teased. "Robert it would be an honor to have you propose to my mother. I think I will take my drink and go to the garden for a stroll." He stood and walked from the room. Troy found Penny and Timothy out in the garden. They were a little surprised.

"Troy, I'm surprised to see you out here and with your drink. You usually sit and drink in the parlor."

"The parlor is being used right now for a proposal."

"Mother and Robert! Oh Troy, I'm so happy for them." She ran to him and hugged him.

"It makes my heart feel lighter to see such a close family. I can't wait to be part of it officially," Timothy said.

"In due time, Timothy. I want to enjoy my sister for a while before I send her off. But I know she will be in good hands." He clapped Timothy on the shoulder. "I do believe it's time for lunch." He turned and went to the dining room. Lady Matilda and Robert were there waiting for the others.

Troy went to Robert and shook his hand. "Welcome to our family."

They all sat down to enjoy the meal. Troy spent a little time with the family after lunch. When he felt it was appropriate, he made his excuses and left the room. He went to the library and started looking at some of the books. This would be a good project to occupy his time while he waited for word on Aspen and for the end of the season. He would start tomorrow. He went up towards his room. He stopped in front of Aspen's room again. He couldn't resist. He went in and laid on her bed again. He just wanted to be close to her. He wanted to smell her scent. He fell asleep holding her pillow again.

He awoke the next morning and went to his room. Bailey was waiting for him. "How may I help you this morning, my lord."

"You can get me some breakfast Bailey and then please sit with me for a while."

"Yes, my lord. I will return shortly." He bowed and left the room.

Troy got dressed and went onto the balcony. Bailey returned and joined him on the balcony. Troy poured them each a cup of tea. He sat back and tried to relax.

"I'm sorry, Bailey. This is so very hard for me. I have to keep up a good front for my family while I am breaking apart inside."

"I do understand, my lord. It's extremely hard. I had a similar experience."

"I'm so sorry Bailey. I never knew. Tell me about it. Then maybe I won't feel so sorry for myself."

"When I was about your age, maybe a tad younger, I was engaged to a lovely woman but she was killed. She was run over by a wagon while crossing a street in London. The driver of the wagon was drunk and ran right over her. I saw it happen. We were to meet at the corner of the street. She was trying to get across when the wagon went straight for her. I only hope you will not have to suffer like I did and will get Lady Aspen back quickly."

"I refuse to think of her as dead, Bailey. But I feel terrible for you. Have you not found anyone since?"

"As you know, my lord, it is not easy when you find the love of your life and have to go on without her. I have had a couple of interests but it has never worked out."

"I feel like our hearts are connected. I feel I would know if her heart was no longer beating. I don't feel that. I feel her heart still beating right along with mine. Am I crazy, Bailey?"

"I don't think so, my lord. I felt my heart stop the second Aimee's did. So I know what you are saying. I believe like you do, my lord."

Talking to Bailey helped Troy so much. He knew in his heart that Aspen was still alive somewhere. "Thank you, Bailey, you have helped me tremendously. I have been sleeping in her room to be near her scent. It helps me sleep peacefully. Otherwise I have horrific dreams."

"I thought so, my lord, so I did not disturb you."

"Thoughtful as always, Bailey. Thank you. Lady Matilda is now engaged to Lord Robert I don't know when the wedding will be. Penny is still two years from her marriage. I'm hoping Slick will come through for me. Have you heard anything from him?"

"No, my lord. But he is thorough in his investigations so I do believe you will hear from him when he has information to impart with you."

"I agree. It is hard being so patient, but that is what I have to do. Leave it to someone who knows more than myself. I have decided to go through the library and update it while I wait."

"I understand, my lord. It does help to keep yourself occupied. After my ordeal, I started working for your father. It helped keep my mind off my sorrows. In time it got better. It will for you also. If you will excuse me, I do have some work to do."

Troy went down to the library and started going through the books. Some were really old. He decided to start at the top and work his way down. The bookshelves took up two full walls of the room. There was a desk in the middle of the room with a couch and some chairs. One of the outer walls had two large windows celling to floor with French doors between the windows. The French doors led to a small patio on the side of the house. The other wall had two windows looking out to the front of the house. All the windows were covered with red and gold colored draperies. Troy opened the drapes to get more light in the room. He decided it would be better to look at the desk first. He started going through the drawers. He was thinking of his father sitting here. He heard a sound and looked up. Lady Matilda was in the doorway, her one hand over her mouth and the other over her heart.

"Mother!" he cried running to her. "Come and sit down. Do you want some sherry or brandy?"

"Brandy please, Troy." Troy got her a brandy and brought it to her. "I'm sorry, Troy. I came looking for you. When I came into the room, I thought I was seeing a ghost. Your father used this room so much. I would find him in here sitting at the desk. When I saw you sitting there, I almost had a heart attack because I thought it was your Father. I didn't mean to scare you. I'm so much better now."

"You did really scare me. I didn't realize what you were seeing. I'm so sorry."

"It's not your fault, you look just like your father. I'm really glad you do. As I said before, it's like still having him with me. I love you for you but you are special because you are so like your Father."

Troy came over to her and kissed her. He took her hands in his and squeezed them. "Thank you, Mother. You are very special to me too. I love you with all my heart. To change the subject a little, when is the wedding?"

She started laughing. "We are not there yet, my dear. We have to discuss a lot of issues. Penny's wedding has to be planned. You have to find

Aspen. We have to decide where we will live and to combine our incomes and a whole lot of other issues."

"Thank you for including Aspen. But please don't let that deter you from getting married again and being happy. Penny's wedding can be taken care of anywhere. I'm aware that protocol dictates the engagement needs to take two years. Surely you're not going to wait for two years for your happiness."

"No, and you're right. I might be dragging my feet a little. I love Robert. He is very kind and gentle. In some ways he is the total opposite of your father and in other ways he is just like him. I'm not sure I'm ready to get married again, but Robert is ready now. His wife passed away ten years ago. He has grown children with grandchildren. I want to meet them before we get married. I don't want problems down the road. We have to work out the issues and then I will let you know first so you leave me alone with that question." She laughed up at him.

"That is the sound I want to hear from you and Penny. When I find Aspen and we are married, you will hear it all the time from me. Until then I'm trying to get by." He stood and gave his mother a kiss. He went back to the desk. "What did Father work on at this desk?"

"I have no idea. He was always sitting there. He loved this library."

"I plan to update it. I want to go through the desk first." He started pulling out drawers. He noticed a bundle of folded papers in the bottom drawer. "What is this?" he said more to himself, forgetting Lady Matilda was in the room. He pulled them out. "These are letters addressed to Father." Troy opened one and looked at the name at the bottom to see who they were from. He looked up at his mother. "Mother, these are letters from you."

"Oh dear, he saved all those letters. Those are personal, Troy. I would like to take them."

"Absolutely, Mother. I will have a servant bring them to your room."

"Thank you, love. I think I will retire now before Robert comes."

Troy rang for a servant and had the letters delivered to Lady Matilda's room. He kept going through the desk. He found ledgers from Battingham

Castle and the house here. It was interesting to see the figures as compared to now. He found other letters in his desk from businessmen. He was surprised to see one from Oliver Braxton. He was offering Troy's father the same as he was offering Troy now. Troy would have to find out if he knew his father. They have never really had the time to talk. He tired of looking at all this miniscule writing. He turned to the books on the shelf. He took the ladder to the corner of the room. He climbed up and started looking. He was surprised to find so many first edition books. He was wondering if he shouldn't have someone come in and catalog the collection. He didn't know enough about this to make a difference. Just then the doorbell rang so Troy decided to go to the parlor and play his part in the family.

Troy walked into the room. "Robert," he said. "Good to see you again. Can I get you something?"

"Yes, I could use a drink, a whisky, please."

Lady Matilda walked in then wearing a lovely white muslin gown with the empire waist. Troy made her a sherry and handed out the drinks. He made himself a bourbon and sat to chat with them.

"Did you have a bad day, Robert?" asked Troy.

"Not really a bad day, just hectic. My daughter Amelia came with her children. I love my daughter and I love my grandchildren, but I miss the peace and quiet. My grandchildren are five, four, and three. They can be a handful. I'm not used to having someone slide down the bannister or scream at the top of their lungs. But I would do anything for each and every one of them. My daughter has decided to present a ball and she wants to do it next week. Her husband will be here by then. She is wondering if you could help her, my beloved," he said looking at Lady Matilda.

"I will certainly help her. I do believe next week will not be feasible. We have the Braxton's second ball. Unless she wants to make it a couple of days before theirs. But the invitations would have to go out immediately. I will accompany you when you leave and talk with her."

"Thank you, my love. I can't tell you how I was not looking forward to dealing with this."

"What does her husband do, if you don't mind my asking?"

"He works for a shipping company, The South Shore Shipping Company. He organizes the shipment of all kinds of products."

"Interesting," said Troy. "Lord Braxton has a wharf on his property and is asking me to come see it. In fact, Mother, I found a letter from Lord Braxton to Father on the same subject. What a small world we really live in."

"Really, dear. I didn't know your father was acquainted with Lord Braxton."

"It is something for me to ask Lord Braxton when we meet tomorrow. For right now, I will go back to my library and see if I can make sense of things." Troy stood up.

"What kind of problems are you having in the library, Troy?" asked Robert.

"I may have to find a cataloger to see what I have. It appears I have several first edition books and heaven only knows what else in there."

"I believe I can help you there. When I inherited the house from my father, I was faced with the same type of problem. The cataloger I used was very efficient. I will send you her name."

"I will be quite indebted to you for the information. And now I will take my leave."

He went back to the library and kept looking through the books. Lady Matilda and Lord Robert had left. Penny was spending the day and evening at the Braxton townhouse. Troy was all alone. He kept trying to keep his thoughts away from Aspen but couldn't. *Where are you?* he thought. *Are you okay? I would give up wanting you back if I only knew you are okay. I would give up my life just to ensure you have yours. I love you so much it hurts.* He had to get his thoughts onto something else. He looked around to find an interesting book to read. All these books and not one is more interesting than Aspen.

Troy decided to give up and go upstairs. He went to Aspen's room just to look around. He found small stuff that she had left. He found a book on her table that she had borrowed from the library. He opened it. There was a flower in there that he had handed her the first time they had strolled in the garden. He found a ribbon she had used in her hair the day he proposed to her. All the little signs of her. He would leave this room just as it is until the day they had to leave. He needed to leave it so he had someplace to come and feel her presence.

There was a knock on the door.

"Enter," he said.

Bailey walked in. "May I get you some dinner, my lord, and bring it up to your room?"

"No, Bailey. I'm not hungry tonight. Is there any word from Slick?"

"No, my lord. Not yet."

"Thank you, Bailey. That will be all for tonight." Troy went to the balcony for a while and then laid down on her bed. He fell asleep and did not wake until the next morning.

When he woke the next morning, he went to his room. Bailey had breakfast waiting for him.

"You are too good a groomsman to be wasted on the likes of me, Bailey." Troy said.

"No, my lord. Your father trained me well and I am honored to serve you as well."

"I'm going to the Braxton townhouse today. I will be gone all day. I will need my horse readied for me. I should be able to leave in about an hour's time."

"Yes, my lord. I will ensure it is ready for you."

Troy got dressed and sat down to eat some breakfast and drink a cup of tea. He was looking forward to today. It would give him something to do other than waste time. He was interested in the Braxton holdings. He wanted more information. This was probably the best time to make more money. There was a knock on the door and Lady Matilda entered the room.

"Good morning, Mother. Would you like to share some breakfast with me?"

"Yes, I think I would, Troy." She sat down with him at the table. "I brought you the information you asked Robert for. It's written down on this paper."

"Thank you and please thank Robert for me. I will be spending the day at the Braxton townhouse. I will probably escort Penny home this evening. When is the Gatsby Ball?"

"It will be the week after next. The Braxton Ball is next week. I do believe we are winding down. We only have a few other balls and it will be time to pack up and head back to Battingham Castle."

"I'm looking forward to that. But I also want to stay here in London to find Aspen. I just wish I would hear something from Slick. I do believe I'll stay until I hear something."

"Hopefully you will hear something soon. I can't believe it has been more than a month already."

"My feelings exactly," Troy answered.

"I believe I will rest in my room for a while before Robert comes. Do have a good day, Troy, and give my best to the Braxtons."

"I will, Mother. I will talk to you later." He kissed her as she left the room.

Chapter 27

*T*roy *rode through the streets of London.* It felt so good riding. He must find some place to ride more often. It was good exercise. He soon found the Braxton townhouse. He dismounted and went to the door. After a few minutes, the door opened. A butler led him to the parlor. Penny was there with Timothy. It caught him by surprise to see her in this different environment. He realized soon she will not be with him any longer.

"Good morning, Troy," she said coming to kiss him on the cheek. "Come and sit down with us and chat."

Troy took a seat.

Timothy bowed to him. "May I offer you some refreshments?" he asked.

"Some tea would be nice. How are you this morning, sis? You are looking especially lovely in that gown." She was wearing a pale-yellow empire waist gown with ribbons flowing around the skirt making the dress very allusive.

"Thank you, Troy. I have been having such a good time getting to know Timmy's family. He has such adorable brothers and sisters. It will be easy fitting into this family as well as keeping my own favorite brother." She smiled at him.

"We are going to love having her join our family," came a voice from the doorway. It was Oliver. He went to Troy and shook his hand. "How are you this fine morning? It is wonderful seeing you recuperated. I do hope things are getting better for you."

"In time, Oliver. Thank you for your well wishes. I found something yesterday while going through my father's desk in the library. I found a letter from you offering Father the same as you are offering me. I'm curious if you knew my father."

"We had met, but nothing came of our acquaintance. Your father returned to Battingham Castle and we never met again. I was truly sorry to hear of his passing. He was a fine man."

"Thank you. I imagine he was taken up with his responsibilities at home and just never got around to working with you. However, I'm here to remedy that. I'm very interested in talking to you about your holdings and to see what we might work out."

"Excellent. Shall we retire to the study where we can talk undisturbed? I hear the sounds of little ones waking up."

Penny and Timothy laughed. They hurried upstairs to help Timothy's mother with the younger ones.

Troy and Oliver moved to the study. They poured over the holdings for a few hours which Oliver had accumulated. Troy was impressed. He wanted to learn all the details. They worked for a couple of more hours. Troy stopped and stood up to stretch his muscles.

"Everything is impressive. I'm sorry my father didn't partake of this venture long ago. We will have to see how my input can help, where my talents would fit in."

"I can think of several areas your input would be a big help," Oliver stated. "I believe it might be time to see if lunch is ready. I don't know about you but I could use a drink to get through the rest of this."

"I agree, Oliver. I think I need a little time to digest all of this information."

They walked to the parlor and Oliver made them each a drink. They continued to talk about Oliver's holdings until lunch was announced. Troy was surprised to see such a gathering at the table. Penny and Timothy were seated next to each other. There were two other girls seated at the same side and four boys seated at the other side of the table. Their ages ranged from Timothy, who was twenty, the next girl just turned seventeen, then two boys came in at fifteen and fourteen, the other girl came next at ten, and the last boy was eight. They were very well behaved and had impeccable manners. Troy found a seat next to the eight-year-old boy.

"What might your name be?" Troy asked.

"Daniel, my lord," he answered quietly.

"It's a pleasure to meet you Daniel. Do you help your father at his work?"

"No, my lord. I'm too young to work at the wharf."

"A big strong boy like you!" Troy feigned. "No Daniel, I'm sure you would be capable of helping your Father."

"Can I Father? Is there some way for me to help you?"

Oliver looked at Troy. "We'll see what we can do."

Daniel turned a big smile up to Troy. Penny was watching the exchange. Her heart broke because she knew just how good a father Troy would be. *Why was fate so cruel?* she thought. She turned to Timothy with tears in her eyes.

"Whatever is wrong, my love?" he said.

"Nothing. I think I just got something in my eye. Maybe we can go out to the garden in the light and you can take a look."

"Come, I will take care of you."

Troy watched that exchange and wondered what was going on.

"Penny, I will be about another hour with Oliver. Am I taking you back to the townhouse?"

"I'll let you know in an hour, Troy." She left with Timothy. When Penny and Timothy made it outside. Penny started crying.

Timothy held her. "What is it, my love? You are crying like your heart is broken. I'm here."

Penny clung to him. When she was calmer, she was finally able to talk. "Did you see the exchange between Daniel and Troy? Troy would be such a good father. It breaks my heart that he has lost Aspen. He should be married right now and extremely happy. I feel so guilty being happy with you when he is so miserable."

"It will all work out. He will find Aspen. They will be happy yet. Give it a little time and don't feel guilty that you are happy and he is going through a rough time."

"I want to keep our engagement low-key until Troy is better. Promise me," she said unexpectedly. "I don't want to see him hurt because of my callousness."

"I promise, my love," and he pulled her into his arms and held her.

Troy and Oliver returned to the study.

"I have been given quite a bit of information this morning but need to think through all of it. We are returning back to Battingham Castle in about three weeks. I need to get caught up with everything back there and then I would like to come visit you and go through your holdings in person. I would like to pay you a visit for a couple of months if you won't mind. I would like to see your day-to-day operations."

"That would be outstanding. I would love to take you through the entire process. I'm sure we will be working together by the end of your time with us. Maybe you can bring your sister along for a visit. I'm very pleased our families are joining together. Penny is such a sweet girl. Timothy is head over heels in love with her. I wish them a life of happiness."

"As I do," Troy said and shook Oliver's hand. "I must go see if Penny is coming with me or coming home later, I assume with Timothy."

They shook hands and parted. Troy went looking for Penny. She was still in the garden with Timothy. Troy could see she had been crying. He wanted to ask about it but then knew what love at this stage could do to a couple so he decided to stay out of it.

"There you are Penny. I am about to leave. Am I to be your escort home or is this handsome boy going to be?" he said, winking at Timothy.

"I think I would like to wait for Timothy, Troy, if that is alright with you."

"Of course, it's alright with me. Remember, I just went through all this myself. I must leave now." He gave Penny a kiss on the forehead and said in her ear, "Don't give him such a hard time."

She hit him on the arm and smiled up at him. He turned and left.

Since he had some extra time, he decided to stop by the store front of the book cataloger. He maneuvered the streets of London until he finally found where he wanted to be. He dismounted his horse. The store front wasn't anything spectacular. Nothing stood out about it. It was a book store. Once he opened the door and stood in the doorway, he saw it was overcrowded with books. Books were everywhere. There were book shelves, tables stacked with books, and books all over the floor. He was not sure he wanted to do business here. He was about to turn and leave when a woman about his age came out of the back room.

"Are you going to stand there with the door open and let all the flies in?" she asked in a crisp voice.

"Sorry," he said as he closed the door.

"How may I help you?" She was an average height woman dressed in clothes that were not rich but not poor. The dress she had on was a flower print with a waist and the skirt which hung down to the floor. It did not flow out as the ladies of fashion wore their dresses. She had a pretty heart-shaped face. Her hair was dark and her eyes were hazel. She was a very pretty girl.

"I'm looking for Martha Shelton."

"She isn't here right now. What is it you need from her?"

"I'm in need of a book cataloger at my townhouse. Can you tell me how long it normally takes to catalog a library of approximately a thousand books.?"

"I believe it would take approximately a week to complete such an assignment."

"Do you know if Miss Shelton would be available for such an assignment?" He was becoming irritated that this person was purposely making him pull out any information from her.

"I can't speak for her, but I also catalog books. Would I do if she is not available?"

"And pray tell, who might you be?" he asked derisively.

"I'm her daughter. My name is Mandy Shelton and you are?"

Troy realized he was being rude. "I apologize. I should not have been rude. I'm Troy Bowling, Earl of Battingham Castle. I'm residing at Bowling townhouse. Here is the address." He wrote it on a piece of paper. "Would someone be able to come around tomorrow at nine o'clock in the morning to take a look at what I have?"

"I will be there, my lord," Mandy said as she curtsied to him. "I also apologize for acting so smart."

Troy laughed and took her hand to kiss. "We were both mistaken. Until tomorrow morning."

He turned and left. He rode back to the townhouse in a better mood. When he reached the townhouse, he dismounted and gave the reins to a servant. He went into the house and went to the parlor. Lady Matilda and Robert were sitting and talking. Troy went to the cupboard to pour a drink. He asked if anyone wanted something. He then poured everyone a drink and distributed them. He sat down to join the conversation.

"Thank you for the information on the cataloger. She is coming tomorrow morning at nine."

"Anytime, my boy. I'm so glad I could be of help. Maybe you can return the favor and help me with your mother. I can't get her to commit to a wedding date. We are going around in circles."

"We already did discuss this, Mother. I told you not to hold up on your happiness. What seems to be the problem now?"

Lady Matilda stood and walked over to the fireplace. "I just don't know if I'm ready. I love you, Robert, and want to be your wife. I guess I'm getting cold feet and don't know if I'm doing the right thing. This is so hard. I loved Troy very much. We were supposed to be married for a lifetime. Why did he have to leave so soon?"

Robert went to her and held her. "I understand completely. I went through it with my wife. It should not happen this way. We should be able to live with our first love for the rest of our lives. But sometimes they are taken from us and we must go on. That shouldn't stop us from enjoying the rest of our lives. If you had passed first, would you want to Troy to stay single the rest of his life even if he met someone he loved?"

"Yes," she replied anguished. "I'm selfish." Then she smiled and re-laxed. "No, I would never want to hold Troy back from loving again. I see your point. My children are grown and will have lives of their own. I didn't like being the third man out at the beginning of the pre-season. It has been so lonely by myself at the manor. So I'm very thankful we met. I do love you, dear Robert." She put her hand up to his face.

"Well then how about a date?" Troy asked.

"Let Robert and I talk a little more and we will let you know when the date is set in stone," Lady Matilda laughed.

"Good I'm going to my room." Troy turned and left the parlor. *Love!* he thought.

Troy opened the door to his room. Bailey was there. He told Troy that Slick was waiting for him in the garden. Troy ran down the stairs and out to the garden. He found Slick and shook his hand.

"Tell me where she is. I will help you rescue her."

"Me lord, I don't know where she is. We found who had kidnapped her, but someone stole her from them and no one knows who."

"What do you mean, 'No one knows who'?" he cried out. He took hold of Slick by the collar and started shaking him. "Where is she?"

"Me lord, I don't know. We did work with the sheriffs and had the group arrested for kidnapping her in the first place. They only had her for a day and someone stole her from them. We have searched and searched. There is no clue as to who has her or where they have her. We can find no clues."

"This can't be!" Troy said anguished. He let go of Slick. "There must be some sign as to where she is."

"This is what has taken so long. Whoever it was, is a professional. We have searched everywhere. No one saw anything or heard anything. It is like she just disappeared."

"I can't believe it. There must be some sign, some clue somewhere." Troy was pulling at his hair. "I know you Slick. I know you leave no stone unturned. But man, there has to be something."

"Me lord, I feel as if I have failed you, but my men and I and your men just cannot find even a shred of a clue. We have no one or no place. It is like she didn't exist."

"She existed alright and she is the woman I love!" Troy sat down and put his head in his hands. "I can't comprehend this."

"I didn't want to leave it like this, but we have searched all over London and can't find her. We combed every area and dug deep. I knew you were waiting for news so I thought I must come, finally, and tell you. I am so sorry I failed you, me lord." Slick slipped away.

Troy sat in the garden for a long time. He was trying to wrap his mind around the thought of her being gone. Where was she? Who had her? What could he do now? If Slick couldn't find her, what chance did he have of looking and finding her? Lady Matilda and Robert were taking a stroll in the garden and came across him.

Lady Matilda saw his expression and sat beside him. "What is it, Troy? What has happened?"

"They can't find her, Mother. She is gone. They can't find who has her or where they have her. She just disappeared. I can't believe it. She is somewhere. She is out there somewhere and there is nothing I can do. I am helpless." He sobbed a desperate sob. "Help me, Mother. I don't know what to do. I don't know what to think. I'm lost, totally lost," and he started crying with a desperation of a lost soul.

Lady Matilda started crying with him. She held him close to her. "Oh, my poor baby. I am so sorry to hear this news."

She held Troy until he finally was in control again. But he was like a dead man walking. He had no soul left. He stood up and squeezed his mother's hands and walked into the house. As he walked away, Lady Matilda went to Robert. He held her close and tightly.

"Oh, Robert, what can I do? I can't stand to see him so desolate," she said, also sounding grim.

"Sweetheart, there is nothing you can do. He must work his way through this. It is his life and there is no way to help except to be there if he indeed needs someone. I know you. I know you will be there for him if the need arises. You have a big heart and Troy takes up a big part of that heart." Robert held her close again. He did wish there was something he could help but he knew Troy had the best help he could find in London. If they couldn't find Aspen, she was truly gone.

Troy went up to his room and told Bailey to get him a full bottle of bourbon. He then went into Aspen's room, sat in a chair by the fireplace, and started drinking the whole bottle. He wanted the hurt to stop. He wanted his heart to not feel anymore. He did manage to sleep a little.

Chapter 28

When he got up in the morning, he dressed and went down to the library. He poured himself another drink and quickly finished. He was sitting in a chair starring out the front window. He saw Mandy Shelton arrive. He had forgotten about hiring her. He tried to pull himself together but didn't have much success. He waited for her to enter. When she entered, she curtsied to him.

"Good morning, my lord," she said in that sweet voice of hers. She was surprised to see him looking so haggard.

"Good morning," he said lifelessly. "Have a look around and see what needs to be done." He went to the cupboard and poured himself another drink which quickly disappeared. He poured another and sat back down and started starring out the window again.

She was perplexed but did as he asked. She found the ladder and climbed up to start locking at the books. She was impressed and excited at what she was finding. She worked and forgot that Troy was even in the room. He was that quiet. She had been taking a few books down from the shelves and started making piles of them. Troy had started walking around the room. She missed the last step of the ladder and started falling. With his quick reflexes, he caught her. He had his arms around her and looked into her hazel eyes. He bent and kissed her an urgent kiss. She started to protest and then she was overcome with desire. His kisses were more and more demanding and she couldn't resist. He felt her fire and it flamed his even more. His desire grew beyond control. He couldn't stop now nor did he want to.

"Oh, Aspen I love you," he said.

Mandy went cold with shock. He could feel the change and all of a sudden reality returned to him. It was like being doused with a bucket of cold water. He looked at her and was surprised. He jumped up and fixed his clothing. She did the same.

"My utmost apologizes, my dear lady. Let me explain and maybe you will have it in your heart to forgive me."

After they fixed their clothing, he motioned for her to sit and he explained the whole story of Aspen. His anguish and desperation came through in his voice. She started crying for him.

He sat beside her and took her hand. "I am truly ashamed of my behavior. I promise it will never happen again. I finally have my senses back and can't apologize enough for putting you through such an ordeal. I just hope you can accept my sincerest apology."

"I feel, my lord, I just happened to be in the wrong place at the wrong time. I do wish it had not happened, but I do have an understanding. We must ensure this never happens again. I forgive you once, but never again."

"So noted. How about I go get us some tea and we can discuss what needs to be done here. The door will be kept open at all times."

"Thank you, my lord. I feel that will be fine," she said with a little laugh.

Troy stood and left the room. Mandy was a little beside herself. She was not only surprised at Lord Bowling's actions but her own. How could she give in so quickly? She had never felt like that before. She had dated a few men, but she had never felt what she had for Lord Bowling. She was ashamed of her own reactions.

He returned. "The servant is bringing us some tea. So what is your impression of the books so far?" he asked.

She was having a hard time forgetting the feel of his hands on her body. Her face was beet-red but she ignored the feeling. "I'm very impressed.

You have quite a number of first editions. The type of books is quite exten-
sive. You have both fiction and non-fiction books. I was just starting to
make up piles to separate them into categories."

"I think in the future, I will be the one climbing the ladder and taking
down the books. You can start at the lower shelves."

She blushed again and nodded. He tried hard to ignore the loveliness
of that blush. He was beginning to become a little uncomfortable.

"If you don't mind, I think I need to go find my mother and explain
what we are doing here. I will return shortly." He stood and bowed to her
and left to go out into the gardens and stroll around to clear his head.

He couldn't believe what he had done to that poor girl. He hoped he
hadn't traumatized her. How could he do such a thing? He loved Aspen
with all his heart. But for a few minutes, he imagined this girl to be Aspen.
Maybe that explained it. He sure hoped so. Mandy was a beautiful woman
but she wasn't his Aspen. He was shocked at his actions towards Mandy,
but he was just as surprised at Mandy's reactions. He didn't think she was
one of those women, but he was learning a new lesson in the relationships
between men and women. Both have strong desires and circumstances can
have devasting consequences. If he had not stopped when he did, he
would have had to marry Mandy for respectability's sake, not love. That
was not fair to either of them.

He would have to be much more careful in the future and not let his
grief get so out of control. He took a few deep breaths and returned to the
library. Mandy was gone. She left a note saying she had to leave but would
return tomorrow. He decided to start clearing the shelves of the books. He
decided to have a few more tables added to the room so Mandy would not
have to bend over or sit upon the floor. It took him most of the day to complete this duty. He was pleased with his progress. He was also happy that
his mind was occupied and not filled with Aspen.

He went to the parlor and poured himself a drink. Lady Matilda and
Robert were sitting by the fireplace.

"Would anyone like something a drink?"

They both declined since they were each holding a drink.

"Sorry," Troy said. "My mind is somewhere else."

"We understand," Lady Matilda answered. "Are you doing alright? Is there anything we can do to help you?"

Troy turned to them. "The best thing you can do is to live your lives to the fullest. Set the date for your wedding."

"We have," Robert answered. "It is to be one year from today. We do have a few things to work out and it shouldn't take more than a year to complete everything."

Troy went over and kissed his mother. He turned and shook hands with Robert. "I am so relieved. I do hope you are very happy, Mother, and you are welcome anytime to Battingham Castle. It will always be your home."

"Thank you, Troy, for those kind words. Robert and I will visit as often as possible, but it is your home as bequeathed by your father. I am happy you have inherited everything from your father. You deserve it."

Just then dinner was announced.

"I believe I will be going to my room, if you will excuse me," Troy said.

"Troy, you must eat. Please come join us. Penny and Timothy are here and will join us."

"Thank you Mother, but I really have no appetite at this time." He kissed her on the cheek and let Robert escort her to the dining room. He went to the cupboard. He scolded himself and reminded himself to take it easy on the bourbon. He did not want to repeat what happened this morning. He took his drink out to the garden. He sipped his drink as he strolled around. He was surprised to see Slick.

"Slick, what are you doing here?"

"I's that worried about you, me lord. Yous was in terrible shape when I left yesterday."

"I'm doing the best I can. Have you found out anymore?"

"No, me lord. It saddens me to say there is no way to find out where the lady is, but I will never stop looking. Do you want your men to stay and help or do you want to send them back? I did forget to tell you one thing the other day. Yous was so upset it flew right from mes head."

"What is it you forgot to say? I thought you were very thorough in your reporting to me."

"When they got the lot of them thieves, they also got the ringleader. The one giving all the orders and finding out the information. It was a Lord Louder. He was behind the whole thing. When the thieves was thrown in gaol, theys gave him up as quick as that. Do yous know him, me lord?"

"Well, I had my suspicions, now I have the proof. Wait 'til Mother hears about this. Send my people back. If you have investigated as deeply as you say, and I do believe you, then there is nothing more for them to do. I do hope I did not hurt you last night. I was out of control."

"No, me lord, I totally understood. You didn't try to hurt me. You were hurting yourself."

"If you want to continue looking Slick, come here tomorrow and I will set up for you to get paid on a regular basis."

"I'm not looking for more money, me lord. You have been more than generous. It has been a pleasure to serve you. I will see you when I do have information." He bowed and left.

Troy sat on the bench and sipped his drink. He was going to have to make some decisions. First off, what was he going to do with his life. But life without Aspen just didn't seem possible. He thought he would have to get over that fact before he could do anything about his life.

Penny came out to see him. "Oh, Troy," she started. "Mother told me what has happened." She put her arms around him. "I'm so sorry. We have to hope she is alright and will be returned."

"I do have that hope, Penny. But I must also continue on with life as it is. It's not easy. All I want to do is get drunk and hide in Aspen's room. But that is not how I can act. I have to go on and cope as best as I can. At least I have the knowledge that those responsible in the first place are behind bars. They found the ringleader, the one behind the corruption. It happens to be our own Lord Louder. I knew he was crooked. He is in gaol with the others."

"Oh my," she said stunned. "I would never have believed it of him. I'm shocked."

"I had some suspicions. He took life too frivolously. He didn't seem to take anything seriously. I always thought that quite odd. But they are all in gaol now. That is but a small satisfaction."

"What can I do to help you?"

"You can be happy with Timothy and love him with all your being."

"I already do. I can't believe we have to wait two years to be married."

"You are both young. You have much to learn. Maybe it's not such a bad protocol to follow. Penny, I know your emotions are going haywire with Timothy right now. Believe me I went through it with Aspen. But life is so much more. You need to get beyond just your feelings when you are together. You truly must love with you heart as well as your body. When you get there, your marriage should be just like Mother and Father's."

"When did you become so smart?"

"I grew up, Penny. I believe I'm finally an adult. I grew up fast, but now that I have lost Aspen, I see life so much differently. I would give my life to have her back."

"I know, dear brother. I love you so much. I will take your advice to heart and will do the best I can to be your beloved sister." She stood and kissed him. She then turned and ran towards the house.

Troy felt it was time to go to the house. He went straight to Aspen's room. He laid down on the bed and held her pillow. He let himself have a good quiet cry and fell asleep.

Chapter 29

When Troy awoke the next morning, he went to his room, cleaned himself up, and changed clothes. He asked Bailey to have breakfast brought to the library. He then went to the library and waited on the patio for Mandy. He didn't have long to wait. She walked into the room and was totally surprised. She saw him sitting on the patio and went to join him.

"Good morning, my lord," she said as she curtsied. "I see you are feeling much better than yesterday."

"Please don't remind me. I was a terrible cad and again I apologize. I am sorrier than you will ever know. I'm not that type of man and hope to prove it to you."

"Well that remains to be seen. I see you have been very busy."

"It's part of my campaign to prove to you who I really am." He stood and bowed to her. "Please partake of some breakfast with me before we start working."

"Thank you, my lord. I would love some."

They sat and talked for a while. She was trying to educate him on how to catalog a book.

"The first thing to do is to separate the books into categories. Is it a mystery, a novel, a biography, an autobiography, a reference book, etc. I would also like to place the first editions in a separate pile and then categorize them."

"And you can do all of that within a week?" he said amazed.

She started laughing. "Once you get started, it doesn't take long."

"Well, let's finish our breakfast so we have the strength to do all this work as quickly as you say it can be done."

They both laughed and drank some tea.

Lady Matilda was coming to the library when she heard the talking and laughter. She went into the room to see Troy entertaining a woman on the patio. She was very surprised. She also noticed the library was a mess. Books everywhere.

"Good morning, Troy," Lady Matilda said.

Troy turned to her and gave her a kiss. "Good morning, Mother. May I introduce our cataloger, Mandy Shelton."

"Good morning, my lady," Mandy said as she stood up and curtsied.

Lady Matilda nodded her head as she sat down at the table. "I see you are preparing to help us with the inventory of the books."

"Yes, my lady. Your son has been very kind to remove all the books from the shelves so I can start sorting through them today."

"I plan to stay here and help her," Troy stated.

"That is good. It will keep you busy and out of trouble," Lady Matilda smiled at Mandy.

Mandy blushed and it made Lady Matilda wonder what had gone on between these two. But Troy was broken up because of Aspen. On the other hand, what could help most is another woman to help mend his heart. We would have to wait and see.

"Robert will be here soon and I must finish getting ready for him. We are going to spend the day at his house. I'm helping his daughter with her ball next week. All the invitations have gone out. I should be home by dinner. Will you be joining us tonight?"

"I don't know yet, Mother. We will see this evening. Will Penny be here or at the Braxton townhouse?"

"I do believe she will be staying with Timothy and his family. Their ball is tomorrow night. Do not forget." She stood to go.

Troy stood to give her a kiss. "Be kind to Robert today," he said with a twinkle in his eye.

Lady Matilda patted his cheek and left.

"Your mother appears to be a very kind lady," Mandy commented.

"She is," he said a little mistily. He turned to her, "Shall we get busy?"

He held out his hand for her to take, out of habit. He saw the gesture and retracked his hand immediately. She saw the move and decided to ignore what happened. She stood.

"I'm ready even if you're not," she said laughing and went into the library. She took one look around the room and made some decisions. "It appears to me the majority of the books are on history. Let's empty the table with the least number of books and put those here on the couch. We can then start stacking the history books on the table."

Troy did as she suggested and before long, they had a table full of history books.

"Let's now find the first edition books and put them on this table. There are quite a few but appears it will be the smallest group of books. My but you do a fair amount of reading, don't you?"

"This is not my collection. It is my father's. I inherited it when I inherited the house upon his death."

"I'm so sorry. I was not aware."

"It's alright. He passed five years ago. I still miss him tremendously, but I have adapted. It was hard being thrown into an Earlship at the age of twenty. I had a lot to learn and not much time to do it. But I feel I'm a decent earl. I take care of my people, the tenants and my family."

"I can see what a good job you do of it, my lord. I see how much your mother respects and counts on you. It says a lot about you."

"Thank you and please start calling me Troy. 'My lord' is too much since we are working so closely."

"Yes, my lord, but it keeps us in our places."

"And what place is that, pray tell?"

"I am a shopkeeper. You are an earl. There is a big divide between us."

"I don't like the way society tries to keep everyone in their places. If I fall in love with someone in a lower station than mine, it wouldn't change the love I have for that person." He was thinking if Aspen was the daughter of a servant, it would never matter to him. His love for her was complete.

Mandy saw the faraway look on his face and wondered about this Aspen that he called out to while he was making love to her. There must be more to the story. Oh well, she would never know so it made no difference.

Troy shook himself and returned to the present. "How about some lunch before we continue this afternoon?"

"That sounds good. We need a break from all this work. We accomplished a good deal of work this morning. We work well together."

Troy smiled at her and escorted her to the patio leading to the garden. He asked the servants to bring a light lunch with some tea. They took a stroll before sitting down to lunch.

"Your townhouse is quite exquisite." Mandy was looking around.

"Again, it is part of the inheritance. I'm not far enough into all that I have inherited to know what to do with everything. I have been concentrating on my people. However, I do believe I would like to keep this house so the entire family can come here for a season. My sister will have her family after she marries and if I ever marry, I will have mine. Mother will have Robert's townhouse but she may stay here with us sometimes. Anyway, that is how I see things going. My sister's fiancée's family is very large so I believe Penny will enjoy having a place of their own to go to."

"So you do intend to marry someday?"

"It is my obligation to produce an heir to the family. It is the only area where I feel I am lacking. It will take me some time to believe I will never see Aspen again, if ever. I still feel we will be together. I'm sorry. How about you? You never did tell me about your life."

"There is not that much to tell. My father passed away before I was born so I never knew him. My mother worked hard for us over the years. I owe her a lot. She gave me my passion for books. She is a really great lady."

"How about you? Aren't you as much a great lady? I have put you through so much and yet you bounce right back."

"It comes with the territory. A working woman, it seems, must be from the seedier side of life. Some so-called gentlemen think a working woman is for their pleasures. I've had my hands full. That is why I came off so gruff the first day we met. I was thinking 'another dandy' when you came into the store. I find I was quite wrong."

"Are you sure? I put you through a lot of grief. I do wonder about something though. Why made you react to me the way you did? I'm just wondering, you don't have to answer, but what made you give in to me?"

She blushed, "I do hate to think about it. I don't really know. You were a complete stranger. I was appalled at my reaction to you. I have never done anything like that in my life. I have been courted before and have never reacted. You were quite demanding, my lord."

"I was completely out of my mind. I can't even think of how I could have done such a thing to one as innocent as you. I do apologize now. We really shouldn't be talking like this, so intimate. Please forgive me."

"Why not? Can't we at least be friends? Don't good friends help each other out in any circumstances? Right now, I'm someone you can open up to. Isn't that helping you?"

"In a way it is. I can't talk to my mother or sister. They feel my pain too deeply and they get upset at how I feel. You are different, but you are a woman and I should not be talking of this with you. Society states it as so. A man and a woman can only feel and work through those feelings. That is what I have been doing ever since I met Aspen, but I feel we finally got there and then she disappeared. Enough of this we should get back to work."

In both their minds, they were remembering the feel of another's touch. Mandy was remembering his touch and he was remembering Aspen's. This was not going to be an easy task for either. It appeared they would both be fighting their demons. Troy's were doubled now that he almost dishonored Mandy.

He escorted her back to the library. She asked him to put the history books in alphabetical order. She went on to separate the rest of the books into piles. They worked steadily until just before dinner. Troy heard voices in the foyer. He knew his mother and sister were probably home.

"Would you like to stay for dinner?" he asked.

"Thank you Troy, but I must go home. My mother will be home by now."

"Tomorrow you must tell me about your life."

"We will see." She gathered her things and left.

He went to the parlor to spend time with the rest of the family. The four of them were sitting and talking about weddings. Troy wasn't sure he wanted to stay and listen. Penny changed to subject to the ball tomorrow night.

"Troy, maybe you should invite that cataloger. You two seem to have hit it off," Lady Matilda stated.

"I don't believe she would go with me or anyone. She made it clear that her station is below mine."

"That's nonsense," Robert blurted.

"I agree, but I can't argue anymore. I have argued with Aspen and now Mandy. I give up."

"Troy, darling, let me try," said Penny. "I will come and talk to her tomorrow morning."

"If you want, sister. That is up to you. I will not argue anymore. Robert, are your daughter and son-in-law attending the ball tomorrow night?"

"Yes, David arrived today so they will be attending tomorrow night. I will stay with them tomorrow during the day and join you at the ball."

"Excellent. I am looking forward to meeting your son-in-law. I understand that he works for Lord Braxton. It is getting to be a small family we have here between the three of us."

"Yes, I know David Knoell," Timothy said. "I didn't realize he was your son-in-law, Lord Robert."

"Yes indeed, it will be a small family. I didn't realize we were all associated in some manner. Interesting."

Chapter 30

Troy again had breakfast waiting for Mandy when she arrived. This time Penny was waiting with Troy. Mandy walked in and spotted Troy.

"You are starting to make a habit of this, Troy," she said walking to the patio. She stopped short when she saw a beautiful woman sitting at the table with Troy. She curtsied to them both.

Penny jumped up. "Good morning, I'm Penny, Troy's sister. And you must be Mandy."

"Thanks sis for letting me make the introductions. Mandy, sit and have breakfast with me. Penny imposed herself on us this morning." Penny playfully hit him on the arm. "The abuse I take around here," he laughed.

They started talking small talk while they ate their breakfast. Mandy relaxed and enjoyed talking with Penny.

Finally, Penny breached the subject. "Mandy, we would like to invite you to come with us to the ball tonight."

"That is very kind of you, but I cannot go."

"Why not?" Penny asked softly.

"For one thing, I have nothing to wear. For another, I am a shopkeeper. I'm not from gentry."

"There are those who attend who do not have titles or lands. We are not that snobbish. We would be honored to have you attend with us. I will introduce you to all my friends. Poor Troy has no friends."

"Thank you, sister. You make me sound so lively." He laughed at her.

"But even if I did say yes, I still have nothing to wear, so I must decline your kind offer."

"That's no problem, she can wear a gown that Aspen left."

"NO," shouted Troy. "No one will touch her things."

Both girls looked startled at him. He immediately was remorseful for being so forceful.

"Penny, please. I can't see anyone else wearing her clothing."

Penny was immediately contrite. "I'm so sorry, Troy. I didn't mean to be so insensitive. Of course, you don't want to see anyone else wearing her clothes. Mandy, we can look at my closet and we will find something. We are the same height and build."

"I really couldn't."

Troy could see there were tears beginning in Mandy's eyes. "Penny, go to your room and start looking. I will bring Mandy up in just a minute."

Penny got up and left.

Troy sat next to Mandy and took her hands. "It would be an honor if you would allow me to take you to the ball. I'm so sorry for shouting before. It's too soon for me to make a break with Aspen. I hope you understand my feelings. It had nothing to do with you or my wish to escort you to the ball. I would truly be honored if you would allow me to sponsor you."

She looked up into his troubled eyes. "I really don't know, Troy."

"Please," he said and her heart melted.

"Alright. I will attend this one ball with you."

They stood and Troy took her to his sister's room. He left them there going through all the gowns. He didn't want any part of this so he went down to the parlor. Lady Matilda was there.

"Mandy is attending the ball tonight. She is with Penny looking at gowns."

"I'm glad you have someone to take."

"I will escort her and sponsor her, but I do hope she finds someone there to interest her. She is a lovely girl."

"I do believe she is more than a girl, Troy. Have you not noticed?"

"Yes Mother, I noticed, but you well know my heart belongs to another."

"I will let it go for now, dear."

Troy sighed a big sigh of relief. He stood and went out to the garden for a stroll. He really didn't mean to upset Mandy. He would do his duty this evening and then let her go and hopefully she will meet someone who can love her as he loves Aspen. Aspen is the world to him and he can't forget her. It has been more than two months and he still can feel her and taste her kisses. He came close to making one mistake and will never do that again.

He decided to go to his room and see how Bailey is making out. The household has started getting ready to leave and go back to Battingham. Aspen's uncle was still there and was doing so much better. Troy told Matlock to keep him there. Troy had also set up an account for Slick and would put money in it each month. Slick deserved it. He had really worked hard for Troy. He was going to have Bailey find Slick and give him the information. Slick should be taken care of for life. Troy was planning to leave London the week after the Gasman Ball. There were more balls, but the season was winding down. His family was set so there was really no reason to stay. He would spend a month at Battingham and then go to the Braxton estate and work with Oliver for about two months. After that, a quiet life at Battingham. He decided to lay down and rest for a bit. He went to Aspen's room and laid on her bed. He was soon in a relaxed sleep.

He woke several hours later. The house was quiet. He stood up and went down to the parlor. He went and made himself a drink. He sat in a chair by the fireplace. He was thinking he would like to be here in the winter sometime to sit by the fireplace while it was full of fire. Troy thought he would have to give some thought into when he wanted to come back here.

Lady Matilda walked into the room.

"Good afternoon, Mother. Did you have a good rest?" he said, giving her a peck on the cheek.

"I did Troy. And how was your rest? You slept for a long time."

"Yes, I didn't sleep well last night so I caught up with it today."

"I have noticed you are sleeping in Aspen's room. Her wedding gown is still on the bed."

"Yes, I sleep better in her room with her scent. It helps me relax and makes the horrible nightmares stay away. I feel close to her."

"I do understand completely. I would have horrible nightmares, seeing him fall from that horse time after time. At first after your Father passed, I wouldn't let anyone change the sheets. His scent was all around me. I would wake from those nightmares and smell his scent. It would immediately calm me. After a while, the nightmares subsided and I was able to get a good night's sleep. Of course, we had been married for twenty years. I do understand what you are going through, Troy."

"I'm sorry, I didn't realize what a hard time you were having when Father passed. You didn't show it to Penny and I."

"I had responsibilities to take care of. Two almost grown children and you had to take on the brunt of all those responsibilities. I tried to be there for you."

"You were. You were such a big help to me. I will never be able to repay you."

Penny walked in with Mandy. They took a seat on the couch. The talk changed to the ball tonight. Mandy seemed uncomfortable.

"I do hope you are not having second thoughts, Mandy," Troy said.

"No, my lord, but I am a bit nervous."

"Let's have some tea and then we can go and start getting ready," Penny offered.

Mandy nodded. Penny had helped to plan the ball and was telling Mandy about it. Troy just sat and listened. As soon as tea was over, everyone rose and went to their rooms to get ready.

Troy was the first one ready, as usual. He waited in the parlor for the others to join him to await the carriage. Lady Matilda was the first female ready. She looked spectacular in a rose-colored gown with the wire hoop petticoat underneath. It was especially low cut for her. Troy had never seen her wear a dress that low cut. She wore a pair of ruby and diamond earrings with a ruby and diamond necklace. The ruby necklace was made of a large stone surrounded with tiny diamonds and it dipped down to her cleavage. She looked stunning.

"Mother, I'm impressed. Robert is going to faint when he sees you. You are absolutely gorgeous. I can assuredly see why Father fell madly in love with you."

"Thank you, my dear. You look dapper yourself. May I have a small sherry while we wait for the girls?"

"Right away."

Troy went to the cupboard to make her sherry and he made himself a small bourbon. He was handing her the drink when the girls arrived. Penny came in first wearing a stunning yellow gown with sprinkles of gold throughout it. It sparkled every time she moved. She wore it without any hoops. It was very low cut and went straight down her body. Troy knew that Timothy's eyes were going to pop out. She was wearing her diamond necklace and earrings. She was no longer wearing a dance card around her wrist, but she had a golden fan attached. Her hair was swept up in a soft bun held with a gold comb.

Troy went over to kiss her. "You look beautiful. Timothy will not let go of you tonight." Then he turned to Mandy. "Miss Sheldon, I am amazed at your beauty. I knew you were beautiful before but you stand in front of me as a shining sun."

She was dressed in one of Penny's yellow gowns with the wire hoop petticoat underneath. The dress was low cut, but a tad higher than Penny's and Lady Matilda's. She was wearing a necklace of amethyst. It looked so beautiful lying between her breasts. He could remember the feel of them and had to shake his head. Mandy's dark hair was swept up into a soft bun and held together with a comb of amethyst.

She curtsied to Troy. "Thank you, my lord. You are very kind."

"Not kind, Miss Shelton, truthful." He bowed to her.

The carriage was announced and they went to the Braxton townhouse for the ball. They were taken to the reception line. Troy introduced Miss Shelton and they went to the ballroom. Mandy's eyes grew big looking at all the glimmer and shine in the room. They took a seat and Troy got them some refreshments. Some boys came up and asked if they could sign her dance card. Troy said any dance but the first dance, which he claimed. Robert was beside himself with Lady Matilda. She had hold of his arm and he kept his hand on top of hers the whole evening. They did dance a few dances. They made a remarkable couple.

After Troy danced the first dance with Mandy, Oliver came over to speak to him. Troy kept an eye on Mandy but let her enjoy herself. He was going to take her to dinner, but a couple of the boys took her off with them. She really seemed to be enjoying herself. He and Oliver were staying in a corner talking most of the night. He did see the two boys try to take Mandy out to the garden. Troy went over to intervene.

"You know better than that, Mr. Carlson and Mr. Smithers. The lady must have a chaperone to go into the garden. Do you want to go Miss Shelton?"

"I would like a bit of fresh air," she replied.

Troy took her arm and led her outside. Mr. Carlson and Mr. Smithers followed and each took one side of Mandy. Troy then walked behind and watched them. They took a spin and returned to the ballroom. Mandy was claimed for the next dance. Troy went back to the corner and Oliver joined him. By the end of the ball, Mandy was tired but had about four gentlemen wanting to know where they could come to see her. Troy gave them his address.

"But, my lord, I can't intrude on your kindness any longer. This is too much."

He took her hand. "I don't mind sponsoring you. I hope you find the love of your life."

They all went out to the carriage. Penny decided to stay with the Braxton's that night. Timothy would be bringing her home tomorrow. Oliver was so happy this event was finally over. They were staying in London for a month longer than Troy. They would arrive at their estate shortly before Troy planned to join them. Troy talked to Oliver about sponsoring Mandy after they left. Who knew? Maybe she would be engaged before Troy left.

Mandy spent the night in Penny's room. Troy went to his room. He poured himself a drink and sat out on the balcony. Bailey was there to help him undress and get ready for bed. Bailey took his clothes to ensure they would be cleaned, pressed and ready to go for the next ball. Troy finished his drink and went to bed.

Chapter 31

Troy was up early the next morning. He dressed and was going down to the library. He met Mandy in the hallway.

"You are up early, Mandy." He offered her his arm. "We will go and have breakfast and then start working. I have a feeling you are going to be busy for the rest of the day."

"But Troy, I can't overlook my responsibilities to you. I must complete my work according to our contract."

"I'm not worried about the work getting done. We will be here another two weeks. By the way, I spoke to Lord Braxton last night. He wants to sponsor you after we leave if you are not engaged by then."

"Again, you are too kind. I doubt I will be engaged within two weeks. I can just tell the suitors to come to my mother's home."

"And who will chaperone you? No, I think you will be in good hands with Lord Braxton. I just had an idea. I know Penny would like to stay here when we leave so she can be with Timothy. You and Penny can stay at this house. I will work out a suitable chaperone for the two of you. Maybe Lady Matilda will want to stay and she can chaperone you and Penny. I will come up with something. It will be properly done."

"I don't want to even think about that. I want to get to work so I can help you with the cataloging."

They ate some breakfast and then started working. Troy was still going through and alphabetizing the different categories of the books while Mandy had started making a list of all the books accordingly. They were hard at work when they heard the doorbell ring.

"I do believe you will have your first suitor. We should go to the parlor and meet him."

"If we must, my lord," she sighed.

They walked to the parlor. Mr. Carlson and Mr. Smithers were both standing there. Mandy bowed to each and took a seat on the couch. The gentlemen each took one side of Mandy. Troy smiled at her. He ordered some tea. Lady Matilda entered. The gentlemen both stood and bowed to Lady Matilda. She sat in the chair by the fireplace. The doorbell rang again and Robert entered. Lady Matilda served tea to everyone. The doorbell rang again and soon the room was full. Lady Matilda and Robert went for a stroll in the garden. Troy was left with six gentlemen and Mandy.

Finally, the gentlemen began to leave. Mr. Carlson was the last to leave. He and Mandy were talking raptly and both forgot about everyone else in the room. Mr. Carlson appeared to be taken with Mandy and she appeared to return the interest. Troy just sat and listened. It appeared Mr. Devon Carlson was very interested in books. Troy cut in and made a comment that maybe Mandy would like to show Devon his library. Of course, he accompanied them and sat at his desk while they looked and talked about the books. Devon Carlson stayed for another hour and then took his leave.

"Well?" asked Troy.

"Okay, I believe you are right, Troy. I'm interested in Mr. Devon Carlson. I'm really impressed with his knowledge of books."

"We'll keep an eye on him. Will you be staying for dinner tonight?"

"I really must get back to see my mother."

"Why not ask her if you can stay here for the next two weeks?" We have a spare room you can stay in. We can work between your beaus coming to see you and the balls."

"Troy, you are doing too much. I can never repay you."

"The payment you can give me is to see you happy." He bowed to her.

She turned and left before he could see the tears in her eyes. Troy went to have dinner with Lady Matilda and Robert.

Troy was interested in talking to his mother about Mandy. He broached the subject as soon as the moment presented itself. "Mother, I was wondering of your plans when it is time for us to leave for Battingham."

"I don't understand your question, my dear. What is it you mean?"

"I'm thinking of Mandy. She is just starting and the season is about over. She has met a beau that interests her. It is Mr. Devon Carlson."

"I have heard of the Carlsons," Robert spoke up. "If I'm not mistaken, Devon is the second son and not in the line for much of an inheritance. I believe they only have the two sons. His father is a merchant with quite a large holding. The older son is married but has no children."

"Devon, it appears, is an avid book enthusiast. He and Mandy are hitting it off already. But with the season almost over, their time together is quite shortened."

"Spit it out, Troy. What are you thinking?"

"What I am thinking is that we close up about half the house. If you and Penny would like to finish out the season here and be chaperones for Mandy, then she could complete the cycle and find a good husband. I'm sure Robert and Timothy would be happy to watch over the two of you in my absence. Then Robert might like to take you back to Battingham and stay there while I am at Braxton's estate. I could take Penny to Braxton's or she could travel with them. I will bring Penny home to Battingham when I leave there."

"That is not a bad plan," Robert chimed in. He looked at Lady Matilda in a sly manner. "It would give us lots of time to be together."

"I'm sure Penny wouldn't disagree either. She would love to stay and finish out the season."

"I will hire extra guards for around the house to ensure your safety. I wouldn't want anything to happen to my best two girls."

They finished their dinner and went to the parlor.

"One other thing," Troy started. "I would like for Mandy to have a new wardrobe. Do you think you could have the seamstress come again?"

"I think a trip to the seamstress' store might be in order," Lady Matilda answered.

"I would love to accompany you, my dear," Robert said.

"Mother, I will leave it up to you to decide what from the house will stay and what will go. You know best. I'm sorry I'm putting so much work on you. But I will be gone soon." Troy stood and bowed to them and made his departure.

Troy went to his room in search of Bailey.

"There you are, my good man," Troy said when he found him.

"Yes, my lord. How may I help you?" Bailey replied.

"Leave that stuff for later. Come and have a drink with me. I need to have a talk with you."

Bailey did as he was ordered. He poured two drinks and went out to the balcony to sit with Troy.

"I have made some decisions concerning our leaving. Lady Matilda and Lady Penny are going to stay here for the rest of the season. Lord Robert will escort Lady Matilda back to Battingham in a month. I will pick up Lady Penny on my way to Braxton. I would like you to stay here and be in charge of their safety. Lord Robert and Lord Timothy will be taking care of the ladies as well. They will be escorting them wherever they need to go."

"Do you want me to hire more men to be around the house?"

"Yes, but please make sure they stay inconspicuous. So far you have done an excellent job with our security. I don't want the ladies disturbed at all. Miss Mandy Shelton will be staying here as well. I believe I'm giving you enough time to make the arrangements. I took on sponsorship of Miss Shelton, but I really don't want to stay here in London any longer than I have to."

"Will you be wanting me to go to Braxton with you when you return or go back to Battingham?"

"I'm not sure yet, Bailey. More than likely I will want you with me in Braxton. I will be looking at some different types of investments and hope for your input."

"I will plan on that, my lord. I will have everything set for the house before you leave." He stood and bowed to Troy then turned to leave.

Troy sat back and relaxed. He had done all he could do. He would finish out the last three balls and then head for home. He was looking forward to getting back into his own element. He missed the hard work and riding his horse out in the wilds of the lands. He felt so confined here in London. He just wanted to feel free again. He decided to go for a stroll in the garden before getting ready for bed. He walked around and came to the infamous rose garden. How Aspen had loved it here. It still bothered him but he was beginning to put it aside for a while. He was beginning to sleep in his own bed and not have those horrible nightmares. He was finally on the mend, but his heart would never mend, not until he found out the truth of what happened. He was tired. It had been a full day. He decided to go to bed.

He woke early and got ready for the day. He went to Aspen's room. He found the maid and said he wanted to speak to the housekeeper. He asked to see her in the library. He also went and ordered breakfast and was waiting for Mandy. The housekeeper came in and Troy gave her orders to start packing up Aspen's room. He wanted everything packed as if it was crystal. He didn't want one thing broken. She said she understood and would take care of everything. Troy finally relaxed back into his seat. It was not long before Mandy appeared.

"How is your mother?"

"She is doing quite well, thank you, my lord. She is not sure I should be accepting all that you are giving me, but she is also thankful."

"Have you mentioned Mr. Carlson?"

Mandy blushed. "I have mentioned him. Mother is very pleased. She is getting up in years and was worried about me. Now she has you to thank for my possible future."

"No thanks are necessary. You are very deserving of a good life. If I can help in any way, I'm happy. Well are we ready to tackle this job again?" Troy said standing up.

"We have really made good progress. At this rate we will finish right on time."

"What needs to be done? I think I have alphabetized all the books. I don't know what else I can do."

"Actually, I will need to write them all down in alphabetical order under each category. Then you will have to decide what you want to keep and what you want to sell. I will then look for buyers for your books. I do believe your father invested a lot of money in this collection. I am hoping to get you a very good return on that money. I can advise you as to which books to keep and which books you might want to sell. I can also advise you as the best books to sell for the most amount of money."

"I am not looking to make a lot of money off of these books. My father bought them for a reason. Maybe he enjoyed reading them. I will never know. It will be more of what can I do with all these books. I may use this house more than my parents did but right now I just don't know what the future will hold."

"I understand Troy and I will advise you as best I can. Now if you can find something else to do, I will get busy on cataloging all this."

"Would it bother you if I stayed here and worked at my desk? I have some correspondence to catch up on."

"Of course, it would bother me. How do you expect me to get any work done with you here?" she teased him. She started laughing and he joined in. They both started working at their chores.

It seemed to be just a few minutes before they heard the doorbell ring. It was actually a couple of hours.

"It does seem they are coming earlier and earlier," Troy commented.

They finished what they were doing and Troy escorted Mandy to the parlor.

Chapter 32

Mandy was surprised to see Lord Michael Brentwood. He bowed to Mandy and took her hand to kiss. Troy asked if anyone wanted anything to drink. He offered to order tea. Lady Matilda entered the room just then, as beautiful as ever. She was dressed in a flowery dress of empire waist and straight skirt. She took her seat next to the fireplace after the gentlemen all bowed to her. Her stance was always so regal.

"Thank you, Troy, for ordering the tea. It will be delightful. And who is this gentleman? You look a little familiar. Tell me who your parents are," said Lady Matilda.

Lord Michael bowed to her. "I am Lord Michael Brentwood. My parents are Lady Noel and Lord Stewart Brentwood."

"Yes," said Lady Matilda. "You look just like your mother. They have land close to Leicester. We have known them for years. I don't remember seeing you earlier in the season, Lord Michael."

"We were held up by some crimes being committed around Leicester. I know we have basically lost the whole season but I am here now. Mother and Father stayed home at Norsdom Castle to handle what has been going on."

"May I enquire as to what has been happening?" Troy asked.

"Yes, my lord," Lord Michael answered. "At first we were having some of our tenants attacked and then there was a problem at the ancestry home of the sister to the Dowager Queen of England. My father went to help. I didn't hear of the details but it had to do with her brother, Charles."

Troy knew what he was talking about but didn't want to get into that now. Since Lord Michael wasn't aware of the details, he was going to let it go.

"I will have to go and meet your parents when I return back to Battingham Castle. They sound like neighbors I would like on my side." Troy turned to Lady Matilda and engaged her in conversation so Mandy and Lord Michael would have a chance to talk.

The doorbell rang about an hour later. Mr. Carlson entered the room. He stopped short when he saw Lord Michael. His expression was not very kind toward the lord. Mr. Carlson bowed to everyone in the room. He then came and kissed the hand of Lady Matilda and Mandy. He took a chair beside the settee. Lady Matilda offered him a cup of tea which he accepted. He started asking Mandy about the cataloging. Mandy answered his questions. Then they talked back and forth. Soon the doorbell rang again. Two more suiters showed up. Mandy was encased by suiters. Troy tried hard to hide his smile, but he couldn't hide it completely. Mandy caught the smile and smiled back. Robert finally came and whisked Lady Matilda off to the garden, leaving Troy with a room of four suiters and Mandy. Troy finally went over to the cupboard and poured himself a drink. Lord Michael came over and joined him.

"May I bother you for one of those, my lord?" he asked.

"Certainly, is bourbon alright?" Lord Michael nodded. "I'm a little surprised we have never met before. We live so close."

"I do know your lovely sister, Penny. I'm a few years older than she. I used to watch her running around with all the other boys from around there when she was much younger."

"She wasn't very lady like back then. Thank goodness she has grown up into a beautiful lady now."

"I'm almost sorry I missed the season with her. But I hear she has made an excellent catch. I wish her nothing but happiness."

"Thank you, my lord," Troy said and took a sip of his drink.

"I say I'm almost sorry I missed her. If I had been here earlier, I would have missed your beautiful Miss Shelton."

"Oh, she is definitely not my Miss Shelton. She is a lovely lady and I'm honored to sponsor her."

"I'm curious about the relationship, my lord. You don't have to answer of course."

"I hired her to catalog the library left me by my father. I saw how beautiful, kind, and generous she is. I took an interest in her and her future. I want to help her in any way possible. She is a true lady."

"She is certainly all you say. I can't help but confide in you that I am very interested in her. She is everything I have ever wanted in a wife. I do believe I'm falling in love with her. She is the sweetest girl I have ever met."

"Then you will have to work on winning her. You two just might be meant for each other. And I wouldn't mind having her as a neighbor."

Troy and Lord Michael clinked glasses together. Mandy stood up just then.

"I do believe I must go for a walk," she said. "I'm getting stiff sitting around here."

She went over to Lord Michael. He offered her his arm and they started walking out of the room. The other three suiters followed behind. Troy went along to keep an eye on all of them. He kept his distance. He couldn't wait until he was done. He did enjoy watching all of them vying for her attention. She seemed to only have eyes for Lord Michael. The last two suiters finally said goodbye to Mandy and left. Lord Michael also said he must leave. He bowed to Mandy and kissed her hand. He turned and left. Devon Carlson was the only one left. They kept strolling around the garden. Finally, it was just about dinner time. It would be rude not to invite him to join them.

Troy finally made the invitation. "Would you care to join us for dinner, Devon?"

"I would love to, my lord," he answered.

Mandy seemed to sigh. "Why not go to the library for a while? I can continue working while we talk," Mandy offered.

Troy followed them to the library. He sat at his desk and resumed his work from earlier. He could hear them behind him working. Devon was calling out the names of the books and the author and Mandy was writing it down on her list. Dinner was finally announced.

They all joined Lady Matilda and Robert at the table. Penny and Timothy had shown up also. They had a lively dinner conversation. The next ball was tomorrow night. Devon was asked by Mandy not to come courting tomorrow afternoon since she would need to rest. Lady Matilda had asked the seamstress to send over some ball gowns for Mandy to try. Penny and Mandy made arrangements to go through them after dinner. When dinner was over, all retired to the parlor. Devon stayed for a while longer then took his leave. Troy asked if Mandy would like to take one last stroll in the garden before she and Penny went upstairs. Mandy agreed.

Mandy took Troy's arm and they started walking. "Well, I see you have a dilemma, my dear Mandy."

"How so, my lord?"

He chuckled, "You know what I mean. You have fallen for Lord Michael. I can see it in your eyes. Poor Devon, I think he saw it too and is desperate to keep you."

"Why I don't know what you mean? I like Lord Michael, but I also like Devon."

"And you like Lord Michael just a little bit more. I am wise to you women." Troy laughed.

Mandy blushed. "I'm not very good at hiding my feelings, am I? Lord Michael just does something too me. His touch is electrifying. My stomach gets all jumpy. I don't know exactly what is happening, but I like it. I don't feel that with Devon. I like him and am comfortable with him, but I don't feel with him what I feel with Lord Michael."

"You, my dear, have been bitten by the love bug."

"It's too soon. I just met both of the gentlemen. How could I have been bitten? That doesn't make sense."

"I found out the hard way, love doesn't have to make sense. It just is."

"I'll have to think on that one. It doesn't make any sense to me. I am getting tired.

I believe I will go and see if Penny is ready to look at the dresses. I can't thank you enough again for your kindness, my lord. I really do not deserve all of this."

He stopped and turned to her. "Yes, you do. And I want you to stop saying thank you. You deserve all of this and more."

He took her back to the parlor and said his good nights. He went to his room. But he stopped in Aspen's room first. The servants had started packing up her belongings. He would take them back to Battingham with him from there he wasn't sure what he would do with them. He wanted them put in his room but was too afraid he would have to pack them up later and move them again. He didn't want to do that. He just wanted Aspen back. He went on to his room. He saw Bailey.

"Come and have a drink with me Bailey. I like having the company."

Bailey made the drinks and joined Troy on the balcony. "I have started lining up a few security people today and I saw our dear friend, Slick. I was finally able to give him the information on the bank account. I never thought I would see him cry and I didn't this time but he kept wiping at his eyes."

Troy laughed. "I can see him putting on a show. He deserves this and more."

"I agree," Bailey said. "But also, you are a very kind lord, my lord. It is an honor working for someone so aware of the feelings of others."

"I do what I can, Bailey. I'm just very happy I have the means to do so."

"I will just finish up and leave you for the evening, my lord." Bailey stood and went into the other room.

Troy relaxed back into the chair. He closed his eyes and just let his mind wonder. He did help others and was helping them have better lives. It made him feel good. Maybe that is how he can honor Aspen's memory. She was always so sweet and kind to others. How would she feel about Mandy marrying Lord Michael? It was proof that stations could cross. Neither Mandy nor Lord Michael seemed to have the same reservations that Aspen had had. If only he could have proven it to Aspen. Someday there would not be these disinclinations between the stations in life. Maybe he should run for parliament and try to bring such a thing to fruition. He was afraid that would be like hitting one's head into a stone wall. It would happen when the time was right. Now the decorum of the elite was too strict. It was making his head hurt thinking about it. Troy went to get ready for bed and fell into the bed.

Chapter 33

*T*roy *awoke the next morning and went down to the library.* He still had-n't been able to finish his correspondence from yesterday. He started working on his letter to Mr. Blake. He was hard at work when Mandy appeared.

"I'm glad you are here, Troy. I would like to start going over some of the books with you. I will have to check with my mother on some but I think I have an idea of where we stand with the book's values."

"I'm ready for some breakfast first," Troy said. "When we return, we will go through your figures."

They started walking towards the dining room when the doorbell rang. They were right by the door so Troy went to answer it. Lord Michael was waiting outside. Troy opened the door wide in invitation to enter.

"I'm sorry for intruding so early, my lord. I just had to come and spend a little time with Miss Shelton before this evening." He saw Mandy and bowed to her. He then bent and kissed her hand.

"We were on our way to the dining room for breakfast. Would you care to join us?"

"If it isn't an imposition, my lord."

"No imposition on my part, Lord Michael." He led the way to the din-ing room.

Lady Matilda and Penny were just seating themselves. They both looked surprised when they saw Lord Michael.

"We have some company for breakfast this morning," Troy explained. They all sat.

"Lady Penny, it is good to see you again," Lord Michael said, bowing to her and Lady Matilda.

"I'm afraid you have me at a disadvantage, my lord. I don't remember you."

"You were a little too busy running with the boys back then. I must say you have outgrown your habits in a very beautiful way."

Penny was laughing. "Oh my, my past is coming to catch up to me. Where were you when I was playing with the boys?"

"I was on the sidelines watching." He was laughing with the rest of them.

"I always told you Penny, you should have been more lady like back then. But you wouldn't listen to your big brother."

Lady Matilda was laughing also. "This is too funny. I never could control her when she was a child."

They had a very lively breakfast and it made everyone be in a good mood for the day. After breakfast, Lord Michael asked if he could take Miss Shelton for a walk in the garden. Troy followed them but kept his distance. At one point he saw Lord Michael take Mandy in his arms and kiss her. It brought back so many memories of Aspen. He just let it go for a short time. Then he caught up with them and pretended he had not seen anything. Mandy's cheeks were flushed. Lord Michael was smiling warmly down at her.

"Lord Troy," Lord Michael began, "I would like your permission to court Miss Shelton."

"Mandy, what do you say?" Troy asked.

"I would like that very much, Troy."

"Then you have my permission, Lord Michael. I hate to break up a happy time, but we do have some work to complete so this lady can get some rest this afternoon. We will meet you at the ball tonight, Lord Michael."

"'Til then, my lady," Lord Michael bowed and kissed her hand. He turned and left. Mandy sat down.

"Oh Troy, I never thought it could be like this. I will be honest with you. I thought I was in love with you after what happened between us. I thought that is why I responded to you so quickly, but now I see I'm completely in love in Lord Michael. I don't understand how it happened so fast but I'm in no doubt of my love for him."

"Once you find the one you love, there is only your love for each other. I learned it and lost it. Hold on to yours."

"It makes me feel even more sad for you. I'm so sorry, Troy." She started crying. "I want you to be as happy as I am."

He held her in his arms. "I still believe she will be brought back to me. I just have to have patience. Don't worry about me. It will work out."

She wiped her tears away and they went into the house. Penny came and took her by the arm.

"Has Troy been making you cry? You come with me. We have to have a talk." Penny took her up to her room.

Troy looked at Lady Matilda. "We are not going back to me being wrong all the time, are we?"

"No Troy, but it seems whenever you are with a woman, they are either angry or crying. I'm starting to wonder myself." She laughed.

"For your information, Lord Michael has asked permission to court Mandy. I gave my permission. She was so happy, but my circumstances made her terribly unhappy and she started crying. I didn't say anything wrong. I just told her to be happy."

"I'm so excited for her. She will definitely be engaged before you return to London."

"You will have to give him permission to ask for her hand then and I won't have the responsibility."

"You've done your job very well, Troy."

"I didn't do anything. Mandy and Penny did it all with their beauty inside and out. I'm going to attempt, one more time, to finish my correspondence." Troy bowed to her and kissed he on the forehead.

Troy finally finished his correspondence to Mr. Blake and started one to Matlock. He finished that and thought it time to go to his room and rest. As he passed Penny's room, he heard the girls laughing. He really loved that sound. He went on to his room and was able to lay down and take a nap.

He woke up and started getting dressed. He was the first one down as always so he went to pour himself a drink. He poured one for Lady Matilda thinking she would be the second one ready. She walked in as he placed her drink by her chair.

"What a dear boy you are, Troy," she said. She was dressed in a black velvet gown which was empire waist and hung straight. She was wearing a diamond tiara and diamond necklace and earrings.

"I never thought you could be more beautiful than the last ball, but you keep surprising me. You are more and more beautiful," he bent and kissed her.

The girls came into the room and again he was surrounded with beauty. Penny was dressed in a gold gown sprinkled with diamond dust. The gown was low cut and bellowed out from the waist. She was wearing a string of gold chains and a gold tiara. Mandy was dressed in a low-cut red chiffon ball gown with a wire hoop petticoat underneath. She wore the ruby and diamond jewelry. She was wearing a red silk shawl around her shoulders.

"I don't know if I can stand such beauty. No one will even notice me with my new wig. But those who do notice me will envy me being the one who escorting the three most beautiful women at the ball."

Their carriage was announced, so they left for the ball. Troy escorted all three women to the ballroom. Lady Matilda went directly to Robert who bent and gave her a resounding kiss. Penny saw Timothy and went over to him. Jewel was there with her betrothed and with her parents. Penny,

Timothy, Jewel, and John joined together and spent the evening in each other's company. Lady Matilda and Robert joined Lady Judith and Thomas. Mandy saw Lord Michael and he came to take her to a seat. Troy was left alone. That was fast he said to himself.

Troy walked around for a while keeping his eye on Penny and Mandy. He drank a couple of drinks and ate some food. He wasn't hungry and he wasn't interested in the ball. He was ready for all of this to be over. He walked around the garden, following Mandy and Lord Michael. It was finally time to take their leave. Penny again left with Timothy. Lady Matilda and Mandy left with him.

The days took a routine. Mandy went over all the books with Troy. For the moment they returned all the books to the shelves putting the most expensive books at arm's reach. The ones Troy definitely wanted to keep were arranged higher. This task was completed in time for the second ball. This ball followed much the same pattern as the last ball. Troy was meticulous at keeping to his appointed role as chaperone. Mr. Carlson was none too happy with the outcome of himself and Mandy. However, Mandy was extremely happy to be on the arm of Lord Michael.

Then the night of the final ball for Troy. It was the Gatsby Ball. Lady Matilda had spent the night at Robert's house so she could help with the details. She was becoming close to Robert's daughter and her family. Lady Matilda adored the children. Robert's son, Lord Anthony, and his family of three children were supposed to arrive last night. Troy would meet them all today before the ball. He was looking forward to the amalgamating with them all.

He woke early and went to the Gatsby house. It was already in an uproar. There were six children running around while the servants were trying to put the final touches on the house for the ball. Troy walked into the house and was escorted to the parlor. He was introduced to Robert's family. The parents of the children finally were able to calm down all of the children. Lord Anthony was a very handsome man, tall with a confidence and stature. He was dark haired like his father and looked like a younger version of Lord Robert. He was also very easygoing and gracious. Troy liked him immediately. His wife Elinor was also dark haired and had a heart-shaped face. She was tall and slim with a grace of nobility. She was a doting mother. His children were a little older than Amelia's children. They were aged ten, eight, and seven. They were all boys. Troy mingled with the children more than the adults. He was in his glory being with so many children at once. Finally, breakfast was announced. All went to the dining room. The meal was the most rambunctious Troy had ever attended. Everyone was talking at once. The ladies were all excited about the ball. The men started talking work and holdings.

Troy spent an enjoyable three hours with them and then took his leave. He returned to the house to find Lord Michael with Mandy in the parlor with Penny and Timothy. After talking for a while, Lord Michael took Mandy for a stroll in the garden. Troy decided to give them a little space. After lunch, the gentlemen left and the ladies retired to get some rest before the evening. Troy went to his room. Bailey was busy getting things ready for Troy's evening. He went to Aspen's room. It was nearly empty now, only a few odds and ends remained. He strode around the room and looked at the things that were left. He then laid down upon her bed. He could still smell her scent. He hoped he would never lose that scent. It was so calming to him. He fell into light sleep. He woke rested and decided it was time to get ready for the evening.

He dressed in his most exquisite attire. He was dressed in black breeches that came to the knees over white stockings. His waistcoat was of green silk over a white silk ruffled shirt. The ruffles extended to the cuffs of the shirt. This was to be his wedding attire. He decided to get some wear out of it. He put on his buckled shoes and went to the parlor to await the ladies. He poured himself a drink and started pouring a sherry for Lady Matilda then realized she was not in attendance here. He sat and waited for the ladies. Soon he heard them. Penny entered with Mandy. His breath was taken from him at the sight of the two stunning girls. Penny was dressed in a yellow gown with diamond sprinkles scattered over the entire dress. She was wearing her wire hoop petticoat to make her dress flow all around her. Her hair was swept up into a bun with a yellow gold comb holding it in place. Mandy was dressed in a coral colored gown also with the wire hoop petticoat. She was wearing the amber and diamond necklace and earrings. Her hair was also swept up and held with an amber and gold comb. They looked so striking.

"Again, I will definitely be the envy of the evening," he said standing and kissing each girl on the cheek.

The carriage was announced and they made their way to the door.

When they arrived, they went through the reception line. Lady Matilda stood next to Robert tall and stately. Her smile beamed when she saw her family. She introduced Penny and Mandy to Robert's children. Troy looked around for the grandchildren and saw a couple of faces through the bannister of the winding staircase. He escorted the ladies into the ballroom. He handed them over to the counterparts and then made a beeline for the stairway. He gathered the children and took them to one of their bedrooms. He played with them until they became tired. He knew the ladies and their gentlemen were downstairs dancing, so he didn't worry about them. He finally returned to the ball.

Oliver was there and they retired to a corner to talk. All of a sudden there was a commotion on the dance floor. It appeared Mr. Carlson was making a drunken spectacle of himself, trying to get Mandy to dance with him. He started calling her all kinds of names. Troy made a fast dash over to them. Mandy stood there red-faced and a look of shock on her face. Troy took Devon by the arm and escorted him out of the house. Devon finally came to his senses and fled the premises. Troy went back to find Mandy. Lord Michael had taken her to the garden. Troy found them in each other's arms.

"Mandy, are you alright?"

She was crying and Lord Michael wouldn't let go of her. "Lord Troy, I was going to ask this of you later, but I feel I must speak now. I wish to propose marriage to Mandy and I ask your permission to do so."

"I give my permission for you to ask Mandy the question. I will leave the two of you alone for a while so you can talk."

Troy went back to the ball and everything had gone back to normal. At the dinner, Penny found him and wanted to know how Mandy was. Troy explained that she was in the process of being proposed to. He thought she would be just fine. As he predicted, the couple came back all smiles. They both stood erect as if daring anyone to make a comment about the earlier encounter. They mingled with their friends and everything turned out just great. Lord Michael ended up taking Mandy home, Penny was escorted by Timothy, and Lady Matilda stayed overnight with Robert's family. Troy made the short trip home by himself. He saw a long road of loneliness for himself.

Chapter 34

*T*roy spent the next week preparing to leave. The day before he left, he took Mandy into the library. He sat her down in a chair across from his desk. He sat at the desk and looked at her. She was lovelier than the first day they met.

"I would like to have a talk with you. How is your mother taking your engagement?"

"She was very surprised at first, but then was ecstatic for me. We have discussed a little of the wedding but it is too soon to make formal plans."

"I want to present you with a gift," he said. He went to the bookshelf and took down the two most expensive first edition books. He handed them to her. "I wish to give these to you. Maybe they can help you pay for the wedding of your dreams."

"Oh, my lord. I couldn't take these. They are too valuable and anyway, you already paid for my services."

"These are gifts from a friend. Call them a wedding present. I know Lord Michael is an honorable man and will take very good care of you. But with these books, you will have your own money. I know how important it is for you to feel a little independent. It is my wish and you must accept it as a gift."

Mandy was overwhelmed by his generosity. She jumped up, went around the desk, and gave him a big, profound kiss. He started responding to the kiss, then pulled away. She looked at him with love in her eyes, but not the love of a lover relationship more of a special friend or brother. He sighed and accepted the knowledge.

"I want to be at the wedding," he told her.

"It would be an honor if you would give me away, Troy. I know I will be very happy with Lord Michael but the best part will be having such a dear friend so close. I will miss my mother and some of London, nonetheless, I am looking forward to living in the country. I can hardly wait. Michael wants me to come and meet his family soon. He is trying to make the arrangements now."

"I look forward to seeing you there when the time comes. Take good care of yourself. I must go now to finish the details of my trip back to Battingham." He kissed her on the cheek and left.

He found Bailey in his room. The room looked a mess. However, it was an organized mess. "Will this be ready for tomorrow?'

"Yes, my lord. If you can leave me to my chores, I will have all this packed and placed in the wagon by day's end."

"Is that your way of saying get lost, my lord?" Troy laughed.

Bailey laughed with him. "Yes, my lord. It is."

"I'm gone then. I'll talk to you tonight." He turned and went down to the parlor.

Everything was in place for Lady Matilda, Penny and Mandy to stay here for the next month. He would return in one month's time to escort Penny to the Braxton estate. Lady Matilda would travel with Robert, his daughter, and her family to Battingham.

Lady Matilda was in the parlor with Robert. Troy bowed to Lady Matilda and gave her a kiss. He shook hands with Robert. "How are things going on the wedding plans? Is there anything you need my help with?"

"No darling, everything is moving along smoothly. When I need your help, I will definitely let you know."

"I'm sure of that." They all laughed and relaxed.

Penny, Timothy, Mandy, and Michael entered.

Penny kissed her mother and turned to Troy. "Finally, you are learning to make women laugh and not cry," she said, hitting him on the arm.

They all laughed again and spent the day talking and laughing and having a very good time. Troy would intermittently check on the progress of the loading of the wagons for the trip back. He especially wanted to ensure the picture of his mother and father from Lady Matilda's room was well protected. Finally, it was time to get some rest for the long haul back to Battingham.

Troy was up bright and early the next morning, but he didn't rise early enough to beat the others. They were all waiting for him in the dining room for their last meal together. The conversation took up where it left off yesterday. Troy finally said he must leave. They followed him outside to say good bye. He kissed Mandy and Penny on the cheek and shook hands with Michael and Timothy. He went to his mother and Robert.

He shook hands with Robert. "Take good care of her. She is very precious to me."

"I promise, Troy. She is very precious to me also."

Troy turned to his mother. "When you travel, don't forget your pillows."

She laughed and cried at the same time. He kissed her on the cheek.

"Be safe my son and send word back upon your safe arrival that you are alright. I will worry about you."

"I will Mother," he said softly.

He turned and mounted his horse. The convoy of wagons had already left. He spurred his horse to catch up with them. He waved to everyone and they waved back. It took them four days to return to Battingham. The voyage was smooth and unencumbered. He was so very happy to return home. He saw Matlock first

"I have missed you so," he said, dismounting and went to hug him. "How are things?"

"Much better since those crooks were arrested. Things have been running in a usual manner. Charles is still here and is waiting to see you."

Troy went into the house with Matlock. They went to the parlor and found an older gentleman sitting in the seat by the fireplace.

"Charles, I presume. I am Lord Troy Bowling of Battingham Castle. I want to say how sorry I am about Aspen. She wanted to see you so desperately."

"I'm beside myself and only hope to hear something of her soon."

"My wishes also, sir."

"Please dispense with all of that. I'm Charles. I would like to sit and talk to you about Aspen and what her life was like before she was kidnapped in the first place."

"I want to hear all about it, but I must beg your pardon first so I can clean up from the long journey. I will return soon and maybe we can have some refreshments."

"Indeed, my lord. I will await your return."

They each bowed to each other. Troy went to find the housekeeper. He talked to her and gave her the discretion to have the wagons emptied and everything placed in its proper place. He had made the decision to have Aspen's clothes to be brought to her room. He then went to his room and cleaned up. He changed into his casual clothes of the country and enjoyed not having to dress in proper London attire. He assigned a servant to help get his room arranged in the absence of Bailey. It was strange having to take care of all the small details that Lady Matilda had always done. It would be a challenge keeping up with everything and everyone. Lady Matilda did an excellent job of hiring the best servants to ease the process.

He finally went downstairs to relax with Charles. They went to the dining room to partake in some lunch. Charles started telling Troy of Aspen's story. He began before she was born.

"Aspen's mother was married to the King of Denmark. Her life was not all that she had wanted it to be. The king had a lot of issues. He had been abused as a child by a tutor and his mother had known about it but ignored the abuse. The king grew up with a lot of resentment towards women. The queen endured a lot but was strong and was able to protect herself from any abuse from him other than verbal and discarded treatment. A few times they did their marital duty and Aspen was conceived. The queen was afraid for Aspen when she was born. She was not sure how her husband would treat a female child but the queen knew that some of his cohorts were into abusing little girls. So the queen secretly sent her daughter to live with the queen's mother in England. Everyone was told the child died. My sister took the child and raised her. The story went about that Aspen was the result of an escapade between the queen's maidservant and the king, which made Aspen appear to be the illegitimate child of the king."

"Was there such a servant? What about Aspen's sister, Leslie?"

"The king did indeed impregnate the servant girl and the result was Leslie. The queen sent the baby to her mother to protect that child as well. The servant girl became the maid of my sister. The girls grew up, but Leslie was always aware there was a difference between them and was always jealous of Aspen. Aspen was treated differently by my sister and her servants. When Leslie was old enough to understand, her mother, the servant maid, told her the entire story."

"So Leslie knew that Aspen was actually the princess of the King and Queen of Denmark? That is why she tried to destroy Aspen."

"You are correct. Leslie decided to do a season in London and talked Aspen into joining her. We never saw Aspen again. My sister was heartbroken. Leslie told us that Aspen had met someone and that they had gotten married, but my sister knew in her heart that it was a false story. She sent some men to find Aspen but was never successful. I can't thank you enough for rescuing her. I am sure you made her very happy."

"We were to be married. Two days before the wedding I was struck on the head and she was whisked away. We found the culprits, but never Aspen. I am very glad to say that Leslie is behind bars. She is finally getting her due. I'm so sorry, Charles, that I didn't take better care of her. I have been beside myself with worry about her. I only wish I could find her. She was stolen from the culprits who stole her from me. I have had some very good investigators looking for her, but she has vanished without a trace."

"I have been kept appraised of all you have tried to do to find her. I have some thoughts of what might have happened, but I have no facts so I would rather keep my thoughts to myself. I also want to thank you, my lord, for all that you have done for me. I owe you my life. I'm finally back to the best of health I will ever be thanks to your doctor and your wonderful staff. I am forever indebted to you."

"I'm just happy I could have been of service to you, Charles. Aspen was worried about you and wanted to come be with you. I apologize. I talked her out of it because of my duties in London and my selfishness to keep Aspen by my side. It is one of my deepest regrets because now I have lost her completely." His voice cracked with the desperation he felt. "You are welcome to stay here with me for as long as you like. I would truly enjoy your company. My home is your home."

"Thank you, my lord. I am enjoying the home that you have created. Since my sister has passed, I too am quite lonely. My deepest regret is that I was taken before she passed and was not given the privilege of spending time with her before her last days. I'm deeply indebted to you for ensuring the incarceration of those responsible for wrecking all of our lives. May their souls rot in hell."

Troy felt his anguish but had to put it aside. He stood and went to Charles. He took him in his arms and hugged him tightly. No words were needed.

Finally, Troy pulled himself away. "I must go and take a look around the property. Please from now on call me Troy. I will return in a couple of days. I have a large area to get too. But I want to ensure my tenants are well taken care of."

Troy left and called for his horse. He met Matlock.

"I am going to take a tour of the property."

"Would you like some company?" Matlock asked.

"If you think you can keep up with me," Troy laughed. "I have been cooped up too long in the city. I want to ride hard and fast. I want to feel the free open air again."

Matlock grabbed his horse and they rode off together. They had a fun time together. They saw the tenants and slept under the stars. It was chilly at night, but they had thought ahead to bring blankets with them. Troy was able to talk to Matlock about all that had happened. He was able to cry with his anguish and desperation. It was as if Matlock was truly his father and he didn't have to hold back any feelings. He even told Matlock his first encounter with Mandy.

"I was so embarrassed. How could I react to a total stranger in that manner? I'm glad we got beyond the embarrassment. She will soon be a neighbor of ours. She is marrying Lord Michael Brentwood."

"His father was a big help to us in rescuing Charles," Matlock said. "I can't wait to meet this Mandy. Sometimes in our grief our mind plays tricks on us. You had just lost Aspen and here was a woman in the flesh. Our bodies react to what is in front of us. It is called unavoidable desires. Her reaction is a little bit surprising, but then sometimes emotions just get out of hand. Thank goodness you were able to stop short of making a horrific mistake."

"Would it have been a horrific mistake? I could easily have fallen in love with her if it hadn't been for my love of Aspen. In fact, when the episode was happening, I called Mandy by Aspen's name. That was like a douse of cold water. Almost like a jump in the river. She went stiff and I woke up. It saved us both. Yes, if my heart hadn't already been given away, I would have lost it to Mandy."

"You have been living quite the interesting life in London, my lord."

They both laughed. They enjoyed each other's company for the whole two days they were gone. They returned with a much closer relationship. The days slipped into a routine. The household was put back together. Troy made sure he had breakfast, lunch, and dinner with Charles. They were becoming fast friends. A week before he was to leave for London, he told Matlock he was going to the west side just beyond the forest to mend some fencing for the tenants. Matlock was tied up and couldn't accompany him.

Chapter 35

Troy rode out early in the morning and was enjoying the ride. He broke through the forest and was crossing the meadow when he spotted a carriage on the road. It was a very ornate carriage and his curiosity was peaked. Who in the world could that be? He saw the carriage stop and a figure got out. He then saw the figure of a woman picking up her dress and running in his direction. He looked but couldn't believe his eyes. Aspen was running towards him. Was it his imagination? He had already dismounted his horse. He started running in her direction. As he got closer, he could see it was Aspen. He ran faster. He caught her and twirled her around. He started kissing her. He kissed her hair, her eyes, her cheeks, and finally found her mouth. He was enthralled, he was dreaming. He wanted to keep dreaming. He held her to him. He refused to let her go.

"Aspen, my love. I have waited for this moment for so long. I can't believe it is really you. Pinch me hard so I know I'm not dreaming."

"You are not dreaming, my love." She reached up and pulled his head to her and kissed him.

They fell to the earth and kept kissing. They got so heated, he had to force himself to stop. She groaned and he groaned with her. They clung together. They laid there for a long time just holding each other. Neither of them wanted to part.

"Please tell me what happened. I have been filled with despair and desperation. I couldn't find you. Slick looked everywhere. He said you were stolen from the ones who stole you from me and then just disappeared. No one knew where or by whom you were taken. I have been so frantic." She heard the hopelessness in his voice. "I didn't know if I would ever see you."

They clung together again.

"I hate that you had to go through that. The last time I saw you, you were crumpled on the ground. I was worried sick that you were dead. But I did get word that you were alive and well. There was no way to get a message to you."

They finally sat up but he pulled her to him. He didn't want to let her go. She turned around and laid back into his arms. She told him what had happened to her.

"When my mother heard about what Leslie had done to me at the end of the season, she had special guards put around me. No one knew they were there, even me."

"I know the story of your birth. Charles told me all about your life."

"So you know the King and Queen of Denmark are my true parents. The guards stole me from Leslie's clutches and whisked me off to Denmark to be with my mother on her deathbed. I was hidden so no one knew I was there except my mother and her maids. Since she was dying, no one wanted to be around her anyway. I spent the last months with her. When she finally passed, the guards whisked me away again, for my protection. I didn't want any part of the intrigue of the politics of the court of Denmark or anywhere else. The guards wanted to put me in hiding somewhere in Denmark. Since I knew no one knew of me since my mother covered my birth, I felt I wanted to return and take up my life here with you. I was finally able to talk them into bringing me back here to you. I'm no princess. All I want is to be your wife."

He held her tight and started rubbing her body. She turned to him and they kissed a passionate kiss. They again had to pull themselves apart.

"We must go back to the castle," Troy said. He grabbed her and went to his horse. He mounted and pulled her up into his lap.

She started laughing. "I see our emotions match."

She clung to him and he kept his arm around her. They leisurely rode back to the castle. They kept kissing and feeling each other. They should have been husband and wife already. Their separation had been for too long. Neither had any inhibitions about touching each other. They couldn't get enough. When they finally returned to the castle, Matlock saw them coming.

"I didn't hear you say you were going fishing," he laughed. He helped Lady Aspen to the ground. He gave her a kiss and held her back. "And what a fine catch you made, my lord."

"Hands off, Matlock. She is my catch and one I will keep forever."

He kissed her again in front of everyone. All around the people started cheering and laughing.

"Go get the preacher and tell him it is an emergency," he said to Matlock.

Matlock jumped on his horse and rode off. The carriage which brought her back to Troy was in the courtyard. Servants were unloading the carriage. Aspen saw her uncle and took off running. Troy spun around. He didn't want to let go of her. She grabbed her uncle and hugged him. Troy went to them and led them into the parlor holding her hand. He sat her down and went to the cupboard and poured a drink. He downed the drink and poured another.

"Would anyone else like a drink?" he asked.

Charles asked for a bourbon and Aspen asked for a sherry. He poured the drinks and dispersed them. He took his drink and stood behind Aspen. He kept his hand on her shoulder.

"I have sent for the preacher. We are to be wed as soon as he gets here. I have your wedding dress in your room if you would care to wear it," he said to her.

"If you don't mind, my love, I would like to freshen up but I care less what I am wearing. I only want to be your wife."

He bent and kissed her a passionate kiss. Charles would have normally been embarrassed, but he totally understood. He just turned his head.

"Do you need my help, love?" he asked.

She laughed that delightful laugh he remembered. "I believe I will be better served with a maid, my lord," she mocked. Then looked up into his eyes. "I think a maid will be able to help me more right now. Later I will allow you to try out for the position as my maid," her eyes twinkled.

"As you wish, my lady. But I don't think you really know what you are missing."

"I'm sure I will find out. Let me explain to Uncle Charles what has been going on and then I will go prepare myself."

Troy bowed to her. He didn't want to leave but wanted to give her time with her uncle. He bowed to them both and left the room. He went to the kitchen and found Marple. He told her he wanted the most elaborate dinner possible. It was to be his wedding feast and all within the house and the grounds were to be invited. Marple turned and kissed him on the cheek.

"I will take care of everything," she said.

Troy returned to the parlor. Aspen was already upstairs preparing herself. Troy waited patiently downstairs. He finally went upstairs to dress himself. He was all dusty and dirty from rolling in the tall grass with Aspen. She was in her room for the last time preparing herself so he was able to clean himself and dress quickly.

Word was sent up to both that the preacher had arrived. Troy went down first and awaited his bride. He was falling in love with that word and more in love with the person behind the word. He turned and saw Aspen in the doorway. She had found her dress and decided to wear it. His breath stuck in his chest. She was a vision of sheer loveliness. She was surrounded by layers upon layers of golden chiffon with diamond dust covering the skirt. She wore a gold comb in her hair. She walked as if she was in a cloud. He starred at her as if he was in heaven. All the people of the household and grounds were standing around but when they saw her, they all "ah"-ed. The women started crying. Charles stood straight beside Troy. He was so proud of her.

She came to stand beside Troy in front of the preacher. They said their vows and all cheered them on. Troy told Matlock to serve the drinks to the men. There were kegs of rum in the basement. Some men went to get them and took them outside. The women had busied themselves setting up a buffet outside also. Marple was able to make a wedding cake and the whole celebration was perfect. Troy declared the next day a day off for all the servants. Troy and Aspen celebrated for a while with their friends and family, as they felt everyone was, and then stole off to Troy's room.

"Now do I get to apply for the job as your maid?" he asked kissing her. He gently started undressing her. "My goodness, you are still wearing an ungodly amount of under-skirting. I don't know if I can find you."

She laughed and helped him. She also helped him undress. They were finally together and were kissing and feeling each other. She was amazed at his manhood.

"I have been saving up a long time for this," he said kissing her and carrying her to the bed.

The servants had readied the bed for them and had filled them with rose petals. He gently laid her upon the bed and joined her. He made love to her feeling her entire body. She groaned and pulled his lips up to hers. She leaned into him. She moaned even more as he kept up his prelude to the realization of the marital duty. They made love at fever pitch. They came together and held on to each other until the entire experience subsided. They kept hold onto one another after.

"Now I know how it feels, my love, I will never be able to stop."

"I won't ever want you to stop," she started kissing him again.

They made love all night. They finally went down for some refreshment. The house was all cleaned up. They were finally able to part without the desperation or fear of being parted. They were sitting in the parlor after breakfast.

"How are Lady Matilda and Penny?" Aspen asked.

"They are very well. Lady Matilda and Robert have set a wedding date. Penny and Timothy are planning their wedding. Mandy and Lord Michael just became engaged."

"Mandy and Lord Michael? Who are they?"

"I'm sorry, my dear," he said. "I forgot you didn't know about Mandy. I found someone to catalog the books in the library. I started going through them and couldn't make heads of tails out of what I was doing. Robert gave me the name of a cataloger he had used. I went to the book store and hired the daughter of the cataloger Robert had used, Miss Mandy Shelton. Mother, Penny, and I thought she deserved to go to the balls. So I sponsored her and she was the hit of the balls. I was the most envied person at the balls escorting the three most beautiful ladies attending."

"Just how beautiful is this Mandy?" Aspen asked.

Troy turned red but got control of himself quickly. "Not near as beautiful as you, my love." He went to her and kissed her deeply. "Maybe I could interest you in a little nap," he said hopefully.

She smiled at him and took his hand. She had more of an assurance of herself since she had been taken away from him. He liked that. They went to his room and he started undressing her. She was simply dressed this time.

"How am I doing as your maid?" he said, nuzzling her neck.

"Very distracting," she answered him and kissing him.

They made it to the bed and made passionate love. They finished and laid in each other's arms.

"Now tell me just how beautiful this Mandy is?" she asked again.

Again, Troy turned red.

"There is a story here and you have to tell me or I will believe the worst."

Troy told her the story of what happened.

"You brute," she said hitting him. "How could you do that to that poor girl?"

"I was out of my mind with sorrow, my love, because the one I loved with all my heart had been taken from me. Yes, I got drunk and no I had no idea what I was doing. It all stopped when I called her by your name. She went still and I came to my senses. Thank goodness! I was a cad. I was despicable and I felt every bit of that, but we made amends. She really is very beautiful and kind and giving. Much like you, but you more so. Now she is engaged to a wonderful man who by the way is our neighbor. And I am married to the woman of my dreams." He kissed her and she kissed him back. "Am I forgiven?" he asked, kissing her.

Her answer was to give into him again. They finally rose and dressed. They met Charles downstairs and went into dinner together.

Their lives took on a routine. Aspen met with the housekeeper and they spent time getting to know each other. Mrs. Trundle showed Aspen around the manor house and informed her of all that Lady Matilda had set up to run the manor. Aspen was introduced to all the staff within the manor. She soon had taken over the duties of the lady of the manor. Troy and Matlock worked closely to ensure all the tenants had what was needed for a well running of the estate. Troy told Matlock about the Braxtons and how he would be going there to see the holdings involved with the Braxton estate. He informed Matlock of how he and Bailey would be looking into dealings with Oliver Braxton and might well start working with them. Troy and Aspen spent as much time as possible together. They were getting to know each other in special ways that was making their love of each other grow. She took care of her responsibilities and he took care of his but together they took care of all. Aspen wanted to tour the estate with Troy to meet all the tenants. They took a week riding around the five hundred miles of the estate. They spent time with all the tenants. Aspen was amazed at all that Troy was responsible for. She could understand how sometimes the welfare of the tenants could become overwhelming especially when there were problems such as the thieves that had tried to hurt the tenants. She loved watching him intermingle with them and how gentle he was with everyone. He was so complimentary to all even the wives and children of the tenants.

Chapter 36

*T*roy *told Aspen about his plans to go to Braxton Estates* with a stopover in London. They started planning for their trip. It would be much lighter this time because all they needed was their clothing. Charles decided to stay at the castle. He had no interest in going back to the house he shared with his sister. They left early the following week after their tour of the Battingham Estate. Troy was taking his horse but would ride in the carriage with Aspen for the trip. They made good time to London. They would kiss and love on each other while in the carriage and make passionate love each night. They were in good spirits when they arrived at the Bowling townhouse. They rang the bell and had the butler announce them.

They stood outside the parlor as the butler announced Lord and Lady Bowling. They entered the room to shocked expressions. Everyone was stunned when Troy walked in with Aspen on his arm. Mandy was looking at the most beautiful woman she had ever seen. There was a very brief flair of jealousy, then she looked at Lord Michael and everything was in even kilter again. When Penny and Lady Matilda saw Aspen, they each ran and grabbed her and started kissing and hugging her. They were so excited to see each other. They were all talking at once. The men met over by the cupboard. Troy made them each a drink and they just stood there watching the ladies. After about an hour, lunch was announced. Troy and Aspen had to explain everything that happened between them. It made for a very lively dinner.

"So, you finally stopped making Aspen run away from you," Penny laughed.

"I sure did. I finally caught her and she isn't going anywhere. We are stuck together for life now."

"I'm so sorry we had to miss the wedding. You couldn't wait another week and have the wedding here?" asked Lady Matilda.

"No, Mother, we, or at least I, couldn't wait for another minute. We got married the day she came back to me and I'm very glad we did."

Aspen blushed. "We are very happy, Lady Matilda."

"We can give them a reception," Penny piped up.

"What a grand idea," Lady Matilda replied. "You must postpone your departure for another week, my dears."

"But Mother, the house is all packed up. We can't have the servants unpack and then repack when we are ready to go."

"We can have it at our townhouse," said Robert. "We don't pack up our residence. We don't move as much as you do because I use my residence year-round."

Troy looked at Robert and groaned. Everyone laughed.

"It doesn't matter where we go, my lord, as long as we are together," Aspen said to Troy.

He looked at her and sighed. "I bow to your judgement, my love. Alright, we will stay one more week. We will leave for Braxton one week from today."

Penny jumped and kissed Troy on the cheek. The ladies left the table to go to the parlor to start making a plan. They started the invitation list. Penny sent word to the Braxton's to see if they could stay another week. Timothy said he would rush it to them so they would get it in time. Troy came in and made himself, Robert and Lord Michael drinks and they went out to the garden.

"It is very nice of you to do us the honor of hosting a party," Troy said.

"If I had not, I would never have heard the end of it. You are beginning to understand the makings of a woman, aren't you, my boy?"

"Yes sir, I am. But on the other hand, my lord, I wouldn't have it any other way. Marriage is all I expected it to be."

"Yes, you are beginning to understand." Robert and Troy laughed together. "This boy will learn soon."

Robert went back into the parlor to be with Lady Matilda.

Mandy, Lord Michael, Aspen, and Troy went for a stroll in the garden. Troy was talking to Michael so Aspen had a chance to talk to Mandy for a few minutes.

"I'm so glad we get to meet," Aspen said. "Troy has told me the whole story of your relationship. I'm so sorry about what happened to you. But I'm sure you realized how kind Troy really is and he was just overtaken by sorrowful madness at the time."

"The whole story?" Mandy asked. Aspen nodded. "He is so in love with you. And I can see why. You are the most beautiful woman I have ever seen. I'm so dismayed for all the troubles you two have had. You are truly meant to be together. I can see how much in love the two of you are."

"Thank you Mandy and I hope you and I will become really good friends. We'll be neighbors after all."

They hugged and cemented their friendship right then.

Troy finally made his way to his room while Aspen went to hers to get some clothing. Bailey was there.

"My Lord, I'm so happy for you. A happy ending it has become all the way around."

"Yes, Bailey, it is." Troy smiled.

"Which room will you be using, my lord, yours or Lady Aspen's?"

"For now, leave my things here and I will see which room Lady Aspen prefers. We will be staying for the next week. It appears we will be having a wedding reception here in London before we travel on to Braxton. And I would like you to go to Braxton with us. I will need your help more now that Lady Aspen is accompanying us."

"Yes, my lord." Bailey bowed and left Troy sitting on the balcony.

There came a soft knock on the door shortly after Bailey left. Troy thought Bailey was back with another question.

"Enter," he said.

Aspen came in and out onto the balcony.

Troy stood and took her into his arms. "You don't have to knock, my love. My room is your room. Unless you decide you want to stay in your own room, then I will move my things to your room."

"I prefer this room. It appears larger than my old room and I like the smell of this room. It smells of you." She kissed him.

He kissed her back with a longing so intense it surprised him. They started taking off each other's clothes and went to the bed. They made passionate love and fell asleep in each other's arms. When they woke, Troy kept holding her and moved his hands all over her body.

"Do you know where I slept when I lost you?" he asked, kissing her neck. "I slept in your room because of your scent. When I slept here, I would have terrible nightmares. But when I fell asleep with my arms around your pillow, I was at peace."

She turned to him and held him and they kissed. They made love again, but this time it was gentler. They both came to complete fulfillment. They laid for a while in each other's arms and then decided to get up.

"We should make an appearance at dinner."

"Yes, we should, my love. You really don't mind about the wedding reception do you, Troy?" she asked.

"No, my love. I want the world to know you are mine, now and forever."

They kissed and got out of bed. They dressed and went down for dinner. Troy saw Bailey and told him to have Aspen's things moved to his room. They entered the parlor and Troy went to the cupboard. Lady Matilda and Robert were there along with Amelia, David, and their three children, Penny, Timothy, Mandy, and Lord Michael. When the children saw Troy, they ran to him and hugged him. Aspen was quite surprised. She liked seeing the interaction that was happening. It gave her another insight into Troy's personality. Troy went to Amelia and David. He gave Amelia a kiss on the cheek and shook David's hand.

"I would like to introduce my wife, Lady Aspen." He brought her forward.

She curtsied to them and kissed each of them on the cheek. "I understand we are to be family soon. I'm so thrilled. You also have such lovely children." Aspen bent down to get closer to them. "May I have a hug?" she asked them.

The youngest stayed back until the other two hugged her, then he hugged her also. She was smiling at them and hugged them all again. Dinner was announced just then so they all went to the dining room.

Dinner was such a delightful time. Troy got the children to laugh, everyone was talking in groups over each other. The women were talking about the party. The men were talking business and politics. It was a good thing all the men agreed with today's politics. At one point, Troy sat back and looked at all the faces and what they were doing. *This is family,* he thought. *Months ago, it was three, then four. Now look at it.* He decided right there that when he returned to Battingham he would enlarge the dining room so it could accommodate the Bowlings, the Braxtons, the Gatsbys, the Brentwoods, and the Knoells. In fact, he just might have to build a whole other building just so the families could get together. He saw Aspen looking at him from across the table, he smiled at her and jumped back into the conversation with the men.

After dinner, the women retired to the front parlor while the men retired to the back parlor. The ladies were all talking about the party and finalizing their plans while the men were drinking cognac and smoking cigars. Amelia and David were the first to leave to get the children down for bed. Robert went with them. Penny and Timothy wandered out to the garden. Lady Matilda said she was exhausted and went to her room. Troy and Aspen stayed in the front parlor. Lord Michael left and Mandy went to her room.

"What were you thinking when you sat back and relaxed?" she asked. "You had a funny look on your face."

"I was thinking Battingham Castle is too small for this family now. When we left, it was only four. Now look at us. I may have to enlarge the castle."

"Yes. The family has quite grown since I left."

"Not really, my love. You knew Robert, not his family, but him. You knew Timothy, again not his family, but him. Now you have met Robert's family and will meet his son Lord Anthony and Lady Elinor and next week you will meet Timothy's seven brothers and sisters and his parents. You have already met Lord Michael and Mandy and she only has her mother. So you only have a few more to meet."

"I also saw your interchanges with the children. They adore you."

"Just before I first met you, I was at a tenant's abode and his youngest child was about ten. He sat on my lap and I realized just how much I do want children. Yes, I love having children around. At the last ball I attended, I threw chaperoning to the wind and stayed upstairs with Amelia and Lord Anthony's children until they went to bed. Then I picked up my chaperoning duties. I loved every minute spent with the children." He stood and pulled her into his arms. "I hope you don't mind having a houseful of children," he said as he bent to give her a passionate kiss. They went up to their room to retire.

The days went by quickly. Mandy's mother Martha Shelton came and stayed at Bowling townhouse. Troy talked Lord Michael into closing his house and staying with them. Lady Matilda took care of Martha and ensured she had the appropriate attire for the party. Troy saw very little of Aspen except for bedtime. Then they made up for their being apart all day. The ladies were all helping to ensure the best party of the season.

The night finally came. Troy dressed in his elegance and departed the room to allow Lady Aspen to prepare. He took his wig with him to put it on when it was absolutely necessary. Troy, Aspen, and Lady Matilda were to be at the party early to greet the guests. So he had Bailey escort the other women and their beaus. Troy went to the parlor and poured himself a drink. Soon Timothy and Michael joined him. They sat around with their drinks and relaxed before all the commotion would start. Timothy and Michael were really getting along very well. They were becoming fast friends. Troy felt like the father of them all instead of almost the same age. Life had aged Troy into manhood.

When they had first left Battingham Castle, he was very young and naïve. He and Aspen have been through so much. He learned about the emotions going haywire and wanting just sex, then he learned about women and what they go through. He finally got to the stage of being able to control his emotions and enjoy the company. After which he went through hell which he hoped no one would ever have to go through. Now he was content and hoping for a long and loving life with the woman he loved more than life itself. What he had gone through made him grow up and made him stronger.

Aspen and Lady Matilda were the first women to appear through the doorway of the parlor. Timothy whistled and Anthony almost swooned at the beauty of the two. Aspen was dressed in her wedding dress with her hair piled on top of her hair with a diamond crown given to her from her mother. Lady Matilda was dressed in gold. A gold gown with an empire waist and the material flowing to the floor. Her hair was piled high on her head with a gold tiara. Troy went forward and bowed. He then took Lady Matilda's hand and kissed it. He turned to Aspen and kissed her passionately in front of everyone. She turned bright red due to the fact she returned his kiss just as passionately.

"I loved you in the dress the first time I saw you and I love it even more now. Are we ready to go?"

They both nodded and they turned to leave just as Penny, Mandy, and Martha came down.

"Your beaus will swoon at your beauty as well," he said, escorting Lady Matilda and Aspen out the door.

The Gatsby house was decorated so elaborately. Candles were everywhere. There was an ice sculpture of a dove at the end of the room next to a huge wedding cake. Champagne was flowing from the dove and filling glasses as it flowed down. All the guests were so impressed. It truly was the best party of the season. The reception line seemed never to end, but it finally did. Troy, Aspen, Lady Matilda, and Robert were finally able to join the guests and dance. The dinner was exquisite. Troy and Aspen cut the first piece of wedding cake then the servants cut it and passed it to the guests. Troy danced almost every dance with Aspen. The party was perfect., but it finally ended about five o'clock in the morning. Everyone went home and fell into bed exhausted.

Chapter 37

*N*obody stirred in the Bowling townhouse before noon. Troy woke up but didn't want to disturb Aspen so he quietly got up and dressed. He tiptoed out of the room. He went to the parlor and rang for tea. Between the champagne and the dancing last night, he felt very sluggish this morning. He knew Aspen had a wonderful night. It will be a remembrance from their wedding. He was ecstatic about that. He believed she had the wedding she wanted. He wanted to leave for the Braxton estate today, but he would postpone it one day. Everyone needed time to relax.

Lady Matilda walked into the room. "Oh, you are such a sweet dear. The tea is waiting for me. You spoil your mother."

Troy laughed and kissed her on the cheek. "No more than you deserve, Mother. And thank you for a magnificent party last night. It was unforgettable. It was just what Aspen deserved."

"What did I deserve?" Aspen asked as she walked in the door. She went to Troy and kissed him. He held her in his arms.

"You deserved the magnificent party last night."

"Oh, Lady Matilda, it couldn't have been better. It was so enchanting. Thank you for giving us these memories."

"You are both welcome, but I wasn't alone in planning the affair. I had lots of help. Even you, Aspen, helped with the planning but I was very pleased at the outcome. I agree, it couldn't have been better."

"And we will thank everyone that was involved with the whole affair." Aspen poured herself some tea and sat down on the settee.

Troy sat next to her. Mandy and Martha were the next ones to enter the parlor. Lady Matilda served them each some tea.

"While we are together," started Martha, "Lady Matilda and Lord Bowling, I want to thank you for all you have done for my Mandy and myself. I am very humbled by your generosity."

"Mandy is a beautiful, kind, and generous person and she owes it all to you," Troy replied. "We have only helped her reach her full potential and by doing so it will help you also. We are very pleased with the outcome. Besides, you will be our neighbor now."

"I'm in love with Norsdom Castle," said Mandy. "I love the country and Mother is coming to live with us. We have the bookstore up for sale. As soon as it sells, we will be moving to Norsdom Castle and Michael and I will be married."

"Not before me," Penny said from the doorway. "Now Mother, I refuse to be the last one married simply because London protocol. It isn't fair."

"But Penny," Troy jumped in, "You are the youngest of the group. Shouldn't you let your elders go first?"

"Elders!" all the ladies in the room exclaimed together.

"Uh oh!" Troy said. "I don't believe it. This time I made ALL the ladies angry."

They all busted up laughing.

"My poor son," Lady Matilda was trying to get her breath, "I don't know if you will ever learn."

Troy sat down with Aspen and tried to keep his mouth shut until everyone could calm down. Lord Michael entered with Robert and Timothy who had just arrived and wanted to know what had made all the ladies laugh so hard. The ladies finally got control of themselves.

Lady Matilda looked at Robert, "I will explain a little later, my dear. Would you like some tea?"

All the gentlemen nodded.

Troy stated, "I think I will go out to the garden for a walk. Would you care to join me, dear wife?"

Aspen smiled at him with the twinkle in her eye. "Yes, I would love to join you." She stood. "We will see everyone later."

They strolled through the garden. They finally got to the rose garden.

"What am I going to do with you, my love?" She turned and pulled his face to hers and kissed him. "Maybe I should just keep my lips here so nothing wrong comes out of your mouth." She started laughing and pulled away.

"That might work," he said, pulling her back and giving her a very passionate kiss. She melted into his body. They finally parted and he held her tight. They parted after a while and sat on the bench. "We will be leaving tomorrow morning, my love. I believe Penny will be traveling with Timothy's family so it will just be us again."

"I like the sound of that, my lord. It makes for a very nice trip." She bent into him for another kiss. "Should we think of going back?"

"I can think of somewhere else I would rather be," he said, kissing her again and pulling her to him tighter.

"I agree, but we do have some responsibilities."

"None of them were just married. I think they would understand."

"Alright, we will see them later."

They snuck up to their room and stayed there for the next two hours.

They finally returned to the parlor. Everyone was still there and engaged in animated conversations. Aspen went to sit on the settee with Martha. Troy went to the cupboard and poured himself a drink. He looked around and several were holding glasses so he went to stand behind Aspen. Troy again stood back and watched, proud to belong to such an assembly. Finally, dinner was announced. Everyone adjourned to the dining room.

"Mother, when do you and Robert plan to travel to Battingham?" Troy asked.

Robert answered. "We are planning to leave in a week. There are a few loose ends I have yet to tie up and then we will be on our way."

"Timothy, when is your family prepared to leave?"

"They have already left. I do hope you don't mind Penny and I accompanying you and Lady Aspen on your journey to Braxton."

"Oh, Penny!" exclaimed Aspen. "That will be so much fun. I can hardly wait." Troy gave Aspen a look then sighed.

"Yes, it will be a delight traveling with you and Timothy," Troy said.

Again, the women talked about frivolous things and the men talked politics. Dinner continued on with the conversations. After the men had their cigars and cognac, the women joined them and everyone meandered out to the garden. Each couple ended up taking a different path. Martha returned to her room.

The next morning, Troy woke early. He woke Aspen up with kisses and they ended up making love. Then they dressed and left so the servants could finish packing up their room. They were soon on their way to Braxton with Penny and Timothy. The girls talked incessantly almost the whole way there. Troy got to know Timothy much better. He had one year of schooling left, then he would join his father in his enterprises. He and Penny planned to be married shortly after. They would live in their own home being built on the Braxton estate. It appeared they were all set and moving in the right direction. Troy was very impressed with Timothy. He seemed to be maturing into a fine man. Love must have something to do with men standing up to their responsibilities and taking life in hand. His situation had been a little different, but he still had so much more responsibility than the usual twenty-five-year-old. It didn't matter when a boy became a man, it only mattered that he finally did.

They arrived at Braxton manor about midday. They had been traveling for three days. Oliver and Tabitha were there to greet them. Timothy's younger siblings bounded around Troy. They gave him hugs and kisses on the cheek. Troy and Aspen were then shown to their room. They cleaned up and went downstairs to the parlor. Dinner was served shortly after. Troy ensured he was sitting next to Daniel.

"How have you been, Daniel?" Troy inquired of him.

"Fine, my lord. I have been helping my father just as you said," Daniel pronounced proudly.

"Yes," laughed Oliver, "And a very good job he has been doing."

Daniel went on to tell Troy all that he had been doing for his father. "Father has been letting me sweep up the office and I also get to follow him to the wharves and do little things there as long as I'm careful."

Aspen sat and watched the interchange. Her heart swelled with pride.

After dinner, the men went to another parlor and enjoyed a drink and talked. Then Troy took Aspen for a stroll around to see the Braxton gardens. They found a secluded place and started kissing. They were interrupted by Daniel and a couple of his sisters. They were giggling at what they saw. Troy turned and started chasing them. They were all laughing and having a good time when Oliver intervened.

"It's bedtime for you youngsters. Now go and get ready."

"Yes, sir," they all said and ran to the house.

"I apologize for any inconvenience the children have given you." Tabitha came out and joined them.

"There was no inconvenience at all," Troy answered. "It was a lot of fun and good exercise after riding in a carriage for three days. What is our schedule for tomorrow, Oliver?"

They went off and talked about how to handle things. Aspen and Tabitha wondered around the garden together. They were getting to know one another. After a short time, Troy returned. He apologized for leaving her.

"That is quite alright, my love. I really enjoyed walking in the peace and quiet. I really don't care that much for London. I prefer the quiet of the country and Lady Tabitha and I became acquainted."

"Will you be alright while I conduct business with Oliver for the next month or two?"

"Absolutely. I will also have Penny and Lady Tabitha to spend time with, not to mention two other girls. I will be able to keep myself quite busy."

"I do believe it is time for us to retire." He smiled. He took her by the hand and led her up the stairs.

The days flew by. They appraised the house being built for Penny and Timothy. It was to be a grand house. It would be bigger than Battingham Castle. There would be plenty of room for lots of children. Troy was happy for Penny and felt she couldn't have done better and she and Timothy appeared to be very much in love. His heart swelled for her.

While Troy was busy with Oliver and Bailey, Aspen was kept busy with the girls, Penny, and Lady Tabitha. She was having the time of her life being with so many of the same sex. She learned things she had never known before. Things like a relationship with a loving family, how girls could help one another with fun and gentleness, and just how much fun it was to interact with other women and girls. She was learning to needlepoint. The women and girls were enchanted with stories she told of her heritage. She had been brought up by a loving grandmother and uncle but had to deal with a spiteful and hateful sister. Her life was one of mostly loneliness. Her grandmother had been very loving though. She told them how as a baby her mother had sent her away so as not to have any problems later. But that meant that she had to live in secrecy. She also told them that she was unaware of all of this until recently. She always had wondered why her grandmother had never let any of her family come to their house to visit. Her grandmother had always gone to everyone else's house to visit. She was so happy to be part of a real family and a such rambunctious household.

Troy, on the other hand, was in his element with Oliver. Daniel was at his heals most of the time. He ended up buying into a partnership with Oliver. He also made several deals with David to sell his tenants' products for a much larger profit. He and Bailey worked at making all the deals and arrangements for transport of all the products to the wharfs at Braxton. David, Amelia, and their children joined the Braxtons and Bowlings most nights. It was an eventful and fruitful visit. But all good things must come to an end. Everything was finally in place.

"My love," Troy said to Aspen, "it is finally time for us to go home and start our lives as husband and wife."

They kissed and started walking into the manor.

"I do believe we are also starting our own family, my love," Aspen said softly.

Troy stopped in his tracks. Was he hearing what he thought he was hearing? Was she saying she was with child? He couldn't believe it. He swung her around in circles. Then he took her in his arms and kissed her.

"You have just made me the happiest person on earth."

Penny and Timothy came out to the garden. Penny saw their expressions and was wandering what had happened to make Troy look so ecstatic.

"My dear sister," Troy said and twirled her around. "You are going to be an aunt."

Oh!" she exclaimed. "Timothy isn't that wonderful news?" She turned to Aspen and gave her a hug and a kiss on the cheek. "Mother is going to be so happy."

Penny started jumping up and down with enjoyment. Oliver and Tabitha came out from all the noise. Troy told them and they were over joyed at the news. Congratulations went around to Troy and Aspen. Everyone went back to the parlor to have a toast to the happy parents. Aspen was taken in and made to feel very special. They were finally able to step away and retire to their room.

Troy held her and kissed her gently. "Oh my love, how can I tell you how wonderful I feel right now?"

"Well, I didn't do the deed all by myself, my lord. I did have a little help from my husband."

"The cad, how dare he mess with my love." He kissed her and started taking off her clothes while she started on his. He started nuzzling her neck and they went to bed.

The next morning, they woke together.

"Is it true or was I dreaming?"

"It is true, my loving husband. You are going to be such a loving Father. I can hardly wait," she said kissing him.

They didn't get out of bed for a long while. Finally, Troy said they were going to have to get going soon if they were leaving that day, so they both rose and got dressed. They went down for breakfast.

"There's the happy parents to be," said Oliver. "I thought you might be staying another night."

"Sorry we're so late. We were celebrating," Troy said. Aspen blushed. "We do have to leave today. We've been gone for a very long time and need to get into our own routine with our own home. Are you ready, Penny?"

"Not really," she said crying. "I'll miss you so much Timothy," she said clinging to him.

"As I will you, love, but this is necessary so we can get married and move on with our lives also."

"I know. I just hate this part."

Chapter 38

Troy felt for her. He knew all too well how it felt to be separated, but at least she knew where Timothy would be.

"Penny it's not like you won't know where Timothy is. Just think, you can go home and plan your wedding. You have a dress to have made for you. You are going to be so busy. Time will fly by. It will bring you a life time of happiness."

"You're right Troy. I'm being silly right now. I'll get better." She kissed Timothy. "Remember always that you have my heart."

"I will and I wait for the day we will be husband and wife." He kissed her and they made their way to the front door.

They climbed into the carriage for the long ride to Battingham Castle. Aspen took pity on Penny and spent most of the time with her. After a while, Penny seemed to feel better. They talked about her wedding and the baby and everything was made right. Bailey was riding in the carriage with them so he and Troy talked about all that had been accomplished with Oliver and how it would all be implemented. All in all, it was a productive trip. Men and women were content by the time they arrived at Battingham Castle.

They finally arrived at Battingham Castle after a fortnight of traveling. Lady Matilda was thrilled with all the news. The household was in turmoil with all the activity. The castle wasn't used to having small children along with so many people. Troy walked around the castle with Robert and assessed all the changes he was planning. Robert was very attentive and helped by making suggestions. He said he wouldn't mind staying and helping. Troy was very thankful.

The women were busy planning two weddings and the birth of a baby. Aspen and Troy searched for a midwife. They found one who had been recommended by the doctor. Martha, Mandy and Michael came for a visit. The bookstore had sold for a very beneficial price. Martha was well off in her own right. So three weddings were being planned.

Robert and Troy stayed clear of the house during the day. They found some workers to do the work inside the castle to make more rooms. So between the women working and the men working there seemed to be nothing but chaos around the castle. Troy moved his and Donald Blake's offices to the first floor. They made a couple more bedrooms out of the turrets. That gave them six bedrooms at the top of the castle.

They then went to the third. The servants occupied this floor, but only used about half the rooms. They moved the servants and put up a wall with a door. Then took the other half and made eight very nice bedrooms. They toured the second floor and found that there were twenty rooms there. Troy wanted to make half of those into smaller rooms, but nice rooms. He was thinking of later needing rooms for the children they would be having. One would need to be a nursery until they were finished having children. Plus, they would need a room for a nanny and schoolroom. But for the time being, they could make them into bedrooms for all the wedding guests.

Robert took a little time to take Amelia and the children back to London. He rode his horse back to make better time. While he was gone, the workers were completing the plans Troy and Robert had set in place. Also, Troy took that time to ride out to the tenants with Matlock and check to ensure everything was working as it should. Troy and Matlock also took this time to relax together and stay away from all the chaos at the manor. They enjoyed getting back into the relationship they had cemented during

Troy's trials. They finally decided they had stayed away too long and had better head back.

Aspen was showing more and more with the baby. When Troy got back, he was surprised that she was so much bigger than when he left. He took her in his arms and gave her a big kiss.

She responded to him. "You have been gone so long, my dear. I truly missed you."

"I'm here and see that the little one has grown quite a bit." He patted her stomach. He was surprised to have her stomach hit him back. He laughed. "That was the baby?" he asked incredulously.

"Yes, and you should be on my side when he kicks so much."

"He?" Troy asked "You think it will be a boy."

"Definitely," answered Aspen. "No girl would ever kick like this. He is not stopping."

"I'm not too sure about that. The way Penny was, I wouldn't doubt she was like that within my mother."

They laughed.

"You are right, husband. But I still feel it will be a boy." She kissed him and they retired to their bedroom.

When Robert returned, Troy and Robert looked around the first floor. The workers had made quick progress of the other three floors. They were nearly done. Troy and Robert retired to the study, which had become Troy's office. They started drawing up plans for the first floor.

While they were doing all the reconstruction of the castle, the women were busy with the weddings. Lady Matilda and Robert were the first to be married. They had the seamstress there working on all the wedding gowns and gowns for the others to wear at the weddings. Lady Matilda had decided to keep her dress simple since this was her second marriage. It would be empire waist of silk with an overlay of muslin. She decided it would be a powder blue color. The wedding would be held here at the castle in the garden. Penny was going elaborate. It was her first wedding and she wanted it to be grand. She was also getting married at the castle. But it would be inside so she could come down the stairway as her entrance. Her dress was going to be a silk dress with mounds of chiffon covering the silk underdress. She would be wearing the wire hoop under her gown. She would have a veil with a long train flowing behind her dress. She was using Robert's grandchildren as flower girls with the oldest boy as ring-bearer and the other boys to help the girls throw the flowers. They were going to have to practice throwing flowers gently.

Mandy was using the same seamstress so she and Martha had been staying for a few days at Battingham Castle. She wanted something low key like Lady Matilda. She chose a dress of silk with flowers across the bodice and across the skirt. It was not as straight as Lady Matilda's but flowed out not as wide as Penny's. Her skirt would use a crinoline under-garment to make it stand out a little. Her veil was also to flow behind her dress, but not as long as Penny's. Her wedding would be at Norsdom Cas-tle. They were all getting very excited.

Troy and Robert settled on the plans for the first floor and work began. They decided on widening the dining room to twice its size. However, half of it could be closed off by a wall that could slide open when a larger dining room wood be necessary. There were separate tables made for children and the main table could be enlarged. It was an example of new ideas. They were also able to find room to create a second parlor. For the time being, Mr. Blake was sharing the study with Troy so the two offices had been com-bined. It was actually working out better. Troy didn't have to go and find Mr. Blake very often.

Troy and Robert were able to start sitting back and enjoying life but the women were still in a tizzy trying to have everything done for the wed-dings. The day was coming closer for Lady Matilda and Robert. Robert was ecstatic, but Lady Matilda was becoming more and more nervous. They were walking in the garden one night.

"You are especially quiet, my dear," said Robert.

"Yes, I am," she replied.

"May I inquire what is on your mind?"

"I've been thinking more and more about Troy Senior lately. I think that is only natural since I've been planning a wedding that my first wedding would come to mind. I love you Robert," she stopped to look at him. "But Troy Senior keeps interrupting my thoughts."

She turned away from him. He turned her gently back to face him. He held her in his arms. When he sensed her calming down, he kissed her. He increased his demand on his kiss. He could feel her responding to him. He kept up his kiss and he had her groaning into their kiss. He finally pulled back just a little. She leaned into him.

"Now do you have thoughts of Troy Senior?" he asked.

"No, those thoughts flew right out of my head. I do love you Robert and I want to marry you. I started becoming afraid I would dishonor you with my thoughts of Troy."

"I think I can take those thoughts and put them behind you. Give me the chance and I will guide you into our married life together." He kissed her again a very demanding kiss.

She responded much quicker this time. She was ready to marry him and spend the rest of her days with him. They walked back into the house and went to the parlor.

"There the two of you are. I thought I was going to have to get the sheriff out to look for you," Troy said laughing. He handed his mother a sherry and Robert a whisky. "Just three more days and you will be living in wedded bliss."

"I totally agree," Robert said, looking at Lady Matilda.

Timothy and his family had arrived for the wedding. Robert's children and grandchildren had also arrived at the manor. Martha, Mandy, and Michael were spending the night before the wedding with the Bowlings. Lord Stewart and Lady Noel Brentwood would be coming early on the morning of the wedding. The rest of the gentry in the area were also coming the day of the ceremony. A gazebo had been erected in the garden with chairs surrounding it so all could see.

The morning finally arrived. Aspen had a gown of golden muslin made for her. She knew it was Troy's favorite color on her. It had an empire waist and fully showed her with child. There was no hiding the fact so she decided to show off her body as delicately as possible. She wore her hair up with a comb of gold holding it softly. Troy came in to get dressed and stopped short. His breath was taken when he saw her. She was still the most beautiful woman he had ever seen other than his mother and sister. He went to her and pulled her into his arms.

"Can you get redressed if I undress you now?" he asked, kissing her passionately.

"Don't even think it, my lord. I am not redoing all of this. You my dear, will just have to be patient until after the wedding."

"I bow to you, my love, but we may leave the wedding before the bride and groom do. I can only be so patient when you tease me with your beauty."

She left the room so he could ready himself. She went to check on Lady Matilda. She knocked and heard "Enter." Penny was with her mother and was helping do her hair. Penny was looking beautiful in a gown of baby blue chiffon with an empire waist, but it flowed out from there. She was wearing her diamond jewelry. Lady Matilda stood stately beside her daughter. She was finally ready. Troy was giving her away and Penny was her attendant. Robert's youngest grandson was the ringbearer and all his granddaughters were flower girls.

"Oh, you look so beautiful," cried Aspen. "And Penny you are just as beautiful. You look so much like your mother, Penny!" She went and kissed them both on the cheek. "I'm so proud to belong to this family."

They hugged each other and each took a deep breath. It was time. Aspen went downstairs to ensure everything and everybody was prepared. She nodded to the servant and the ceremony started. Penny came down the stairs and walked out to the garden. Robert was waiting with the preacher. The flower girls and ringbearer came next. Then Troy walked next to his mother. When they reached the gazebo and Troy handed his Mother's hand to Robert, he said, "Finally!" He turned and joined Aspen in the front row. He held Aspen's hand during the entire ceremony. They were finally pronounced husband and wife. Robert grabbed her and gave her a resounding kiss. Everyone applauded and they went into the house. The dining room was set up with refreshments. The house was resonating with joy. Robert had hold of Lady Matilda and never let her go. After several hours, they finally went to Lady Matilda's room and retired for the night. Troy soon followed with Aspen.

"You have been driving me wild all day." He kissed her passionately and she melted into him. He undressed her and they went to bed.

The next morning, Troy and Aspen were waiting in the parlor for their guests to wake up. Lord Robert and Lady Matilda were the first ones to arrive. Lady Matilda looked ravishing. Troy was happy to see his mother so enamored with Lord Robert. Lord Robert had a head over heels in love look on his face.

"Is that the way I looked after we were married?" he asked, laughing.

"Worse," said Lady Matilda. "You looked like you had caught the whole world in your hands."

They all laughed at that. Family members started arriving in the parlor. They went towards the dining room. Everyone raved about how the room looked after the renovations. They loved the sliding door to make the room larger or smaller. The meal was quite the gathering. Troy noticed Lady Matilda was having the time of her life. She had seemed tense a few days before the wedding, but that was all behind her now. She was radiant. Troy was very happy for her.

The next wedding was in two weeks. Mandy and Michael were in the final stages of their plans. Troy and his family would be spending the night at the Brentwood manor. Troy would be giving Mandy away. Their wedding was an indoor one like Penny's would be.

Troy waited at the bottom of the stairway for Mandy. When he saw her, he was so proud that she had become exactly what he knew she could be. A lady in her own right. He offered her his arm and took her to the alter and handed her over to Michael. After the ceremony, Michael kissed her very passionately before the congregation. Mandy blushed and looked even more beautiful. The guests all milled around and started taking their leave after a few hours. Troy gave Mandy a kiss on the cheek, shook hands with Michael, and wished them a life of happiness. From the look on Mandy's face, that part would be easy. They all took their leave and arrived home late in the evening. Penny and Timothy went for a stroll in the garden. Robert and Lady Matilda, Troy and Aspen all went into the parlor.

"How are you feeling, my dear?" she asked Aspen.

"I feel like a big heavy balloon," she replied. "This son of ours is insisting on kicking day and night. I'm finding it hard to sleep."

"Didn't Penny kick you insistently Mother?" Troy asked.

"Yes she did," answered Matilda laughing. "I was sure she was another boy. You did kick worse than she did, Troy. You never stopped. She gave me a break occasionally."

Aspen looked smugly at Troy. He caught her and kissed her and they laughed. They all retired to their rooms.

The following week was the last wedding. Penny had finally reached her goal. She was the last one married, but her wedding was spectacular. Everything was set. As she came down the stairway to Troy, he was amazed at her beauty. His pride for her overflowed that day. Her movements and stance were regal just like Matilda's. Although once they were pronounced husband and wife, Penny is the one who grabbed Timothy and gave him a resounding kiss. He is the one who blushed, but they both looked ecstatic. The dinner was superb. All the guests thoroughly enjoyed themselves. They were all late leaving so it was very late when the household was able to retire to their rooms.

The next day no one saw the bride and groom all day. Evidently they had food sent to their room. Troy and Aspen laughed, remembering their time as newlyweds. The Braxtons, Knoells, and Gatsbys stayed for a few more days and then everyone started leaving. Robert and Lady Matilda were staying until the baby was born. Penny and Timothy decided the same thing.

Three weeks later, Troy and Aspen went for a stroll in the garden. All of a sudden she bent over with a pain. Troy caught her and moved her to a seat under a tree.

He called for a servant. "Go fetch, Lady Matilda."

She came right away. "The baby has started coming. Get her up to her room quickly."

Troy carried her up to their room. She smiled up at him with that radiant smile. Lady Matilda had sent for the midwife. Troy was pacing the parlor, then the study, then the hallway downstairs, and finally the hallway outside their room. It took eighteen hours before they finally heard the cry of a baby. Troy went running into the room. Aspen was sitting up in bed holding a little bundle.

She looked up at Troy. "May I present our son to you, my lord."

Troy went towards the bed. He took the bundle from her arms and held him. He was amazed at how tiny and loveable he was. Troy bent down to kiss her.

"Thank you, my love," he said.

The midwife took the baby and shooed Troy from the room. "They are both tired and need to rest. Go on now."

Troy went down to the parlor. He had wanted to stay with Aspen and hold her while she slept, but also knew she worked hard for this baby. He knew she needed to rest undisturbed. He also knew the baby worked hard to enter this world and also needed his rest. A son, it finally hit him he was now a father. The responsibility hit him like a brick. It wasn't a maybe, it was a reality. He gave Charles, Robert, and Timothy each a cigar and the men retired to the garden to smoke.

"What's his name?" asked Robert.

"I have no idea. We never talked about names. I have no idea."

"Give him a name quick. Don't make him going through life as Lord Baby Bowling," Robert said and they all laughed.

Troy was very happy, but he was also worried about Aspen. He finally went up to see her later that evening. They never had time to get the nursery ready. They had found the bassinet he and Penny used as babies. The servants cleaned it up and they were using it. The midwife was attending to the baby while Aspen was sleeping. He sat by the bed at first, then he got into bed with Aspen and watched her sleep. She finally opened her eyes for a couple of minutes, just long enough to move into his arms and fall asleep again. He held her the rest of the night.

She woke early in the morning. The baby started crying. The midwife brought him to her. He watched her feed the baby. It was a miracle. He was amazed. When she finished, the midwife took the baby again. He held her again.

"We have a slight problem, my love," he said.

"Whatever could be a problem? We have everything now."

"Well, it has been brought to my attention that our son needs a name. He can't go around as Lord Baby Bowling for life."

"I see what you mean. I would like to name him Charles after my uncle. I believe your mother would prefer we name his Troy."

"He is our child, not my mother's. Charles it is. Lord Charles Bowling. That has a nice ring to it. I like it and I love you." He bent over and kissed her.

He ordered breakfast for the two of them and had it sent to the room. They did this for a few days. Lady Matilda and Penny visited Aspen a few times.

Finally after three days in bed, Aspen made her appearance in the parlor. The men rushed over to have a look at him.

"May I present Lord Charles Bowling," Troy announced.

Charles was overwhelmed and thanked Aspen and Troy. Everyone was overjoyed.

Soon everyone started taking their leave. Penny and Timothy left first. Then Robert finally said they must return to London. Lady Matilda was torn about leaving but she knew Troy now had a wife and an heir. He had completed his duties very well. Now it was truly time for them to start their lives and build their future. She returned to London with Robert to take up their new lives.

Aspen and Troy stood outside saying good bye to them. Troy gave Lady Matilda a decisive kiss on the cheek.

"Goodbye Mother. Be happy," he said. "And don't forget your pillows."

She laughed at him and got into the carriage with Robert. They took off.

Troy took hold of Aspen's hand while they turned back to the manor to take up their lives of dreams come true.

The End